THE BELATED BACHELOR PARTY

Ravinder Singh is the bestselling author of six novels and two crowd-sourced anthologies. His books have sold over 3.5 million copies to date. After having spent most of his life in Burla, a very small town in western Odisha, Ravinder is currently based in New Delhi. He has an MBA from the Indian School of Business. His eight-year-long IT career started with Infosys and ended in Microsoft, where he worked as a senior programme manager before deciding to pursue writing full-time. Ravinder has also founded and runs a publishing venture called Black Ink (www.BlackInkBooks.in), where he publishes and mentors debut authors.

Beyond his love for words, Ravinder is also a fitness freak. You can reach out to him on his Instagram handle @ThisIsRavinder or write to him at itoohadalovestory@gmail.com.

RAVINDER SINGH

THE BELATED BACHELOR PARTY

HarperCollins *Publishers* India

First published in India by
HarperCollins *Publishers* in 2019
A-75, Sector 57, Noida, Uttar Pradesh 201301, India
www.harpercollins.co.in

2 4 6 8 10 9 7 5 3 1

P-ISBN: 978-93-5357-072-9
E-ISBN: 978-93-5357-073-6

Typeset in 11/14.7 Sabon LT Std at
Manipal Digital Systems, Manipal

Printed and bound at
Thomson Press (India) Ltd

This book is produced from independently certified FSC® paper to ensure responsible forest management.

No animals were harmed in the making of this book.
Some best friends might have been emotionally tortured, though.

To
Happy, MP and Raam ji
What would you three have become had you
not found me?

Prologue

Hi there!

I am friendship. I know you know me. However, please allow me to introduce myself. It is important, because for the next couple of hours, days, weeks or maybe even a month or longer, depending upon your reading appetite and speed, you and I are going to be in each other's company. After all, I am the one who is going to narrate this story to you.

So yeah, coming back to what I was saying – who am I? Well, to put it simply, I am the most beautiful democratic relationship you get to cherish.

Are you wondering why I used that word – democratic? Let me explain. It's because, unlike other relationships, I am not forced upon you by virtue of your birth. I am a *choice* you make.

You didn't get to cherry-pick your parents, or your grandparents and great-grandparents. And as much as you would have liked, nobody asked you for your sibling preferences either. Let's face it – this sneaky section of humanity around you – all those cousins and nephews and nieces and uncles and aunts among them – simply gatecrashed your life while you were busy doing mundane things like, well, being born and growing up.

And then one day, in the world of your choice-less relationships, I walked in, bringing with me people you could pick for yourself. You became friends by choice and remained so by that very choice. Democratic! Get it?

It's quite possible that at this point, depending upon how you think, you may or may not be comparing me with yet another relationship that you get to choose – romantic love!

If that thought hasn't crossed your mind, then we are sorted; but if it has, then let me rescue you at the outset from giving brownie points to this other relationship over me.

Honestly, romantic love is so overrated. If you don't believe it, ask all those people who neglected me after falling in love, then had their hearts broken only to come back to me and cry on my shoulder. I stood there, rock solid. I wiped their leaky noses, consoled them in their hour of need. I was there to lift them up when love knocked them down. Romantic love. Bah! It's a trap laid for you by the hormones in your body and chemical reactions in your brain.

I am evergreen. You don't have to wait for me till you reach puberty. I come to you in your kindergarten itself, and my lifespan is longer than that of love. What's more, I don't come with headcount restrictions. Unlike romantic love, you can share me with more than one person at a time. You see, I bring you variety.

Like I told you, I am the most beautiful democratic relationship you can ever have.

Please don't get me wrong. I don't envy romantic love. Often, that love comes from me; out of me. Sometimes, it is part of me – a tiny subset – while I am the larger entity. However, I pity the people who claim that romantic love is a more special relationship than me.

Anyway, now that the introductions are done, we can move forward with the story – the story of four friends.

It's not the story of how they became friends, but the story of how they remained so, long after their friendship first began during their engineering days.

I remember the last day of their final semester, how the four of them had stood on the platform of the railway station in Hyderabad. Their belongings were packed in their iron trunks and the bedding hold-alls they had brought along with them four years back. One good look at their faces and anybody could tell that they were dealing with two contradictory emotions in that moment – the joy of finally having finished the last paper, and with it, the gloom of bidding goodbye to each other and their college days.

Finally, the whistle of the train broke the silence, summoning their attention. It was time. I was four years old back then, and honestly, it felt like my end had arrived.

Then, just before the train departed, the four boys huddled together and made a solemn promise – we will meet again!

So often do young people make promises about their future – promises they can seldom keep. After all, years later, geographically disconnected, busy with their lives and their hectic jobs, who has the time to remember the promises made during carefree college days?

But you know what, these four? They kept their promise.

I am twenty years old today, and it's time to tell you all about what happened on their third reunion. What makes this reunion special? Well, it was the first after the last of the four got married. No, the wives weren't invited. Why should they be? They hadn't been part of that promise made all those years ago.

So anyway, here is what happened ...

1

The Movie

On the big screen in the dark theatre, the female protagonist has made up her mind. She is not going to cancel her honeymoon trip to Europe. This, in spite of the fact that moments back her wedding was called off by the very man she was supposed to marry. But she is determined. She will go on her honeymoon. Alone.

What follows on screen is a lot more than just a montage of a solo trip. It's the heroine's journey of self-discovery as she experiences the joy of breaking free, cherishing life and living it on her own terms.

As the drama continues on the screen, transforming the heroine and entertaining the audience, something strange happens in the theatre. The adventurous ecstasy of the heroine reaches out from the screen and enters the mind of one of the spectators as she sits staring at the scene unfolding in front of her.

'Next year, I am going on a solo trip.' Without any warning, she drops the bomb in the lap of her husband sitting beside her. The husband stops chewing the popcorn stuffed in his mouth.

Her right arm is interlocked with his left, but she doesn't even turn to face him when she utters those words. His interest in the movie has disappeared, replaced with anxiety that crawls up his back. He turns his head and looks at her. She's still staring at the screen, and there's a smile perched on the corners of her lips. The black in her eyes shines with the reflection of a woman overcoming heartbreak by celebrating it.

That arsehole ditched her. I didn't ditch you, he says to her, but only in his head.

In the world outside his head, and in a sheer display of temporary bravery, all he manages to say is, 'But why, baby?'

Unperturbed, she replies, 'Because the idea of a solo Euro trip is exciting.'

He wants to remind her that movies are an escape from reality. *Let them remain that. Don't let them become reality.* But now's neither the time nor the place to engage in logical debates.

'Come on, baby! You won't enjoy it without me,' he says warmly, drawing her closer and resting his head on her shoulder.

It doesn't work.

'*That* I will let you know on my return,' she whispers into his ear.

He lifts his head and gazes into her eyes. Anxiety and tranquility have a face-off under the reflection of the fast changing screen lights. He wants to say more, but before he can gather his courage and open his mouth, she has turned back to the screen.

(I had promised myself that I wouldn't interrupt the story while narrating it to you, but I have to pause here and say that I've often wondered how things would have been if he had said something. If they'd picked a different movie. If the heroine on screen hadn't been quite that effective. Anyway, back to the movie hall ...)

Wise men put their brains to use and think of unique ways to retaliate. Others, perhaps the not-so-wise ones, don't have the means to do so. They simply borrow the very idea that bothered them, from the person who bothered them, and then they throw it back at that very person. When someone yells – you are an idiot, the best they can do is retaliate by saying, no, you are the idiot. And that's it.

Something similar happens later that night, when the husband and wife are driving back home after the movie.

Taking a momentary break from humming '*London thumakda*' on loop, the wife says, 'So, baby, it's final. Next year, I am going on a vacation without you.'

'Sure! And I'm going on a vacation without you too!' he says, his eyes focused on the road ahead and a hundred thoughts racing through his mind.

'Really! Where?' she asks.

'Where are *you* going?' he counters.

'I told you na! Europe.'

'So am I!' he says and takes a sharp turn at the T-point.

'Wow!' the wife says, her face turned away from his, looking out of the window. The next second, he hears the soft hum of '*Thumakda thumakda ... London ...*' resume.

But then, she pauses and turns to him.

'Wait a minute! We won't be going on solo trips to the same place in the same plane at the same time, right?'

The husband first chuckles and then shakes his head. 'Not at all.'

'Ah good! Because anyway you have copied my idea, now I don't want you to—'

He cuts her off.

'Hey! I haven't copied your idea. You copied the movie's idea. But chances are that you may copy mine too after you hear what it is,' he says.

'Really? What are you planning to do?'

Now he's scrambling, trying to come up with something that will impress her. After all, he *has* no plan.

'I am not going solo,' he ends up saying.

'Then what?'

'I'm going with ... a ... a ... with friends. Yes! Friends!' he blurts out, with a spark of inspiration.

'Which friends?'

'College friends,' he says, the idea forming as he speaks.

She stares at him. 'The four of you?'

He nods a silent yes as his mind races ahead. What is he doing?

'Are you—' she says before he cuts her off again.

He's had his Eureka moment.

'Yes! We are going on an all-boys trip. To Europe!—*Tu ghanti big baaaaaaaan di, poora ... ting ting ting ting TING!*'

2

The Conference Call

'Sounds exciting, but I have a project delivery scheduled during that time,' a voice said.

'Great idea! However, I got back from a family vacation just last month. Another vacation in six months looks really difficult,' followed another.

The third one pitched in. 'This would have been so much fun. But yaar, I was thinking of visiting India this summer. Maybe the eight of us can do a Euro trip next year?'

Right then the fourth voice interjected. 'Eight? What the hell do you mean by the *eight* of us?'

The four friends were on a conference call, which had been scheduled the very day after the Eureka moment in the car. Sitting in different time zones, they were now discussing the possibility of going on a Euro trip together. But the idea had, for some reason, failed to take off as soon as it was pitched.

'Us eight!' the voice replied to the indignant query. 'Four couples, eight people. A summer Euro trip! That's what we have been discussing here, right?'

'Hold on to that thought, till you get bored of it,' quipped the fourth voice. He paused for effect, and let the implication sink in.

'O teri!' Harprit shouted. 'Rinku veer, are you thinking what I am thinking you are thinking?'

'Well, what do you think I'm thinking?' responded Ravin, or as his friends knew him, Rinku.

'Oh wow! An all-boys Euro trip! Raam ji, are you ready for it?' Manpreet asked Amardeep, using the name they had given their friend during their college days.

In fact, they all had particular nicknames in their little group. Happy was actually Harprit and Manpreet was called MP.

Within the next five minutes, the rigid project delivery date suddenly became flexible, a second vacation within six months didn't seem like that big a deal, and instead of summer, Diwali appeared to be a better time for the next India visit anyway. One by one, all the roadblocks standing in the way of their trip were cleared. Men!

(You see, I have always believed this – where there is a will there is a way. Where there is none, there are excuses. Anyway, let me continue with the story.)

'Okay boys, let's freeze the dates and apply for leave. By the way, we also need to do the research, pick the places, book the hotels, and plan the itinerary. Who's going to do that?' Amardeep asked.

His words led to pin-drop silence, which lasted for about three seconds before Harprit broke it by laughing. Loaded with sarcasm, his chuckles were contagious. Soon, Manpreet and Amardeep joined in and it was evident what their laughter meant.

'No! No way am I doing it this time!' Ravin said before anyone could speak up. 'MP will do it.'

However, Harprit and Amardeep immediately objected. They had zero confidence in Manpreet's administrative abilities, and anyway, history was witness that Ravin was the mommy in their group.

(There's always that one friend, isn't there? The responsible and accountable one; the irreplaceable one. I can tell you that while Ravin protested, he quite liked his place in the group.)

So just like it used to happen in college, more than a decade later, the onus of planning and executing things fell on Ravin's shoulders.

Finally, when all of them were on the same page and equally excited about the vacation, Manpreet asked the most important question, the answer to which would determine the entire foundation of their upcoming trip.

'*Bhaaiyon, biwiyon se kya bolenge?*' (Brothers, what will we tell the wives?)

(To have a wish is one thing. To make it come true, another.)

For these four men, convincing the women they had married to let them go on this trip was the biggest and the foremost hurdle. In fact, it seemed almost impossible. But then, the desire to get some semblance of their old, carefree college days back, to go on a trip of a lifetime as just a foursome, was too strong. And to make their wish come true, they were ready to bite the bullet.

There was one small relief – they had to convince only three women, not four. After all, one of the wives already knew about the plan and was already on board with the idea.

At the same time, they all made a promise to each other, one they would keep – The trip would happen only if all four of them could go. If even one of them, for whatever reason, couldn't, then they'd simply cancel the whole thing.

'Yaar, I'm sure they won't agree!' Manpreet said.

'Yes, but only if you make them believe that it's going to be *too* much fun,' Hapreet said.

'Exactly. And anyway, it's not like we're going on some crazy bachelor party,' Amardeep added, nodding.

'It's a pity that we never went on one of those,' Ravin said drily.

'Seriously, man! Four marriages. Four missed opportunities,' Manpreet complained.

For a few seconds, they were all quiet, contemplating what could have been. And then, a voice – excited, hopeful – broke the silence.

'In that case, how about we let this be our belated bachelor party?'

A moment to process this, and then three voices rose in unison, 'Amen!'

3

The Plan

The final nail in the coffin was hit when Ravin, Harprit and Amardeep collectively reached out to Manpreet's wife; without bringing Manpreet in the picture. Their modus operandi to convince her was to read out an emotional script they had carefully written. '*Bhabhi ji*, the three of us have agreed. It's only your husband who is against the idea of leaving you for this reunion trip. He certainly loves you more than he loves us. Now it's all in your hands, *bhabhi ji.* Only you can push him to go. Else this trip isn't happening.'

(There's no better way to win than making the one whom you want to persuade, persuade you instead.)

The trick worked. They used it twice more and succeeded each time. Their cunning minds were on cloud nine.

Often, men are fools enough to think that they can outsmart women in mind games. While the friends thought they were clever, they never realized their women were cleverer than them. Not only that, but that they were generous too. The wives had well understood their husbands' trick and still agreed to fall prey to it without letting them know.

(Women can read men like an open book, but that's not even the saddest part for men. The saddest part is that most men don't even know they have been read.)

As it turned out, it took very little to convince the women.

(I'm so sorry that I keep interrupting, but I'd like to chime in here and say – did the men think only they needed a bit of ... time off? Come on! But then, guilty pleasures do often make the roads leading up to them appear full of roadblocks, don't they?)

The thing is, a couple of years into marriage, couples aren't usually as possessive about each other as they used to be when things were new. The husbands wanted to step out of the house without their wives, and well, they were happily shocked to realize that the plan suited the wives perfectly. The little time apart would give both parties a chance to recharge and focus on themselves. All in all, a welcome break.

But there was one thing that irked the women. For their husbands, this time would be spent in Europe on a holiday, whereas the women would be stuck at home.

So it made complete sense for them to ask their husbands to pay a price – one that came in all shapes and sizes – gifts and privileges, fewer responsibilities at home, excessive affection in the run-up to the trip ...

And the husbands? Well, they were so glad to be getting their way that they agreed to everything without batting an eye.

By the next weekend, infused with brand-new enthusiasm, the four friends began to plan their trip in earnest.

It began with another conference call.

'So, are we doing all that is supposed to be done on a bachelor party?' Manpreet asked, chuckling.

'Folks, let's not forget that it's a *belated* bachelor party. We've already missed the original bus. The one we are catching now isn't the fully loaded version,' Amardeep, the sage in the club, pointed out.

'Raam ji, I am not sure what you thought I meant!' Manpreet protested. 'I was only wondering if we'd be indulging in getting high.'

'Don't underestimate us, MP! I'm sure there is a lot we are going to offer ourselves, beyond just getting high.' Harprit laughed and then asked Ravin to walk everyone through the plan.

Over the next thirty minutes or so, Ravin laid out an entire buffet of a tempting Euro trip.

He had been thorough in his research. Almost every website with articles and information on the world's wildest bachelor party destinations had been visited; the best locations for trips for married men had been read about online and further verified on YouTube, for simply words can't be believed. Ravin had spent a lot of time trying to make sure that he found only the best options for them. There was no way he was going to ruin such a brilliant opportunity, and so when the Internet had offered up Prague as the best destination for them, he'd looked up a BBC documentary to confirm the claim. The documentary showed how the Czech Republic capital had slowly become the most happening place for a European vacation. Every year, thousands of Europeans, especially Brits, arrived in the city for their weekend getaway parties. To complement it with more fun, Ravin had planned a road trip to Croatia where they would spend the second half of their vacation.

'It is going to be a seven-day trip. We will be spending the first half in Prague and the second in Croatia.'

'Where is Croatia?' somebody asked.

'South of Europe,' answered Ravin. 'Geographically, Czech Republic is in the north and Croatia is in the south, vertically below it.'

'What has the Czech Republic got to do with this?' questioned Amardeep.

'Let me give you a small hint. It is the country Prague is the capital of,' enlightened Ravin.

'I see,' Amardeep replied, completely missing the sarcasm. 'How is it? Prague?' he then asked.

'Wild and notorious,' the James Bond within Ravin replied in style.

'Wonderful,' Manpreet said, satisfied with the answer.

Amardeep spoke again and was about to ask another question, but then unexpectedly he ended up going on an entirely different tangent. 'Guys, talk to my wife.

She wants to ...' He alerted everyone moments before his voice vanished into thin air and his wife took over his call.

'Hellooooo guysssss!' the feminine voice gatecrashed their audio party.

The wonder woman had shut up all the James Bonds with a simple hello.

'Hi! Hello! Hi!' came three responses.

'I thought to say a quick hello to everyone and wish you all a memorable trip,' she said.

'Thank you so much, *bhabhi ji*!' Harprit said, being extra sweet the second he understood the purpose of her snatching the phone from Amardeep's hands and getting on the call.

'So where are you guys going?'

'Most probably Prague,' Manpreet answered.

'How is it? Prague?' she asked, echoing her husband's question from seconds back.

There was pin-drop silence again.

Ravin, fortunately, came to the rescue.

'A ... a ... adventurous and ... and ... liberating.'

Harprit and Manpreet exhaled a long breath.

'Please don't be too adventurous guys, and, come back without broken bones. Have fun and all the best. I am handing over the phone to your friend. B-bye!'

'Bye! B-bye! Bye!' came three responses before Amardeep was back on the call.

'Arsehole! What was that?' Harprit screamed as soon as he heard Amardeep's voice again.

'Sorry guys! She was in a jolly good mood, came chirping in from the other room ... and took over the call. I didn't see it coming,' Amardeep explained.

'Well, as long as she is in a happy mood, there's no threat to you coming on this trip, Raam ji.'

They sighed with relief. It looked like things were coming together.

'Hold on, how exactly did you describe Prague that made her talk about broken bones?' Amardeep demanded.

'Nothing much, Rinku veer found a respectable replacement for the words wild and notorious.' Manpreet laughed.

As per the plan, Prague was going to be their port of entry in Europe. On the fourth day of their vacation the boys were to undertake a twelve-hour-long drive from the Czech Republic to down-south Croatia. The coastal city Dubrovnik in Croatia was going to be their shelter for about two and a half days before they all bid each other adieu and flew back to their respective homes.

'A twelve-hour drive through four countries? That sounds like super fun, man!' Amardeep cheered.

On his laptop, Harprit had opened the map of Europe and talked simultaneously, 'So we will start in Czech Republic, keep going south, cross two more countries – Austria and Slovenia, on our way and then enter the last one and stop—'

Ravin cut him off to finish the route guide narration himself.

'When there is no land left ahead.'

'What do you mean, there is no land left ahead?' Manpreet asked.

'It means we are going to stay in a villa on the cliffs overlooking the Adriatic Sea,' Ravin explained.

On hearing that, Harprit was quick to click the link that popped up on the screen of his laptop. It took him to the glossary of the scenic coastline of Croatia. The next second, so that everyone could see what he was seeing, he dropped a few images from his laptop to their WhatsApp group.

Looking at them, Manpreet was the first one to react. 'O teri! Just imagine the four of us witnessing the sunset while the waves hit the cliffs.'

'And sipping wine in the courtyard of a private villa as night falls,' Ravin added.

'Remember our first reunion, guys?' Harprit asked. 'Drinking by the banks of the river Hooghly in Howrah and looking at the Kolkata skyline ...'

'Those were the days,' Amardeep sighed.

'Ten years later we are going to replace the river with a sea, a domestic location with an international one. So much has changed.' Manpreet had become emotional.

'But not our friendship,' Harprit said and everyone agreed, filled with a sense of deep appreciation for the friendship they cherished.

'Wherever you are, pour yourself a drink right now,' somebody on the call announced. The moment demanded a celebration and a promising reunion trip to look forward to.

While the evening had just begun for Harprit in London, and midnight was near for Ravin and Amardeep in India, a brand new day had just dawned for Manpreet in the US. But since when have emotions cared for the time of day? Manpreet too poured himself a small peg of single malt.

'For the sake of old times, guys!'

'For the sake of old times!' The call ended with a bottoms up!

4

The Visa

Procrastination is an art mastered by many. Unfortunately, these four had graduated from this school of thought.

Slowly, the narration changed from there-is-still-enough-time to shit-I-am-running-out-of-time, and before they knew it, they were at the point of just-enough-time. Any more delays, and their trip would remain a fantasy.

Their trip was scheduled for June; everyone had agreed that summer was the best season to visit Europe. Just a few days before the deadline for their visa applications, in order to be in Europe as per schedule, two of the four friends woke up to harsh reality.

Amardeep realized that there was no Czech Republic visa consulate in Hyderabad. In order to get his visa, he would have to travel to Delhi.

Ravin was scheduled to apply for his visa in Delhi the next day. Amardeep found this out when he gave an SOS call to his friend.

'You arsehole, you are waking up to this now?' Ravin yelled at him.

Amardeep remained tactfully silent.

'AMARDEEP!' Ravin roared.

Sensing that Ravin was serious, Amardeep broke his silence with an 'O *yaar, nahi pataa si* (I didn't know about it).'

'What are you planning to do now?'

'Planning to come to you.'

'When?'

'When are you going to the embassy?' Amardeep asked.

'Twelve hours from now, at ten in the morning tomorrow.'

'Cancel it.'

'Cancel what?' Ravin asked, surprised.

'The embassy visit,' Amardeep said.

'What? Why?'

'*Arre, dono bhai katthe apply karenge na* (Come on! Both brothers will apply together).'

(You see, invoking the bro-code doesn't always work, sometimes it falls flat on its face with a heavy thud. More so when something like an all-boys Euro trip is at stake.)

'No way! *Saaley tere chakkar mein mera bhi visa reh jaayega* (You rascal, because of you, I may not get my own visa).'

'Rinku veeeeeerrrr, please!

'Don't Rinku-veer me.' Ravin was firm.

'*Bhai nahi hai tu mera* (Aren't you my brother)?'

Ravin scoffed. Amardeep realized his words weren't going to do the trick. He switched to plan B.

'*Saaley soch le* (Think about it),' Amardeep said now. 'If I don't get my visa, then none of us is going on this trip anyway. Remember!'

Suddenly Ravin's anger changed to anger plus worry. Amardeep was right. They'd made a pact, and they had to honour it.

'Bhenchod!' he exclaimed. Amardeep knew he had won.

On the other side of the world Manpreet had run into visa issues too. There were some inter dependencies between getting a Schengen visa and his H1B renewal, which was due. He apprised everyone on their WhatsApp group, which they had lovingly named *Yaar Anmulle* after a viral Punjabi song that celebrated friendship. *Yaar Anmulle* literally translated to precious friends.

Manpreet's message ended with a single line: Don't worry, guys, I will find a way.

(I've known Manpreet for a long time, and honestly, the man does always get his way, by hook or by crook. So I knew that he meant it this time too. However, his friends couldn't help but worry, because their trip depended on his success. The what-if-not outweighed the what-if. Human nature! Anyway, I was bothered more about Amardeep than Manpreet.)

'Mayday. Mayday,' Harprit wrote on the group. And then he sent another message in tandem. 'All hands on deck right now.'

Interpreting his message correctly, the friends got on an immediate conference call.

Manpreet was the first one to speak. 'Happy, are you watching some ship-sinking movie right now? *All hands on deck ...*'

'Laugh away, but the joke's on all of us, because guess what is sinking faster than that unfortunate ship? Our Euro trip!' Harprit announced, and then asked, 'Where's Amardeep? I don't see him on the call.'

'He hasn't joined in yet,' Ravin said, and put everyone on hold to call Amardeep. Being in the same country, it often fell to him to call their friend.

In the comfort of his newly bought home in Hyderabad and after delaying Ravin's visa, Amardeep was snoring in deep sleep. Most of the time, it was impossible to get him to respond to messages, or even see them. There were instances when people had to call him to tell him that he had an unread message in his phone that needed a response. This is what Ravin did now as well.

'*Ki ho gayaa, kameeneyon* (What happened, arseholes)?' Amardeep murmured sleepily, his eyes still shut, when he finally came on the conference call.

'Look at the audacity of this guy,' Ravin said. 'Hasn't got his visa, delayed mine too and is now busy sleeping over it!'

'Wait a minute! So does that mean none of you have gotten your visas yet?' Harprit exclaimed.

The cat was out of the bag. A loud silence descended upon the call.

'Guys, come on!' Harprit's tone spoke volumes of his displeasure. 'Well, you need to move your asses,' he said when no one said a word. 'And you need to do it NOW.'

'Right now it is dark. Everything is closed.' Amardeep said, yawning.

Even Harprit could not hold back his laugh at that. 'You pig,' he said to his lazy friend.

'Look who's talking! The one who doesn't even have to lift his butt off the bed,' Amardeep retorted.

After living a couple of years in London, Harprit had secured UK citizenship some time back. He had a UK passport, which bestowed upon him the privilege of travelling to a number of countries without having to apply for a visa beforehand. Unlike the others, he didn't have to go through the hassles of paperwork, photographs, biometric, appointments and interviews. All he had to do was simply walk into the airport and board a flight – as easy as swatting a fly.

'I would if I had to, but for the moment it's you guys who need to,' Harprit said.

'Folks, Happy is right. Our trip is at risk,' Ravin intervened.

Amardeep, who by now was wide awake, said, 'Guys, I am sorry about being late, but there won't be any more delay from my end. I promise you that.'

Manpreet too updated everyone on the call about his visa issue. His H1B was up for renewal. Besides, he had a family vacation to Spain coming up as well. He was now trying to merge things in a way that suited everyone. Of course, he not only wanted to avoid travelling twice to Europe, but also to leverage this opportunity to renew his H1B, which required him to step out of America.

'I have applied for a Schengen visa in the embassy of Spain here. I will land in Spain with my family a week before you guys land in Prague. In Spain, I will apply for renewal of my US H1B as well. Once my family vacation is over, I will see off my wife and kid at the airport. They will fly back to the US and I will come to Prague.'

'As long as you make it to Prague, bhai,' Harprit said. 'Raam ji and Rinku, when are you two going to the embassy?' he asked.

'The day after tomorrow,' Ravin replied.

'MP, let us know once you get the Schengen visa,' Amardeep said.

'Roger that,' came the response.

'Damn! Are we back to salvaging that ship?' Harprit mocked Manpreet's choice of words.

'Looks like it, buddy.'

'Now that we are on the verge of saving the ship, can I go back to sleep?' Amardeep said.

'Yes, go back to sleep, Raam ji,' Ravin said, and then added, '... but say a little prayer before you do, because from where I see it, we haven't quite saved this ship. Not yet.'

'And why do you say that, Rinku veer?' Manpreet questioned.

'Guys, as I speak to you ...' Ravin said and paused before going on '... I am also going through the Schengen visa website for Czech. They have updated their guidelines.'

'So why do you sound like you've swallowed an insect?'

'Because based upon the spike in the summer Europe travel and rampantly increasing visa applications, these folks have increased the time duration between applying for the visa and receiving it.'

'By how many days?' Harprit asked, his voice holding a hint of panic.

'Seven.'

'So if you and Amardeep need your visa in time to make it for the trip, you should apply for the visa ...' Harprit said, trailing off as he counted backwards in his head.

They were silent for a few seconds as reality sank in, and then four voices said together, 'Today.'

5

The Czech Republic Embassy, New Delhi

Outside Terminal 1D of Delhi airport, Ravin had arrived to pick up Amardeep. It took them a little time to find each other amidst the sea of humanity and cabs. The moment they finally traced each other in the crowd, they both felt like an adventure was about to begin. Amardeep walked fast towards the car Ravin was waiting in.

Once he was in and the initial round of pleasantries, shot through with cuss words, was over, they hugged and slapped each other's backs. They laughed at the obstacles their plan had run into. Contrary to what they had thought, dealing with their spouses had been the least of their problems. Dealing with their own procrastination was turning out to be much more difficult. Sitting in the stationary car for a few minutes, they contemplated the possibility of the trip not materializing at all, but then decided to not mourn for a loss that hadn't happened yet. They would read the eulogy at the funeral, if it came to that.

'Let's do our karma and not bother about the result,' Amardeep said in a grave, pious voice.

'You mean our belated karma,' Ravin corrected him.

'I mean the belated karma for the belated bachelor party,' Amardeep said and burst into laughter.

As the car crawled ahead on a clogged road, Amardeep sat back and pulled out his phone, sending an update of their status to the other two friends on *Yaar Anmulle*.

'We have been given a mission to meet the highly placed diplomats in the Czech Republic consulate in the capital and secure two Schengen visas. We have less than eight hours to break into their systems and ensure this visa protocol is initiated in our interest. If we are caught or killed on our mission, the secretary of state will disavow any knowledge of our actions. We choose to accept this mission.'

As the car stalled again, Ravin picked up his phone and read the message notification, before turning to Amardeep with an eyebrow raised.

'*Aa ki hai* (What's this now)?'

'*Bhai, feel achhi aati hai* (Makes things thrilling, bro).'

(Wait a minute. Did I tell you, Amardeep is a big movie buff? No? Well, then I must warn you. You will see a lot more of it as I tell you the story ahead.)

Before Ravin could respond, both their cellphones beeped again. It was Harprit.

'Good luck, Ethan Hunt.'

By 10 a.m., the two friends were standing in the queue outside a window on Niti Marg in Chanakyapuri, Delhi. The blue signboard on the window read – EMBASSY OF THE CZECH REPUBLIC. Though it was still early, the Delhi heat was already unbearable. Unlike other embassies around them, this one was tiny. Unless called for an interview, people were supposed to stand outside the block and communicate with officials through a window.

When their turn came, Amardeep and Ravin collected their respective tokens with a serial number, based on which they'd be called for their visa interviews. One of the many travel agents milling around assured them that it would be at least an hour and a half before their names were called. That left them with enough time to get something to eat. Amardeep was beginning to feel hungry, having had only a cup of tea before leaving his Hyderabad home in the wee hours of the morning.

A while later, as he dug his teeth into a roasted chicken sandwich in an air-conditioned café in Lutyens' Delhi, he said, 'MP played the cards quite well for us.'

Ravin followed his gaze and saw the flight tickets placed on top of the paperwork for their visa applications.

'He is smart,' he agreed.

Due to Manpreet's presence of mind, the foursome had not actually booked their return tickets to Europe. With the uncertainty of timely visa approvals hanging over their heads, spending half a lakh rupees on booking the flight tickets seemed like an unnecessary risk. Instead,

Manpreet had given them the idea of blocking the tickets, something that the men didn't have to pay for.

'I understand blocking hotels, but can we block flights as well?' Ravin had asked while they all were chatting on *Yaar Anmulle* a day before.

'I am not sure about how it works in India, but in the US you can do so at no cost with certain privilege membership cards. I have blocked tickets with my credit card before. The ticket printout will show our names, date of travel, flight number, departure as well as arrival and all the details that the embassy wants to see. However, you can only block tickets for seventy-two hours,' Manpreet had explained.

'And after seventy-two hours?' Ravin had asked.

'Auto cancellation.'

'And how soon can you block these tickets for us?' Amardeep had questioned.

'In the next ten minutes,' was Manpreet's reply.

And so, the boys had strategically booked their tickets hours before the visa appointment.

Amardeep finished his sandwich and, brushing the crumbs off his shirt, asked Ravin, 'What's your gut feeling? Will we get the visa on time?'

'I think we will,' Ravin responded, his voice serious.

'What makes you so confident?' Amardeep asked.

'Death.'

'Death?'

'Yes.'

'What are you up to, bhai?' Amardeep asked.

'Shouldn't you be the one planning? I thought you were going to play mission impossible,' Ravin asked, a grin on his lips.

'Cut the crap and come to the point. Why are you talking in code language?'

'Bhai, feel achhi aati hai.'

A short while later, back at the embassy, Amardeep found himself smiling as he thought of the plan Ravin had laid out for him in the café. It was crazy, but right now, it was their only viable plan of getting the visa on time. Anyway, it was not Amardeep who was going to be the star performer in this act.

There were just three more people ahead of them in queue now, and barely twenty minutes later they both heard Ravin's token number being called.

Ravin walked to the tiny window, and promptly, the door next to it opened. He turned around and gave his friend one final look before being swallowed by the opening.

It was showtime!

Inside, on the other side of the table, a fair-skinned lady who must have been in her early forties was busy putting the papers on her desk inside a folder. Ravin stood next to the chair across from her and she looked up.

'Hello!' she said in a mechanically cheery way.

Ravin replied with a smile, 'Hi there.'

'Please take your seat and hand over your application form.'

Ravin complied.

After glancing through the documents quickly and efficiently, the woman looked up and asked Ravin the main question.

'What's the purpose of your trip? Business or vacation?'

'Neither, actually,' Ravin said, and something in his voice grabbed the woman's attention. Her focus was now completely on the man in front of her. Without asking anything further, she let Ravin talk.

'I don't know how to say this, but ...' Ravin paused, his voice thick with sorrow. He then looked at her theatrically, poised with a ready supply of emotion.

The woman's eyes filled with sympathy as she stretched out her hand to pass the clearly upset man a glass of water.

'... my best friend from college, Happy, is in Prague,' Ravin said, and then paused again.

'Yes, go on?' she said, eager and curious.

'You see ... he is dying.'

6

The Czech Republic Embassy, New Delhi

'Oh! I am so sorry!' the woman exclaimed. She looked both upset and worried, wondering if Ravin was going to break into tears right there. With a still long queue outside her office, melodrama was the last thing she needed.

'He lives in the Czech Republic?' she asked, her voice soft with empathy.

Channelling the Meena Kumari in him, Ravin hung his head and gave one small sob, thus neatly avoiding the need to reply. The woman's anxiety about having a weeping man on her hands increased.

'Cancer?' she asked.

'AIDS!' he replied.

'Jesus Christ!' she said a prayer.

'Mother Mary and Joseph,' Ravin completed for her.

'And you are very close to each other?'

Ravin took his time. He pulled out a handkerchief from his pocket and wiped his nose.

'Very! He is like my brother.'

'Brother!' she tutted, her eyes sympathetic.

'From another mother,' Ravin replied.

'How much time does he have?' she asked.

Ravin stayed silent, focusing with pained eyes on a fancy crystal paperweight kept above the papers on her desk. She was immediately contrite. Of course, asking such a question was insensitive of her.

She changed tack.

'How soon do you want to travel?' she asked, glancing at the tickets attached with his application on her desk.

Ravin finally looked up.

'How soon can I get the visa?' he asked, hope sailing in his eyes.

'Ideally, it would have been nothing less than four weeks at this point,' she said.

'Oh Happy!' Ravin sighed softly.

'... but considering the situation, I will put this on priority. If things work out, you will get your visa by the end of this week,' she finished with a soft smile.

Ravin wanted to jump off his chair and indulge in an impromptu bhangra. But his best friend was dying, so he settled for something more proper for the moment.

'God bless you!' he said in a choked voice. After all, he meant it.

'God bless your friend and your friendship,' she said, clearly touched by his story.

'Amen!' he said, and got up from his chair. The woman got up too, and they shook hands. Then, just before leaving, he said, 'Madam, just one more thing.'

'Yes?' she asked, eyebrows raised.

'Happy is lucky to have another friend like me.'

He paused and let his words sink in.

'Oh! So you are two people travelling together,' she said, connecting the dots.

'We want to. But it's in your hands.'

'Has your friend already applied for the visa?'

'He is next in line after me.'

'Oh I see! Well, don't worry. I will process both your applications in the same batch.'

'You have been very kind. God bless you!'

With those words, Ravin felt a pang of guilt about tricking this kind woman. But then he had no other choice. It had to be done.

'I hope you all get to meet before ...' she said, her voice trailing off as they parted with another handshake.

Outside, Amardeep was waiting for Ravin with bated breath. The moment he saw his friend walk out of that door, he raised his arms in question. Ravin winked in return. Amardeep grinned with happiness, but before he could say anything, his token number was called.

Just as he moved to the door, Ravin pulled him aside.

'There's a change in the plan.'

'What?' Amardeep asked.

'Happy is dying of AIDS, not cancer.'

'What! But why?' Amardeep was stumped.

'Because she guessed cancer.'

'So?'

'I don't know ... I ... I ... felt our case would be more convincing by countering her guess.'

'So you picked *AIDS*?' Amardeep said, his voice rising slightly.

'That was the only other deadly disease that came to my mind.'

'Come on!'

'What? You want me to google a deadly disease in the middle of it?'

Amardeep made a face, but couldn't respond because his number was called again.

As he walked through the door, he realized that in a decade and a half of their friendship, this was the first time they were going to kill one of their best friends, and that they were delighted about it.

7

Terminal 3, Delhi International Airport

Evening had descended upon the city of Delhi, and the soft light of dusk was fast giving way to darkness. Separated by time zones, our four friends were all set to embark on their big adventure, their bags packed and their passports secured with visas.

Earlier in the day, Amardeep had called Ravin from Hyderabad. He was worried about not being worried, a usual state of mind for him before international trips.

'Am I missing something?' he had asked Ravin, his voice anxious.

'What do you mean?'

'All I am carrying is my luggage, and of course, my passport. But that's it.'

'Well, that's all you need,' Ravin assured his friend.

'I don't know ... I feel different ... like I'm missing a lung or something ... I have never felt like this before.'

'That's because you've never had me by your side on your international trips before.'

Amardeep smiled to himself. It was true. Unlike all his previous international trips, this time he didn't have to bother much – from the flight tickets to hotel bookings to arranging forex in card and cash – everything, even the international driving licence, had been handled by Ravin. It was liberating, knowing that someone else was taking care of everything.

As for Ravin, he was more than happy to step in. He knew he couldn't rely on Amardeep, especially after the visa debacle. When it came to applying for the international driving licence as well, Amardeep appeared to be lazy. It was too much of a task for him, because in order to get it, he would first have to apply for a new domestic driving licence. He had lost his some two years back and never felt the need to get a new one.

(I told you, procrastination is an art some master.)

Leaving anything to Amardeep meant jeopardizing the trip, and that was a risk Ravin wasn't willing to take.

By the time Amardeep landed in Delhi and the two friends met at the airport, it was close to 8 p.m. This meeting was very different from their last, when there had been a big question mark on their trip. This time, they could feel their excitement soar as they realized that their reunion plan was finally going to see the light of day.

Spotting Ravin in the crowd, Amardeep began walking fast towards him, and as he did, he raised his left hand in the air and made his shoulder pop up and down, mimicking a bhangra step. In his right hand was his luggage, which rolled behind him.

After a moment of hesitation, Ravin threw both his hands up in the air, imitating his friend and laughing.

Punjabis!

And when that happened, they ran towards each other. It was a scene pulled right out of 1990s' Bollywood movies. Only this time, it was between two grown-up men.

(You understand what kind of scene I am talking about, right? The one in which everything around the two protagonists freezes as they run towards each other in slow motion. And the background music changes to: La-la laaaa ... la laa ... La-la laaaa.)

Amardeep embraced Ravin in a tight bear hug.

'*Le bai mitaraa aa gaye assi* (See my friend, I have come),' he said with an expansive sweep of his arms.

After the melodramatic reunion, when the two finally walked towards their airline counter, Amardeep clicked a picture of them and posted it to their group. Half a world away, in Europe, Harprit's and Manpreet's phones buzzed with the update.

The queue at the Austrian Airlines counter was longer than they had anticipated, snaking up to all the way past the barrier.

'O bete!' yelled Amardeep, and grinned. 'We'll be here forever!'

Ravin quickly joined the tail of the row and pulled Amardeep next to him in line. 'So let's get in line now,' he said.

'How many people are flying with us? Rinku veer, are we flying in an Airbus A380?' Amardeep asked, curious.

For a change, Ravin didn't want to spoon-feed his friend. He decided to let Amardeep take charge for once, and so didn't respond to his question.

Seconds later, Amardeep stepped forward and looked at Ravin's face. Clearly, his majesty wanted an answer.

Taking his eyes off the long queue that was bothering him, Ravin finally said, 'I could ask you the same question.' Shifting his eyes back to the sea of people ahead of him, he muttered under his breath, 'Which plane make are we flying in, he asks.'

Amardeep looked confused, wondering at Ravin's bad mood. This wasn't surprising. Amardeep often missed puns and hints, and his innocent reaction would make the person cracking the joke feel horrible and guilty.

'Relax yaar, relax. No big deal. We will fly in any make of plane,' Amardeep consoled.

There was no way Amardeep was going to move his ass to satisfy his own curiosity. He stood still, changing the subject of the conversation. Meanwhile, a lot of passengers had come to join the queue behind them.

For the next twenty minutes, the line didn't move an inch, and the two began seriously wondering what the problem was. People ahead of them too were stepping out of the queue to look at the counter for any movement. There was none.

Amardeep, shifting impatiently on his feet, finally decided to walk up to the counter and check with the ground staff.

A couple of minutes later he returned with a piece of news that was going to change their entire plan for the evening.

'*Bhai, apni flight cancel ho gai* (Our flight got cancelled),' he announced, sending a tremor through the hearts of everyone in the queue who heard him.

8

Still at Delhi International Airport

'The pilot has fallen sick,' Amardeep said to the passengers staring at him with horrified looks.

'Is that the reason this queue is not moving?'an older blonde woman asked in a British accent.

'*Hanji, maata ji*,' Amardeep responded in the affirmative, and the lady looked baffled at this sudden introduction to Punjabi. Crisis makes people do crazy things.

'*Saala saaddi reunion di kundali vich hi dosh hai* (There's something wrong with the stars of our reunion trip),' Ravin said in frustration.

Before they knew it, the line had scattered, and people began pushing their way to the counter to confirm Amardeep's news. A human sea flooded over the airline counter, but the ground staff, clearly used to the situation, looked calm and unperturbed. They started fending off the onslaught of questions and queries with a handful of boilerplate answers.

'You don't have a pilot on standby?' someone asked.

'Unfortunately today we don't have one, sir.'

'What do I do now?' another voice piped up.

'Sir, you will have to wait till our next flight tomorrow morning.'

'What the hell? What am I going to do till then?'

'Sir, we will be providing you with a night's stay at a five-star hotel near the airport.'

The crowd, dissatisfied with the arrangement despite the promise of a five-star hotel, began losing their cool. Their voices gradually rose and the tone was that of anger. The leftover trolleys loaded with giant luggage bags marked the informal boundary of the crowd engaged in war of words with the airline folks. Anarchy had finally set in.

And cutting through the crowd were half a dozen representatives from different five-star hotels that had desks at the airport.

(You know how it is, friends. When the dogs smell the bone, they begin to dig.)

After all, a cancelled flight with more than three hundred passengers is a treasure trove for hoteliers. And as soon as the news broke, the sales managers had scattered all around like bees, trying to crack a deal with airline officials.

Somebody's loss is almost always somebody else's profit.

Negotiations and counter-negotiations between the officials of various hotels and the airline happened on the spot, right in front of the passengers who were desperate to fly.

'What are they saying?' Amardeep asked Ravin, who stood ahead of him at the crowded counter.

'*Bhai hamaari boli lag rahi hai* (They are auctioning us).'

'What?'

'The hotels are negotiating rates for passengers' rooms,' Ravin answered, his eyes fixed on the proceedings at the counter.

'You are making it sound as if ...' he let the sentence hang mid-air and instead asked, 'which one are you hoping will win?'

Ravin turned to look at his friend and barked. '*Saale, IPL auction nahi chal rahaa hai* (You arsehole, this isn't an IPL auction going on).'

Amardeep laughed out loud.

'We can't afford to miss a day of our reunion,' Ravin added.

'I know, but what do we do now?' Amardeep said.

The question clearly had no ready answers.

Ravin pulled out his phone from his pocket and called up his friend Avantika in Dubai, who was a lead cabin crew in an international airline. A full ring died a natural death without anyone picking the call. He dialed again with no luck. In the end, he typed a couple of text messages. They ended with the words – 'what can be done now?'

Meanwhile, the air reverberated with threats to sue the airline, demands for full refund along with a night's stay and the occasional Delhi anthem of 'you-don't-know-who-I-am'. The airline's ground staff, as part of their routine protocol to deal with such situations, empathized with the travellers, but that made little difference.

Frustrated passengers and eager hoteliers weren't the only people the staff had to deal with. In parallel, they were on the phone talking to some folks about seat availability. Listening carefully to their one-sided conversation, Amardeep wondered what they were referring to.

'Shouldn't they be checking for availability of rooms instead of seats?' he asked Ravin.

'Raam ji, will you forget about the hotel? If we don't get on a flight today, I have my house here. We will go to my home, not a hotel!' Irritated with how things were unfolding, Ravin too was losing his cool. Amardeep, though, seemed calm despite everything going on.

Ravin was wondering how his friend managed to maintain such composure when his phone beeped. He immediately pulled it out, expecting a response from his Dubai friend, but it was a thumbs-up emoji message from Manpreet on their group, in response to their airport selfie picture they had shared earlier. Amardeep's phone beeped too, intimating him about the same message. Seeing it, Amardeep asked if it was time to update the other two about the situation in Delhi.

Taking a deep breath, Ravin acknowledged. 'I guess so.'

Just as he was about to type a reply to all in the group, another message arrived on his phone. 'Sorry missed your call. Check if the partner airlines have seats available. The airline should adjust you in them,' Avantika had written.

Ravin dropped the idea of updating the group and instead passed his phone to Amardeep, who read the message and immediately connected the dots.

'So that means the seats that this ground staff is enquiring about ...' Ravin said and Amardeep finished his sentence, '... are on the partner airlines.'

'I bet they are,' Ravin responded.

They both turned to the counter again, where they could see the ground staff questioning passengers about the purpose of their travel.

As they listened, they realized that there was a pattern emerging. People with medical conditions, senior citizens and women travelling alone or with kids were asked for further details. Families on vacation and men travelling for business were served platitudes and asked to wait on the side.

'I think we're in trouble,' Amardeep whispered.

'Yeah, they are creating a priority list of passengers for the available seats in the partner airline,' Ravin murmured back.

Amardeep nodded in agreement and was silent for a while, lost in thought. Then something seemed to occur to him and with newly discovered vigour, he exclaimed, 'Leave this to me! And later, at the bar beyond the security check, order a martini for me. Shaken, not stirred.'

'I will, double O seven, but what's the plan?' Ravin asked, amused.

'Same old, same old,' Amardeep shot back.

'Kill Happy?'

'Obviously!'

Ravin followed Amardeep to the airline counter. As they walked, he could tell that Amardeep had begun to feel a lot less confident about the plan. He now looked at Ravin and said, 'Yaar! Telling a lie so many times makes me believe it is the truth.'

Ravin controlled the laughter bubbling inside him. It was important to play the part of aggrieved friends.

'Look on the bright side, Raam ji. If you start believing it, then you aren't lying any more. That helps.' Ravin tried to convince his friend.

'This time, shall we change it to cancer?' Amardeep asked.

'Dude, let's stick to what we've said before for consistency. Why change anything now,' Ravin responded. 'And think about it yaar ... it's easier to make them think we're telling the truth if we tell them our friend has the one disease that so many people in the world choose to hide.'

Amardeep nodded his head. '*Sahi keh raha hai, bhai.* '*AIDS hi sahi rahega* (You are right, buddy. AIDS will work better).'

Amardeep slipped through the crowd and reached the counter. 'What happened to the captain?' he asked, showing grave concern.

'Food poisoning,' the lady behind the desk said shortly. She seemed like she'd had a long enough day and didn't want to say any more than she absolutely had to.

'Oh no.' Amardeep made a face.

'Oh yes,' she confirmed.

Amardeep managed to place his elbows on the counter and held his head in his palms, momentarily closing his eyes. 'Why is there so much death and disease in the world?' he murmured theatrically to himself, loud enough for the woman to hear.

'Are you all right, sir?' she asked, alarmed.

'How could I be all right when my friend is on his deathbed and I am unable to travel to meet him?' he said, a sob catching at his throat.

Ravin stood a little away, worried that Amardeep was now overdoing it. Any more drama and the woman would know it was all fake.

But the airline rep clearly appeared to be buying the melodrama. Her body language changed and she leaned forward, her brows furrowed in concern. 'Sir, can't you wait till tomorrow morning?' she asked.

'We can, but he may not,' Ravin drew closer and pitched in before Amardeep could speak.

The lady at the counter looked at the men. 'You two are together?' she asked.

Amardeep lifted his head and looked at her. '*Hanji, behenji*. I mean, ye ... ye ... yes madam.'

Listening to his untimely Punjabi, Ravin whispered in his ear, 'What's wrong with you?'

'What's wrong with your friend?' the lady at the counter asked.

'Acquired Immune Deficiency Syndrome,' Amardeep answered.

She looked at them with questioning eyes. Her face broadcasted the question – what-kind-of-disease-is-this?

'AIDS,' Ravin clarified.

'Oh!' she said, and then again, 'Ohoooooooo … AIDS!'

Her eyes scanned Ravin's face, shock visible on it.

The voices in their immediate proximity, hearing the woman, went silent. Amardeep and Ravin turned around and saw that the passengers behind them were staring at them anxiously.

'Not us. Our friend,' Ravin announced. And then added further, 'He has very little time left and we want to see him before …' he said, maintaining eye contact with a random traveller as he spoke. Tactfully, he left his sentence unfinished.

'And don't worry, it does not spread through touch,' Amardeep said, noticing how a few people in the crowd had stepped back.

The men turned back to the woman at the counter, and she asked them to step aside.

'What? Why? We are not going anywhere,' Amardeep said, reluctant to leave the battleground.

She ignored him and stepped out from behind the counter herself. Seeing her walk away, Ravin shouted, 'You can't do this to us! If one person's food poisoning is a good enough reason for three-hundred-plus passengers not flying, then another person's AIDS should be a good enough reason to make two people fly.'

She stopped and turned around to look at the two men. 'Sir, I cannot fly a plane, or I would have done that for you. Meanwhile, I can only do what's in my hands. Please, I request you to follow me.'

The men meekly did as told, rolling their luggage behind them.

As they matched her footsteps, she said, 'I am trying to help you, sir. I couldn't make it obvious in front of scores of waiting passengers.'

The lady guided them to an empty channel at the Air France counter. She had a word with another woman, who was the ground staff from Air France.

'*Rinku veer, Air France wali di dress zyaada changi hai Austrian Airlines wali to. Nahi* (The Air France ground staff's attire is nicer than the Austrian ones. No)?' Amardeep said.

'*Kanjaraa, dressan baad ch vekh lavaange, pehlaan seataan te focus kar lai ye* (Idiot, we can focus on their dresses later, let's first focus on getting our seats)?' Ravin responded.

After a quick chat, the two women nodded their heads in agreement. It looked like a done deal. The lady from the previous airline wished them luck and then, just before she left, she leaned in and whispered something to the men.

'Next time, please don't fake a death to get on a plane. Have a safe flight!'

9

Yes! Still at Delhi International Airport

The two men watched the confident stride of the woman walking away from them, and then turned to each other.

'She knew!' Ravin said, his voice laced with wonder. 'I wonder why she still helped us?'

'Sab uski marzi hai (It's all as per His will),' Amardeep said, pointing his finger up to refer to the Almighty.

The men now turned to the lady at the Air France counter, and were briefed about their new flight. They were now to take their connecting flight to Prague from Paris instead of Vienna.

What they were also told was that there were only two seats left in the aircraft they were to board. One was in the business class and other in economy.

(Sorry to interrupt the story again, dear reader, but I just want you to notice something. These two had almost lost the

opportunity to fly at all that night. They had had to virtually kill their best friend – yet again. And look at them now. Finally, when they might actually catch a flight that could have taken them to their destination on time, these two smart men decided to pick a fight between themselves instead! Who will get to fly business class?)

'Yaar, I had a long day. You would agree I deserve it,' Amardeep said.

'*Kuttey* (You dog),' Ravin responded succinctly.

'What *kuttey*? Dude, I have come all the way from Hyderabad,' Amardeep challenged.

'Oh! Then you must be the *Nizam* of Hyderabad!'

'Come on, Rinku veer,' Amardeep pleaded.

'*Saale, tickets main book karun, hotel main book karun, forex meri zimmedari, international driving licence meri headache, aur business class mein kaun jayega? Tu* (Rascal, I book the tickets, I book the hotel, I manage to get the forex, the international driving licences are my headache, and who gets to fly business class? You)?' Ravin mocked him.

For a while, the Air France rep looked on as the two men squabbled in front of her. Watching them fight for the business class seat, she found it highly unlikely that the story of their friend dying was true.

After about five minutes, she interrupted them, suggesting that they check in their luggage, take their boarding pass and continue their debate inside the plane.

'Guys, I suggest you move your fight inside the plane rather than here,' she said.

'Why?' asked Ravin, momentarily distracted.

'Because if you don't hurry up, there won't be a plane left to fight for. Your flight leaves in an hour.'

'Exactly,' acknowledged Amardeep and quickly added, 'anyway, alphabetically my name comes first. You check me in first, and put me in business class.'

'What is this, your school attendance register?' Ravin objected.

Taking their passports, the woman glanced at their ages, and then she looked back at them. *Age is no guarantee of maturity*, she thought to herself and let out a deep breath.

'Maybe you could toss a coin, guys,' she suggested.

'Okay,' Amardeep agreed after pausing to consider the idea.

She looked at Ravin. 'Okay,' he said reluctantly.

The three kept looking at each other. A few seconds passed.

Finally, the airline rep had had enough. 'Look, I am not going to fetch a coin for you,' she said firmly.

Ravin quickly drew a coin from his wallet. He was about to flip it when Amardeep interrupted and suggested the lady at the counter should do it for them. 'Just to be fair,' he said.

Looking baffled at what her job had been reduced to, the woman took the coin from Ravin. Her only incentive to toss it was to get rid of them as soon as possible.

'Heads I win, tails you win,' Amardeep announced.

'No, no, no ...' Ravin interrupted and proposed the reverse.

'I knew you would fight over this as well.' Amardeep chuckled and agreed.

The woman flipped the coin. It went two feet above her hand, fell on the desk, spun for a while and then gradually slowed down before falling flat.

'Tails!' Amardeep looked at the result and burst into a laugh! 'I win! I win!' he shouted.

'What?' Ravin shouted. Shifting his serious gaze to the woman, he said, 'Aren't we doing best of three?'

10

Paris, London, Madrid Airports and Yaar Anmulle

It was a bright, sunny morning in Paris. The four friends were now geographically closer to each other than they had been eight hours ago. There was still some time left before they would all be in one place.

Amardeep and Ravin had arrived in Paris. They were starving and had ordered some breakfast at a café in the airport lounge. While awaiting their tea, eggs and sandwiches, they connected their phones to the airport WiFi and let their families back home know about their status. They also sent updates on *Yaar Anmulle* and asked about Manpreet and Harprit's progress.

Amardeep was still hung-over from the war movie he had watched on the flight.

'Delta calling Charlie. Delta calling Alpha. Over,' he wrote, and waited for some response. A minute or two passed and there was none.

He wrote again. 'Team Delta has arrived in Paris. What's your status, Charlie and Alpha? Update with your positions immediately. Delta remains on standby. Over and out!'

Ravin looked at his phone, read the messages and shifted his gaze to Amardeep. '*Tu phir shuru ho gayaa* (You've started that again)?' he said, making a face.

Amardeep didn't say anything. His lips curved into a broad smile.

A short while ago, Manpreet had said goodbye to his wife and daughter at the Madrid Barajas airport, marking an end to the fun-filled week the family of three had spent in Spain. They had divided their time between Seville and Madrid, and it had been the countryside life of Seville that had charmed them more. To not return to the US as a family wasn't ideal, but Manpreet's wife knew what his friends meant to him.

In the heat of the moment, though, Manpreet had ended up saying to his wife, 'I wish I could go back home with you two.'

His wife had smiled and run a loving hand on his cheeks, saying, 'Darling, I might look gullible, but I am not. Go enjoy your trip with your friends. I will be waiting for you when you come back.'

Embarrassed, Manpreet chuckled and his wife laughed with him. He then kissed her and bent down to embrace his daughter, planting a kiss on her forehead.

'Mommy, isn't daddy coming with us?' the little one sang in her American accent.

'Daddy is going to go on a little trip to bring new toys for you. He will come home next week,' her mother responded.

'But I *have* toys at home. Daddy, please come with us,' she said, stretching her arms towards her father, her eyes wide.

'How about candies? They are the best in this part of the world. Do you want me to go and get them for you?' Manpreet asked her.

That made her contemplate. She realized that the proposition wasn't that bad either. Rolling her eyes, she got busy thinking and then in the end, said, 'I think I would like that, daddy.'

Manpreet and his wife chuckled as they listened to her. 'You would like that, my baby?' he repeated her words and gave her another peck.

A minute later, he watched the two ladies walk towards the security check. After waving them a final goodbye, he turned back and moved towards the terminal from where he was to take the flight to Prague.

Around the same time, in the duty-free section of Heathrow airport, clad in a loose t-shirt, smart shorts and white sneakers, Harprit roamed like a nomad from one counter to another. The cap on his head and the sling bag around his torso completed his look of a seasoned tourist. He was on a well-negotiated marital mission – to shop for his wife. Simply put, she had passed on to him a list of branded items that he needed to pick up.

Not that his wife had laid down any conditions, and Harprit could have easily travelled without having to do any of this. However, carried away in the euphoria of going on a reunion trip with his friends, he had joyfully declared to his wife in Shakespearean English, 'I must, on my return, bring for thee, my darling wife, whatever thou wants.'

Now here he was, doing the rounds of the duty-free sections. Never one to put off tasks he didn't like, he had decided to get it over with at the beginning of his journey. Get over with tasks you don't enjoy but must do as soon as possible, he would always say.

Besides, he was a big fan of simplicity. Keep things simple, was the other thing he would often say. He avoided making decisions as much as possible. So, when his wife had been dictating her list to him, and was in the middle of saying '... a beautiful watch, a nice perfume ...' he had interrupted. 'Stop ... stop ... stop. All this is subjective. Be objective,' he'd said.

'What is subjective?' his wife had asked.

'The adjectives you are using – beautiful and nice.'

She'd laughed and then said she wanted him to get what he thought was good. 'I would love it if you choose them for me na,' she'd explained.

'But my happiness is in ensuring you get things as per your taste,' Harprit had responded, his lips curving into a smile. *Oh no, dear wife, I won't let you outsource decision-making to me so that you can hold me accountable if you don't like it,* he'd thought.

So his wife had nodded, smiled and lovingly pulled his cheek. 'I will certainly help you, if you want me to.' *Even better, now I can get exactly what I want*, she'd thought.

Just like Harprit had asked, his wife had picked the products online and sent him screenshots on his phone before he left the house. This allowed Harprit to simply walk down to the duty-free shops and hand over his phone to the salespersons. A cakewalk!

'Do you have this?' he'd ask.

'Yes, we do.'

'I will buy it.'

'Sir, do you want to see more options? Perhaps you'd like to try it ...'

'No,' came the answer, firm and clear.

Chapter closed.

He was a customer any salesperson would pull out the red carpet for. They'd welcome him with garlands and agarbatti. A man who spent almost no time browsing, and definitely made a purchase? A dream come true.

Luckily, Harprit managed to find everything his wife wanted. And though expensive, most of these items – cosmetics, jewellery, perfumes – weren't going to take up a lot of space in his luggage. He could easily carry the lot in his cabin baggage, which was half empty to begin with.

His work over, Harprit plugged the earphones into his ears, bought himself a coffee and finally walked towards the departure gate of his flight. The boarding would begin soon.

Just as he relaxed into his chair, a message on *Yaar Anmulle* summoned his attention. Amardeep had asked for an update, albeit in a strange way. Why was he speaking like an army man? Anyway, Harprit typed out a reply.

'Delta this is Charlie. Heathrow airport perimeter secured. Over.'

In Paris, Amardeep looked at the screen of his phone and smiled. *Good on Harprit for playing along.*

Gratified, he wrote back, 'Welcome aboard, Charlie. Unit Delta to arrive in Prague at 1200 hours. Update with your ETA. Over.'

'1330 hours. Over.'

'All right, Charlie. Over and Out.'

Cheap thrills over, Harprit addressed a message to Ravin, this time sans army talk.

'*Rinku veer, ki ho gayaa apne veer nu* (Rinku, what has happened to our brother)?' he wrote.

'*Saale ne koi world war movie dekh li hai flight vich. Bus odaa hi bhoot savaar hai* (This arsehole has watched a world war movie on the flight. Now, he is fancying himself as one of its characters).'

Harprit first sent a few ROFL emojis and then typed, 'Don't tell me, Rinku, that you agreed to let Raam travel in business class?'

'I had to. This bugger won the toss. And you all know I am a man of my word,' Ravin replied.

Suddenly, their phones pinged with a message from Manpreet, who had finally cleared security and could reply to the texts.

'Alpha coming in. Alpha coming in from Madrid.'

'Oye MP! All good?' Ravin felt a thrill. The trip was finally happening. They were all on their way! The chat on the group felt special, like a curtain raiser on all there was to come.

'All good, bhai. So you and Amardeep didn't sit next to each other on the flight?' Manpreet wrote.

'We did,' Amardeep wrote.

'What? How?' Harprit asked.

'Where there is a will there is a way. One of us gave up his seat for the sake of sitting with the other,' Ravin replied.

'Oh, so Raam ji was generous enough to give up his business class seat to sit next to you? True friendship, yaar!' Manpreet wrote back and added a few laughing emojis.

'No!' Ravin replied. 'He made the person sitting next to him give up his seat, which I took.'

Harprit's mouth fell open and he let out a big laugh. The coffee he had just sipped erupted like a volcano from his mouth. Embarrassed, he looked here and there and when he found no one looking at him, he got back to the chat.

'Are you kidding me?' he wrote.

'Whatttttttttttt?' Manpreet messaged at the same time. His choice of emoji this time was a surprised face with its mouth open.

Nibbling their sandwiches and sipping tea, Ravin and Amardeep glanced at each other. Amardeep scanned the buffet of emojis available and wished the digital chat world would introduce the much-needed bhangra emoji to express thrilling joy.

Meanwhile, Ravin typed the next message. 'The guy sitting next to Amardeep was travelling solo. Amardeep coughed and sneezed and tried to make him believe that he was the cursed carrier of a super-contagious flu.'

'Lol,' wrote Manpreet. Then he added, 'So he freaked out and you guys used the opportunity to shift him ...'

'No ... let him finish,' Amardeep interjected.

Ravin resumed writing. 'That was the plan, but unfortunately it didn't work. The guy held on to his seat.'

'And what was plan B then?' Harprit messaged, curious.

Amardeep responded this time. 'The woman sitting next to Ravin was hot.'

Ravin added further, 'So, Raam ji, unable to scare away the man, instead sold him hope.'

'Which the man paid for with his business class seat?' Manpreet wrote back.

Amardeep only sent a shamelessly smiling emoji in return as an acknowledgement.

11

Prague, Czech Republic

The Delta unit was the first to arrive in Prague.

The airport was significantly less crowded than the one in Paris. Amardeep and Ravin got off the plane, used the washroom, connected to the airport WiFi and got busy on their phones. The next time they found time to talk to each other was when they got to the conveyor belt to collect their luggage.

Later, while Ravin got busy figuring out how to work the currency cards they had brought with them, Amardeep stood beside him. Inquisitively, he looked here and there studying the atmosphere around him.

'Here,' Ravin said, handing Amardeep his card.

Amardeep immediately balked and moved back. 'You keep it yaar, it's safe with you.' He knew that from setting up a new PIN to remembering it and then following more than half a dozen steps to withdraw cash with the card was too much trouble.

Ravin knew how much his friend hated learning curves. 'Oh! His majesty from Hyderabad cannot be bothered with such things, right?' he quipped.

Amardeep shamelessly smiled in return.

'*Bakwaas na kar* (Don't talk nonsense),' Ravin said firmly and slipped the currency card into his friend's shirt pocket before Amardeep could even realize what was happening.

The ATM was a few feet away from them. Ravin walked towards it. Amardeep followed him half-heartedly. At the machine, he pulled out his currency card and looked at it as if it were a liability instead of an asset. Turning to his friend, he tried his luck one more time.

'Rinku veer! How about if we first use up the cash on your card and then use mine?' he asked.

'How about we do it the other way round?' Ravin shot back.

'Sure! Here, go ahead,' Amardeep said immediately and put his card back in Ravin's hand, before turning around and walking away.

Frustrated about falling in the trap his friend had laid out, Ravin shouted, '*Kithe dafaa ho riha hain* (Where the hell are you going)?'

Without looking back, Amardeep pointed at the duty-free alcohol section and shouted his reply, 'To do more important things for our reunion!'

When it came to Amardeep, Ravin had long accepted his fate.

After withdrawing the necessary cash and safely putting both the currency cards back in his wallet, Ravin dropped a status update on *Yaar Anmulle*. There was still some time before Manpreet and Harprit would join them in Prague. As was decided earlier, Ravin and Amardeep would leave for the hotel and wait for their friends there.

Ravin walked up to the cash counter of the duty-free, where Amardeep stood holding two bottles of single malt. Ravin eyed his friend coldly, letting him know that he was displeased with the dirty trick played on him. The look was lost on Amardeep, who only smiled back blandly.

Pissed off, Ravin turned on his heel and walked away from the counter towards the airport exit, his luggage rolling behind him.

'Rinku veer! RINKU VEER!' Amardeep shouted after him.

Ravin stopped and turned around. Amardeep raised first his hands, which were holding the bottles, and then his eyebrows – twice.

'What?' Ravin shouted.

'Let's buy happiness!' Amardeep shouted back. By now, the other passengers were staring at them. The attention didn't bother him. His smile and twinkling eyes remained undaunted.

'So buy it,' Ravin responded.

'You have the money.'

'Oh, so what am I now – your personal treasurer?' Ravin shot back.

Amardeep thought of something and then shouted back. 'Does CFO sound like a better designation?'

Ravin fumed and turned back towards the exit.

'*Achha galti ho gai bhai. Sun ... sun ... abey sun na* (Okay, I made a mistake. Listen now, please)!' Amardeep shouted pleadingly, genuinely contrite.

Ravin turned again to look at him and said, icily, 'Apologize.'

'*Maaf kar de bhai* (Pardon me, brother),' Amardeep responded immediately.

'No. Say it as if you mean it. That too in English so that others get to understand. And stop laughing while apologizing.'

The duty-free salesperson had been witnessing the entire drama unfold in front of his eyes. *Gay lovers!* he told himself, smiling.

Arranging his features in a deeply apologetic expression, Amardeep obliged, and in a pampering tone and a gesture he would otherwise reserve for his wife, he said a heartfelt sorry.

Ravin was finally satisfied, his ego massaged sufficiently, and walked back to the counter.

'How much for these?' he asked the salesperson.

Amardeep looked at the notes in Ravin's hand.

'Bhai, I think you've made a mistake! These are not euros,' he said.

'Four hundred korunas,' said the shopkeeper at the same time.

'*Korunas*?' Amardeep repeated the currency name and looked at his friend for explanation.

Ravin first paid for the bottles, handed them to Amardeep, and then gestured for them to walk towards the exit.

On the way out, he explained, 'The local currency here is called Czech koruna.'

'But shouldn't it be euros, given that Czech is a part of the European Union and we got in here on a Schengen visa?'

'The euro is used here too, but it's not widely accepted. Koruna is the primary currency,' Ravin enlightened him.

As soon as the two stepped out of the rotating glass doors of the silent airport, the hustle-bustle of the Czech capital welcomed them. The city breeze on their faces felt refreshing.

They watched as several passengers greeted and hugged their loved ones. Cars full of happy, chatty people coursed past them. Their trip had finally begun! The day was bright and Prague's very air felt like it was infused with excitement.

'How are we going to the hotel now?' Amardeep asked.

'I hate your guts,' Ravin said impulsively.

'What?'

'I don't know. You tell *me* how we are supposed to go to the hotel.'

Amardeep looked at his friend with puppy eyes. Watching Ravin's grim face, he realized that this time his friend was serious. The next second, he looked over his shoulder and spotted something of their interest. He then said, 'All right, you think I don't do enough? Let me take it from here.'

His words surprised Ravin, who turned his head and followed Amardeep's line of vision. It was a public transport desk, a little distance away from them.

'Come,' Amardeep announced in style and began walking towards the desk.

Ravin followed him and simultaneously shouted, 'Dude, the cabs are on the other side!'

Baba Amardeep turned to his friend and delivered his sermon with a beatific smile on his face.

'Rinku veer, the entire point of being in a new country is to get to see it and experience it, and what better way than to do so by using public transport?'

Ravin was impressed. Amardeep's words actually made sense, and it seemed like he could finally stop babysitting him.

At the transport help desk, they spent a good fifteen minutes trying to understand the public transport system. The mode of communication was broken English. While the local language was Czech, Prague's popularity as a tourist destination meant that the local population had picked up a smattering of English. However, it would be a long while before they became fluent in it.

Once the two friends had understood the routes and prices, they quickly did the maths and plotted the P&L sheet in their heads. The desis then agreed to take a three-day public transport card, which covered all three modes of public transport in the city – buses, trams and metro, which was called the subway here.

The next bus to leave for the city was already waiting at the airport. They quickly got on it and found seats for themselves and space for their luggage. Once settled, they looked at the public transport map they had taken from the counter.

The Czech names on the map were mostly in Latin script and some other graphic symbols. To the two men, they might as well have been a language from another planet. The person at the counter had already helped them by circling on the map their final destination and the bus stop where they had to get down in order to take the tram. They were now left with the business of connecting the dots and understanding the map, also to facilitate the rest of their time in the city.

In order to get to their destination, they had to refer to two different maps, one meant for the city geography and the other for the public transport to chalk out their way ahead.

At one point of time, when they were in doubt, they consulted a gentleman on their bus. The two were happy to know that he could converse fluently in English. After a careful glance at their map, he nodded a yes and helped them with info on which other trams they could take, should they miss the one they wanted to hop on to.

'They all go in the same direction.' He flipped the map and showed them a column that had all the public transport numbers and colour-coded routes.

'Oh wonderful! Wonderful!' Amardeep's voice was strangely accented as he nodded his head in acknowledgement.

'*Tere acent nu ki ho gaya* (What's wrong with your accent, dude)?' chuckled Ravin.

'*Oh yaar, goreyaan naal gal kar ke ho jaanda hai* (Happens to me while conversing with foreigners),' Amardeep said.

Gradually, the bus left the suburbs behind and entered the city. They noticed the vast patches of land making way for commercial and residential blocks. The place around them was green and picturesque to look at. They enjoyed noticing people who got on the bus at various stops. Native women, particularly, caught their interest.

They heard people around them talk in an unfamiliar language and safely assumed it was Czech. Before the arrival of every subsequent stop, the announcements in the bus were also in a similar sounding language. Even though the moving LED marquee in the bus displayed the names of the bus stops, the audio announcement helped them to understand the correct pronunciation of the name. Like kids in school, the two recited the same name twice to get a grasp of it.

The transition from the bus to the tram was not as difficult as they had feared. Besides, there were some passengers at the tram station who confirmed that the two men were on the right track. A twenty-minute run brought them to the stop nearest to their hotel and they disembarked.

The hotel was little more than a five-minute walk down the third parallel street to the one they were on, but there was one confusion.

'Third parallel street on our left or right?' asked Ravin.

'Good question,' Amardeep said and immersed himself in the map he held in his hands.

A couple of seconds later, he pointed on the city geography map and said, 'See, we are here.' And then moving his finger, he added, 'And we need to go there.'

'Well, that's fine, but ...' Ravin stopped midway and then thoughtfully murmured, 'without the knowledge of direction in the physical world, how do we make out if that street is on our right or left?'

'Hmm ...' Amardeep pulled his lower lip with his thumb and forefinger. There were no pedestrians around them. It was a long street and they stood right in the middle of it.

'I can solve our problem!' Amardeep shouted suddenly.

'I can solve it too!' Ravin shouted back immediately.

(Sorry for the interruption, friends, but did you notice that? How intelligence often finds its egoistic reciprocation?)

'How?' asked Amardeep.

'See these east, west, north and south symbols on the map?' Ravin retorted.

'I do. So?'

'All we now need to do is find out where east, west, north and south are in the physical world.'

'And how will you do that?'

Ravin looked up at the sky, as if seeking divine intervention.

Amardeep laughed and asked, 'Looking for the sun? Check the time. It's noon. The sun at this point won't help you at all.' He chuckled and celebrated the win over Ravin.

'Hold on,' Ravin said, not letting the opportunity go. He quickly opened the compass app on his phone.

Amardeep folded his hands, smiled and stared at his friend.

Ten seconds later, Ravin let out a frustrated 'damn!' The stubborn little needle of the compass refused to settle.

'Aww, how will Vasco Da Gama find India now?' Amardeep mocked him.

'My compass needle seems to be drunk,' Ravin complained.

'*Sutt de phone nu apne* (Throw your damn phone away).'

'What's your idea?' Ravin asked his friend.

Amardeep, who by then had perched himself on the bench at the tram stop, said, 'First, concede that you have lost.'

'What?'

'You heard me.'

(Reunion trips! How they make grown-ups regress and behave as if they are still teenagers. I have watched these two quarrel like this for so many years, and it's still going on!)

Swallowing his pride, Ravin grimaced and said, 'Okay, I lose. Does that make you happy?'

'Very.' Amardeep smiled.

'Now, can you tell me what's your idea?'

'Very simple. One of us walks to the end of this street and checks the name of the adjacent street,' he said.

'Oh Eureka! Eureka!' Ravin said sarcastically. 'Dear Archimedes, in case you aren't aware, the point was to find a solution right here, without needing to walk,' he said.

'When did we decide that?' Amardeep protested.

'Wasn't it already evident?'

'Not to me.'

Two seconds of angry silence passed.

'Okay. And who is going to walk to the end of the street to check?' Ravin asked, breaking the deadlock.

'Dono bhai challengey na (Both of us brothers will do so),' Amardeep said.

'No! No! No! No! That's not going to happen.'

'Why?'

'Because we never decided on that either.'

'Oh all right. Keep an eye on my luggage while I go check,' Amardeep said, giving in.

Ravin's eyes followed Amardeep till the end of the street, from where he took a left turn and vanished behind the blocks. Ravin took his seat on the bench and waited. The street remained deserted.

More than five minutes passed and there was no sign of Amardeep. Then a sudden movement at the end of the street caught Ravin's attention. It was a motorbike. He leaned back again, stretched his legs and relaxed, waiting for Amardeep and wondering where he had gone.

Seconds later, he noticed something. The person driving the bike was a girl. But that wasn't what shocked him. It was the person behind the girl – Amardeep.

As the bike got closer, his friend tilted his turbaned head, raised his hands up in the air and moved his shoulders up and down, a broad smile on his face.

What the ...? Ravin thought to himself.

'Hi there!' The bike stopped next to the bench and the girl spoke first.

Ravin looked at Amardeep questioningly, and then back at the girl.

'Oh hi ... hi ... hi,' he fumbled.

Clad in high black leather boots and blue denims, the girl took her right leg off the footrest and put it on the ground.

'Your hotel is on the other end of the third street on this side,' she pointed to the right, taking off her helmet and revealing long and thick blonde hair. Her English was good, the best Ravin had heard since they had landed in Prague.

She pulled off her leather gloves and offered her hand for a shake. Ravin jumped to grab it.

'Oh great! Great!' Ravin continued to stammer, trying to understand. He looked back at Amardeep, who looked completely at ease, as if he got lifts from beautiful bike-riding women all the time.

'So we'll see you there? I'll drop his highness to the hotel on my bike,' she said.

'Oh sure ... wait ... what?' Ravin said, confused.

Not letting him finish, Amardeep quickly grabbed his handbag from Ravin's hands and said in Punjabi, '*Please mera luggage lenda aavin* (Please bring my luggage).'

'*Aa his highness da ki chakkar hai* (Why is she calling you his highness)?' Ravin gripped Amardeep's handbag tightly in his hands, not letting him take it.

'*Baad mein bataata hoon* (Will tell you later),' he said.

'Any problem, your highness?' the woman asked.

'Oh, he is just bothered about my safety. Let's race the accelerator, else he won't let me travel with you,' Amardeep said to the woman, trying to pull his handbag out of Ravin's grip with a tug.

'Awww ... such a caring attendant,' she said and twisted the accelerator.

'Attendant?' Ravin's jaw dropped.

In that split second, Amardeep managed to get his handbag out of Ravin's hands, and in no time, the bike picked up speed and raced away.

Ravin stood shouting at him, '*Bhenchod!*'

12

The Hotel in Prague

'What! You told her you are a prince?' Manpreet's voice was incredulous.

He had arrived in the hotel about fifteen minutes back. Earlier, on *Yaar Anmulle*, Ravin had sent detailed directions for getting to the hotel from the airport, including instructions on how to buy the three-day public transport pass. He knew Harprit and Manpreet would connect to the airport WiFi as soon as they landed.

However, Manpreet had a different plan.

What? Read endless messages just to reach the hotel? Chuck it, he had thought to himself at the exit of the airport and screamed, 'Taxi!'

Thirty minutes later, rolling his luggage behind him, he had entered their hotel room. Ravin and Amardeep had jumped up in order to greet him. The hugs were tight, the pats on the back were loud and the spirits were high. Manpreet's arrival had brought in a new wave to the bonhomie Amardeep and Ravin had been sharing for the past fifteen hours.

That's when the landline phone in their room had rung.

Ravin had taken the call. On the other side of the call, there was someone from the hotel staff. She had a request to make: Could they please not be so loud? The guests in the room next to their's had complained.

Ravin had immediately begged her pardon and promised to oblige.

The three had agreed to tone it down, but that didn't mean the celebrations needed to stop. Manpreet had pulled out the last available pint of beer from the mini-fridge for himself and joined his friends who were already holding their respective bottles. They had raised a toast, cheered and made themselves comfortable on the bed and couch next to it.

Someone had mentioned to check on Harprit's whereabouts. However, at the same time, somebody else had pointed out that they had run out of beer. All thoughts related to Harprit were unanimously dismissed in favour of making a call to room service.

Right after the call, Ravin had mentioned the trick Amardeep had played on him.

'Not *a* prince. *The* prince. *The* crown prince,' Amardeep clarified with immense pride and took a giant gulp of beer.

'And she believed you?' Manpreet was incredulous.

'His turban and beard made her believe him. She thought he was from an Indian royal family,' Ravin said.

'Lucky you. Had this been another place, she might have thought you were a Talibani or from ISIS,' Manpreet said ruefully. He had had such experiences in the US.

'After what he did to me, I wish she had thought of him as one of them only,' Ravin complained.

Manpreet chuckled and looked towards Amardeep to throw some light on what Ravin meant.

'Well, a prince is meant to travel with his servant,' Amardeep said.

'Oh! What! Hahaha!' Manpreet burst out into guffaws, and encouraged by it, Amardeep joined in. As Ravin watched the two having a good time at his expense, his brows furrowed.

'Wait! Didn't she ask you about why you were roaming the streets without a cavalcade?' Manpreet asked after he'd finally stopped laughing.

'I was lucky. She didn't,' he answered, amazed at himself at how easily the woman had believed him.

'And what would you have said if she *had* asked you that?' Ravin asked, curious.

'Hmm ... let me think.' Amardeep closed his eyes for a moment and then opened them. 'That I am a minimalist prince!'

'Bravo!' Manpreet clapped and then said, 'A minimalist pedestrian prince along with his servant. You two make a good story.'

'And I might have to write one to settle scores,' Ravin said, giving Amardeep an annoyed look.

'Talking of writing stories,' Manpreet added, changing the course of the discussion, 'Ravin, please could you turn off the author in you while giving instructions on how to reach from point A to B?'

Amardeep chuckled.

'What do you mean? It didn't help you?' Ravin asked, surprised.

'I didn't even read those chapters you had sent,' Manpreet said, throwing his hands up in the air.

'Chapters!' Amardeep repeated that word, laughing out loud.

'Shut up!' Ravin shouted at Amardeep first and then turned to Manpreet.

'How did you get here then?'

'I took a taxi.'

Just then, there was a knock on the door. Amardeep got out of the bed to answer it.

'Areyyyyyy Raam jiiiiii!' came a loud voice.

The last one in the gang had arrived. Once again, the Punjabis went berserk with their ritual of loud greetings.

(I've observed so many friends. But then, when it comes to Punjabi friends, you see, this breed of human civilization doesn't know how to contain the joy. They have to release it as soon as possible, as loudly as possible. It's as if it is their moral obligation to let the world around them know that they are happy. They can't be privately happy. It has to be announced in the public domain.)

As they were still cheering and whooping, the landline phone in their room rang. The noise suddenly died down. Ravin stretched his arm and pressed the speaker button. It was the lady at the reception, and in her beautiful voice, she proceeded to utter some not-so-beautiful words.

'Sorry sir, but I am going to ask you again to do something you don't like to do, only this time you *will* have to do it.'

'WHICH IS?' Harprit shouted.

'Please don't be loud.'

'Oh sorry!' he apologized and then lowered his voice and repeated his words, 'Which is?'

The others in the room laughed at that. Amardeep explained, 'Dude, she is referring to us being loud in the room.'

'Oh!' Harprit exclaimed, embarrassed.

'Thank God!' said the receptionist.

'We promise to keep it down, ma'am,' Ravin said in a voice that was assuring enough for the lady.

'I hope you mean it this time,' she said before hanging up.

There were two rooms booked in Ravin's name. Each had a king-size bed in it. However, no one bothered to open the second room as it wasn't needed till night fell. They wanted to spend as much time with each other as they could. After all, it had been many years since the four of them had hung out together under one roof.

By four in the afternoon, the boys realized that they were starving. The weather was pleasant and they decided against ordering room service, choosing instead to step out of the hotel.

They looked up the nearby restaurants on Google Maps. The hotel being centrally located, they were close to a lot of highly rated eateries.

Harprit and Amardeep wanted to eat something European, try the local cuisine. However, for the sake of friendship, they found themselves heading towards an Indian restaurant. Manpreet had literally begged for it.

'*Bhai, chhe dino se pasta, pizza aur croissant kha kha ke tatti band ho gai hai. Kuch desi khilwa do, please* (Brothers, six days of eating pizza, pasta and croissants has led to constipation. Let's eat Indian, please)!' Manpreet said, describing the food he had eaten in Spain.

'Thanks for the warning, MP,' Ravin said drily.

And on that note, the conversation then shifted to first figuring out who'd share the room with Manpreet, before an Indian restaurant could be picked.

Everyone got worked up, and the noise increased as each one of the men argued his point.

'Raam ji could share the room with me,' Manpreet said.

Ravin and Harprit looked at Amardeep, who then responded. 'Yeah, I am charming, but not an idiot.'

'How rude!' Ravin immediately grabbed the opportunity to pin him down.

Harprit, who knew that this was the perfect time to get rid of any possibility of sharing the room with Manpreet, pitched in.

'How insensitive,' he said, barely able to hold back his laugh.

'Nice try, you two!' Amardeep mischievously responded to both Ravin and Harprit.

Harprit put an arm over Amardeep's shoulder and said, 'You don't have any sentiments for a guy who shared your hostel room for four years? How many constipations and loose motions have we survived together?'

Everyone giggled. Amardeep shoved Harprit's hand off him.

'I am against sentiments,' Amardeep said, and then asked, 'but if you care for him as much as you say, what stops you from sharing the room with him?'

'I would have. He wants you instead.'

Amardeep playfully shifted his gaze to Manpreet and asked, 'Are you okay with him?'

Harprit crossed his fingers.

'I don't care,' Manpreet said and laughed. It wasn't his worry. He could have had an entire room for himself.

'I don't care that you don't care!' Harprit shouted, sensing that he was seconds away from becoming the victim.

Amardeep first laughed out loud and then said, 'Have some sympathy for the brother you are going to share your room with.'

'Absolutely,' Ravin immediately said. Sensing the shift in the direction of the wind, he had changed his stance and now teamed up with Amardeep.

Harprit looked at him in disbelief and then at Amardeep. 'Says the guy who doesn't have sentiments.'

'I am against having sentiments, not using them in my favour.'

On that note Manpreet and then Ravin hi-fived with Amardeep. The cat for the night was belled. 'Hurray!' the three loudly celebrated arriving at a decision.

'Good, then you will share the room with him.' Ravin announced in a final and firm way, and jumped out of the bed.

Just then the landline phone rang. They all looked at each other and ran out of the room.

The food was delicious. Manpreet was the happiest of all. The visuals of hot tandoori roti making its way on to his plate and the aroma of chicken gravy were the foreplay he enjoyed before he went for the real thing – eating the first bite.

'How is it?' Amardeep asked.

'Orgasmic,' Manpreet answered, his eyes closed.

He ate as if he had not been fed for days. His friends were sympathetic. In fact, the food was so great that all four of them were happy to have discovered the restaurant.

The waiter serving them their late lunch turned out to be from Punjab. His name was Sartaj. He was very friendly and helpful. The jolly Punjabi in him could not hold back his interest when he discovered that the four men had come to Prague for an all-boys reunion.

He smiled at them shrewdly. 'I will tell you all the places where you can find ...' he stopped abruptly to read the reactions on their faces before continuing, '... happiness.'

His wink, which followed his words, was the final nail in the coffin. The four friends looked at each other and smiled.

'We don't need too much happiness though,' Harprit clarified.

'You may be happy, bhaaji, but what about your friends?' With that, he left to fetch them another round of rotis.

In between serving them food, he had left them with a lot of food for thought as well. As the boys ate, they couldn't resist talking about Sartaj's suggestions.

'Bhaaji, don't be shy,' Sartaj said as soon as he walked back to their table with a basket full of rotis. 'Shy people don't come to Prague and people who come to Prague don't remain shy.'

'Okay. Tell us,' Manpreet said, giving in.

Standing up straight with self-importance and puffing out his chest, the waiter gave them a big smile, and asked, 'What kind of fun do you want to have here?'

'Well, what's on the menu?' Ravin countered, smiling back.

13

The Hotel, Prague, Evening

The sun had finally set. A pleasant evening, with the promise of a very exciting first night of their belated bachelor party, was making its way towards the boys, who had settled well in their respective rooms. Harprit was left with no choice but to share the room with Manpreet. Fortunately Manpreet had finally made it to the loo after their lunch. The Indian food, followed by a cup of hot tea in the evening, had helped him.

As per their initial plan, they were supposed to step out at night and get a taste of Prague's nightlife. They didn't want to indulge in anything more than a light dinner. The rest of the night was supposed to be reserved for window-shopping. However, their travel-weary bodies demanded rest. Against all of their wishes, including his own, Amardeep made a suggestion.

'How about we skip stepping out tonight?' he said. He held up the bottle of single malt he had bought from duty-free in his hand.

The promise of their hotel beds lingered, and the boys looked at each other. Amardeep's suggestion was met with silent but unanimous acceptance.

'All right, it's going to be a long night ahead,' Harprit said, jumping out of his bed to fetch four glasses from the cupboard next to the fridge.

Manpreet picked up the room service menu from the bedside table and looked through it. Everything on it appeared too bland to go with the drinks. That's when Sartaj's name popped back into their conversation.

Earlier, in the afternoon, the waiter at the Indian restaurant had gone beyond his call of duty and offered them free delivery, should they want to order something to their hotel. Manpreet recalled his words and pulled out the restaurant's home delivery menu from the back pocket of his jeans which he'd thrown on the couch. Sartaj had handed the same to him right after they had paid the bill along with a generous tip.

The boys decided that instead of a full-fledged dinner, they'd order a number of snacks to go with their drinks.

'*Oye hoye hoye hoye! Yaar suno meri gall,*' Harprit said delightedly while going through the menu. 'Guys, I propose that we order everything. What do you say?'

Manpreet chuckled, looked at Ravin and said, 'He hasn't changed. Has he?'

Smilingly, Ravin shifted his eyes from Manpreet to Harprit.

(I must pause here, friends, to tell you a little about this side of Harprit. Here's the thing about this guy. Like a Ferrari,

his excitement levels go from zero to hundred in no time. And when he is excited, he hates any kind of decision-making. In that moment, he just wants everything. Thank God he has friends to bring him down from hundred.)

'Order everything?' Ravin said, looking at Harprit. 'That's a bold statement,' he added, and snatched the menu from Harprit's hand.

Sartaj's number was dialled from the room telephone. Fish tikka, tandoori murg and seekh kebab were ordered. To go along with them were freshly cut red onions and mint chutney. Sartaj promised delivery within thirty minutes.

However, no one was willing to wait to start drinking till the food arrived. The guys decided to pour a peg each and take it slow till the snacks arrived. Meanwhile, the cashews and chips in the room would suffice. Clad in comfortable shorts and t-shirts, in the cocoon of each other's company, the boys began to unwind.

The wall-mounted lights in the room were turned off. Only the haze of LED lights from behind the false ceiling remained. It filled the entire room with a warm yellow glow and lifted everyone's mood. In contrast to the colourful abstract art of the wall behind the bed, the white bed sheets and cushions appeared more soothing than before. The LED screen on the wall facing the bed was tuned to a music channel. The sound was lowered and worked as soft background music.

'Cheers to our friendship,' they said together as four glasses with single malt in them went up in the air and clinked against each other.

(To tell you the truth, I was overjoyed to hear my name. 'Cheers!' I said to them in a muted voice. I sat there, with them in the corner of the room, watching them celebrate me.)

'Mmm ... smooth,' Harprit murmured, looking at the glass in his hand as the drink went down his throat.

'Indeed,' seconded Manpreet.

A couple of seconds of silence prevailed as they all sat back and enjoyed the feeling of being together. It had been a long while. The last time all four of them were together was at Manpreet's marriage. That was half a decade ago.

'How far we've come,' Harprit said thoughtfully.

Amardeep smiled and said, 'A long way.'

'Seriously, guys,' Ravin said. 'Back in 1999, in one of our hostel rooms, who would have thought that one day we would be sipping single malt in Europe?'

'And that too together,' Manpreet pointed out.

Stretching his arm for a few cashew nuts, Ravin went on. 'Remember the times when we used to take a bicycle on rent to avoid auto-rickshaws in order to save pennies?'

'Those were the days, Rinku veer.' Harprit patted Ravin's back in agreement.

(That's the thing, dear reader. Alcohol makes you time-travel to your humble past, and makes your present look like even more of an achievement. I call this state being nostalgically emotional about the present.)

'Back then, who would have thought that one day we would be able to make enough money to afford ourselves an international vacation?' Manpreet said.

'How could we? When we didn't even know if we would manage to find decent jobs,' Amardeep responded.

'Indeed, we have come a long way, guys,' Ravin said.

'We have!' they all declared almost in unison.

And with that began the walk down memory lane; a walk down those not-so-well-lit corridors of their hostel, where they had danced during the midnight birthday celebrations of friends, those washrooms they had queued up in front of, and those hostel rooms where they had learned more important lessons – lessons on life, something that was not taught in the classrooms of college.

The chill before taking the exams was revisited. Someone mentioned their first mass bunk during Diwali. And while recalling it, they tried to relive all that they had experienced back then – a sense of escape and adventure, a revolt against college authorities and the joy of going back to a place where they had come from and which they called home.

'I was brushing my teeth on the fourth floor when I saw the boys from the Punjab group jumping the hostel boundary wall on the back side. Each one of them was carrying luggage,' Ravin recalled.

'In half an hour's time the warden had informed the principal, who had ordered a lockdown,' Manpreet added.

'But before that could happen, the entire first year had escaped,' Ravin said.

'Seriously man, what a bunk that was. Unplanned, leaderless and yet seamlessly synchronized.'

'Exactly, it was a leaderless mass movement.'

The phone in the room rang and interrupted their sojourn in the past. Sartaj had arrived with the food delivery. Amardeep and Harprit walked down to the reception to collect it. This time, instead of paying a tip, Harprit invited Sartaj to join them for a drink. But since he was on duty and every table back in the restaurant was occupied, he excused himself. But before he left, he reminded them of the information he had shared with them earlier in the day.

'Don't forget to have fun,' he said.

Two minutes later, the room was infused with the aroma of tikkas and kebabs. Ravin rubbed his palms, looking at the mouth-watering delicacies placed right in front of him. Manpreet squeezed a lemon slice on the freshly sliced onion rings. The mint chutney was scooped out on a quarter plate. None of them could wait to have their first bite.

'Mmm ...'

'Wow!'

'What food, yaar!'

They moaned and momentarily closed their eyes as they savoured the taste, before washing it all down with the smooth malt.

As they sat back and relaxed, the conversation changed track from college nostalgia to the current reunion. It was time for them to decide how they were going to spend their belated bachelor party. For starters, Harprit reminded everyone of what Sartaj had told them.

'Rinku veer, what's the plan? What all are we going to do during our days here?' Manpreet asked Ravin.

Ravin answered, 'Depends on what all we agree upon doing. Sightseeing—'

He had only begun when Amardeep cut him off, 'Sightseeing? Have we come to Prague or Agra? Do men come to Prague for sightseeing? We are hairy, true-blooded alpha males and you want us to go sightseeing? What happened to all the wildness and adventure you kept talking about back in India? Isn't this our belated bachelor party? Looks like I'll have better adventures hanging out with Sartaj.'

Manpreet chuckled and patted Amardeep's back.

'Of course, all that too,' Ravin replied.

'Good, then let's put sightseeing on the back burner,' Harprit said. The rest of the boys readily agreed.

Ravin took a good look at their faces and after taking his time finally said, 'Fair enough, pals. Let's do it. Tell me, what sins do you want to commit?'

Ravin's last few words injected an infectious energy in them. A wave of eagerness pulsed through the room. There's something exciting about living on the edge. Contemplating crossing the boundaries and committing a sin.

'Sartaj has given us a lot of options,' Manpreet said.

'I doubt if I will be open to everything he said,' Amardeep said.

'*Bhai, parchiyaan pa linne haan* (Let's decide by picking chits)?' Harprit suggested.

'But are we up for everything he's pitched?' Ravin asked.

'Why kill the fun? Let's have it all on chits and worry about being open to it later?' Harprit said, looking at everyone.

They all agreed. Funny as it may sound, a waiter in an Indian restaurant in Prague had become their guide to the city. Or perhaps they were only trying to shoot their guns from over his shoulder.

So, there they were. Four grown and married men, drinking and writing down all kinds of guilty pleasures they wanted to have on their reunion on tiny pieces of paper. One after the other, they called out all the sins mankind could come up with. Each one raised several eyebrows and gave wicked smiles.

Ravin did the honours of making the chits. Mischievously, he wrote them in creative Hindi. Once they were done, they took a good look at the chits.

Unlike their initial expectations, seeing the words written and laid out in front of them led to a strange reaction. For some reason, guilt bloomed inside them. As if the chits were mirrors they were looking at themselves in, they felt sick. Those wicked smiles now made way for self-reflection. While the propensity for guilty pleasures was strong enough, reducing the purpose of the entire trip to only fulfilling them felt wrong.

'Guys, we are here for fun. But let's not make these,' Amardeep said, pointing to the chits, 'the only source of fun.'

'I agree,' Ravin said and went ahead to tear more paper chits.

'Let's include everything – adventure sports and discovering the city – on this list,' Harprit suggested.

Everyone nodded in agreement.

By the time the new lot of chits was made, the guilty pleasures were just a quarter of the complete list. In their minds that was the best way to have them on the cards and not feel that guilty. Leave it all to luck.

(Sorry to break the flow again, but I have to tell you this. At that point, I could see where this was going. Yeah! Introduce my friend Fate, that poor unsuspecting sitting duck, as a variable and put all the responsibility on it. You can see this, right? Suddenly, it will be Fate pushing them to do what they already wanted to do. People tend to believe what they want to believe.)

As agreed, Amardeep collected all the chits and Manpreet was assigned the task of picking one.

'May the force be with you,' Harprit said dramatically.

Manpreet took a deep breath, as if he was going to compete in a 100-metre sprint, and went for it. He picked up the first chit.

The gladiator nailed it in his first attempt.

He unfolded the chit and read the words: '*Natt-khatt kaam* (Notorious play).'

'O teri. What's this?' Harprit shouted, a bit confused.

Ravin winked and then tapped his nose twice with his forefinger. '*Natt-khatt kaam*,' he repeated, revealing it all. It meant the sin of lust.

Amardeep shifted his gaze on to Manpreet and said, '*O bete, ye kya nikal gayaa* (Oh boy, what have we landed up picking)!'

Looking at Ravin, Harprit asked, 'Is there any other chit that says "*Rangeen raatein*" as well?'

The others let out a big laugh.

Manpreet looked at Ravin, who smiled back with a wicked look in his eyes. Ravin rolled his tongue under his upper teeth and looked at his friends, one by one. The cat was out of the bag. They now had to deal with it.

It was tempting for them to see that even luck had favoured them. The words on the chit thrilled them, but also came with a hint of cold feet. Ever since the idea of this trip was pitched, several times in sheer excitement, they had dropped enough hints that would challenge the boundaries of their marital status, but had never clearly talked about it. But now they could no longer avoid having the discussion they'd been postponing ever since the inception of their trip. It was time to verify whether the trumpets would tout as per their plans at the beginning of the trip or if they would fizzle out tunelessly.

Excitement and discomfort sat together like embarrassed and reluctant classmates.

The sin of lust, written as an option and favoured by luck, now demanded an honest discussion.

'All right, guys!' Amardeep took the lead and in the light of all that Sartaj had pitched, he said, 'All four of us are here together. Prague is indeed wild and notorious. And certainly, we are here to have fun. So yeah, we should have fun, but not too much fun.'

'Differentiate between fun and too much fun,' Harprit demanded.

'You know what I mean,' Amardeep answered.

'Of course he does,' Ravin said.

'Guys!' Manpreet pitched in. 'On a serious note, we all know what we are talking about here. And I believe we all are on the same page. Correct me if I am wrong. This chit is too tempting, but then something within us bothers us as well.'

One after the other they nodded.

'That something is called a conscience,' Harprit enlightened everyone.

The men went on to hold a heart-to-heart conversation with each other. They spent a considerable amount of time discussing it, something they had never planned on. Together, they arrived at an understanding that they didn't want to misuse the freedom they had got. They agreed they wouldn't do anything that their conscience wouldn't allow them. They wanted to have the kind of fun that would not lead to any regrets later. That became their mantra – they would maintain a balance between their desires and their conscience.

'So, this doesn't mean we are going to pick another chit and let go of this. Remember, we *have to* execute what we have chosen. I suggest we cherish this fun with a pact I call don't-drop-your-pants,' a tipsy Ravin said.

'What does that mean?' Amardeep asked.

Manpreet, who by then had decoded Ravin's words, went ahead to explain. 'It means cater to the lust factor without dropping your pants. Isn't it?'

Laughter filled the room and Ravin nodded, smiling.

'Cool!' they all agreed.

'So, you can't have too much fun, but you can have everything around that too much fun?' Harprit paraphrased. He and Ravin high-fived.

Amardeep's brain as usual was slow in processing information. Innocently, he asked, 'What am I missing here?'

'*Abey kaddu! Matlab apni pant nahi utarne deni.* If someone gorgeous isn't wearing it *toh betaa taadd lo* (You are only responsible for holding on to your pants, but you can drool over the gorgeous ones who aren't wearing any),' Ravin explained in a manner Amardeep would understand better.

His brain connected the dots and it all now made sense to him. 'Aaaaahhhh ... I see.' His eyes twinkled and then a wicked smile appeared on his lips.

'You mean a strip show,' he sang, rolling his head in joy.

It didn't require any further confirmation. It was obvious enough. For the sake of clarity, Harprit raised a valid question, 'Anybody against the idea of visiting a strip club? Manpreet?'

'Are you kidding me?' Manpreet said and added, 'I only fear I may not want to come back from there.'

Amardeep laughed so hard that he spilled some whisky from his glass on himself.

'But there isn't anything new in it. I mean, this is something we've all done at least once. Of course, it was long ago, when we were all bachelors and had come abroad on our on-site trips. Isn't it?'

'Agreed,' Amardeep said. 'But we haven't witnessed it together.'

'Maybe we can get a private strip show. I assume so far all of us have only seen the one open to everyone.'

Everyone nodded in response.

Harprit responded to his first point. 'That can be an exclusive thing. If anything of that sort is available.'

'We will need to check on that,' Ravin said.

'Does private mean private for an individual? As in, I get my privacy?' Amardeep asked.

'Don't even think about it,' Ravin laughingly warned him.

'Why?'

'Because I don't trust that you or the others would then keep the pact we just agreed to.'

'And you will be happy to know I hold the same doubts about you.' Amardeep chuckled.

'I know,' Ravin readily agreed. 'Hence, private here means exclusive to the four of us and not just one individual.'

When they were done pulling each other's leg, they resorted to a meaningful discussion.

'On the internet, while looking for Prague, I had come across something that's really classy and sexy at the same time,' Ravin said.

The boys were all ears.

'There's this stylish and luxurious experience of being on a limousine strip tour,' Ravin said and paused.

'We are listening,' Manpreet said, his eyes on Ravin.

'It is Prague's style of bidding farewell to its *exclusive* visitors,' he paused again.

'Go on,' Harprit said impatiently.

Ravin smiled and continued, 'As part of the experience, we will be picked up from our hotel in a limousine and dropped at the airport. Along with us inside the car, there will be strippers. The deal is that you cannot touch them. Only they can touch you if they wish to.'

'Amazingggggggggg,' Manpreet sighed, imagining it all.

'Did you say strippers or stripper?' Amardeep got busy with the nitty-gritties.

'The one with an "s" at the end.'

'Can we have one for each of us?' That was Harprit.

'Mmmm ... guess we can. Will have to check to be sure.'

'Will eight people fit in?'

'The seats of this limousine aren't horizontal but arranged along the sides, facing each other.'

'What do you mean by that?' Manpreet demanded. He was still visualizing it.

'Okay. Imagine how the ambulance is from inside,' Ravin answered.

'You couldn't come up with an example better than an ambulance?' Harprit asked.

'I am sorry about that.' Ravin laughed.

'Continue,' Manpreet said.

Ravin looked at his face and smiled.

'We will have strippers in that limousine waiting for us.'

'Oh boy!' Amardeep sighed.

'There will be a private bar in the car for us.'

'*Oye hoye hoye hoye! Yaar suno meri gall!* Guys, I say let's go on this long drive every night we are here. What do you all say?' Harprit suggested in his typical excited tone.

Others ignored him and waited for Ravin to continue.

'And beyond the lap dances, they also entertain you with some adult games on the go.'

'O teri! What sort of adult games?' Manpreet asked.

'You will find out.'

14

Day 2, Prague

On a bright, laid-back Sunday morning, the boys awoke in their rooms. Harprit was the first to get up. The night before, Manpreet hadn't drawn the curtains on the window on his side. The morning sunrays that peeped into their room interrupted Harprit's sleep. However, he was too lazy to get up and draw the curtains himself. Instead, he kept murmuring and calling Manpreet's name, wanting him to do so, but the latter was in deep sleep. For Harprit's voice to make it to Manpreet's subconscious mind, it had to overcome the latter's loud snores, which was a challenge.

Harprit tossed and turned in his bed, at times covering his face with the bed sheet, but it didn't address the concern. Eventually, he was wide awake and failed to go back to sleep again. So he made his roommate get up as well.

A short while later, Manpreet, his mouth frothy with toothpaste and an electric brush dangling from his mouth, knocked at the door of the other room. He had to tap half a dozen times before Amardeep opened it, rubbing his drowsy eyes.

'*Uth gayaa* (Woken up)?' Amardeep asked, then walked back to his bed and fell on it without waiting for Manpreet to pull out his brush and answer.

'No, I am still sleeping,' Manpreet said sarcastically. His words went unheard.

Harprit had already freshened up by then. Following Manpreet, he too had come looking for his friends in the other room. Used glasses, the empty bottle of single malt on the floor and leftover snacks in the plates welcomed him. The air in their room reeked of alcohol and tikkas.

'Guys, fifteen minutes left for the breakfast counter to close,' he announced loudly as he opened the window to let in some fresh air.

Against the cacophonic backdrop of Harprit's loud persuasion and Manpreet's vociferous electric brush in action, the transition from sleep to reality for the other two humans in the room was slow and steady. Ravin got up and sat on his bed, barely able to keep his eyes open.

Amardeep, noticing that a sound like that of a runningmotor was emerging from Manpreet's toothpaste-frosted mouth, asked, '*Bhai, ye kya liya hua hai muh mein* (What's that baby pacifier you are sucking on)?'

Harprit burst into laughter. Unable to control his own chuckle, Manpreet ran into the washroom to spit and rinse. When he returned to the room, he brandished his hi-tech possession.

Looking at Harprit, Amardeep took a dig at Manpreet. '*Hostel mein daatoon kartaa tha ye*. (During hostel days, he used a twig as a toothbrush) Look at him now. American!'

The dental hygiene session had at least plucked the roommates out of their sleep. One final reminder from Harprit made them jump out of their beds. In a record two minutes, they had washed their faces and brushed their teeth and were now ready to wreak havoc at the breakfast table.

On the ground floor, next to the reception lobby, the breakfast counter was about to close. When the chef apprised them of its closing time, the boys switched to famine control mode.

'*Oye hoye, hoye, hoye! Yaar suno meri gall,*' said Harprit, looking at the buffet spread. Even before he could finish the sentence in his signature style, the rest of the boys jumped in and shouted, 'I say we take everything. What do you say, guys?'

Harprit looked back at them and grinned.

The boys literally picked up everything they saw in one go. By the time they all eventually sat together, their plates were laden with food. The table didn't even have space left for them to place their arms. Manpreet looked at all the food and wondered, 'What are we planning to do after eating all this?'

'Hibernate,' Amardeep said, picking his fork.

'Let's eat,' Harprit said.

It worked more like on-your-mark-get-set-go.

'We need to make space for the eggs we have ordered,' Amardeep said, eyeing the table groaning under plates of food.

'Eat fast then so they can clear some plates from the table,' Ravin said.

By afternoon, they were all ready to step out of the hotel and see the city. Amardeep let go off his turban for the rest of the trip. He instead wore his hair in a man bun at the nape of his neck. He looked cool and flaunted his hairline, which had remained unchanged ever since his childhood. Others in the gang, with their receding hairlines, envied him. The other sardar in the group, Manpreet switched between nice-looking caps and skullcaps for the sake of comfort. He had picked a red cap to match his t-shirt.

The chits they had drawn the night before had determined their activities in Prague. As per plan, they were to go shooting, see the beautiful city of Prague and, of course, experience a strip show in a luxurious limousine. They had wanted to do everything on the same day, but same-day bookings weren't available. When they came to know that every service they wanted to avail needed to be pre-booked a day before, they immediately booked the shooting spree for the subsequent day. Hence, day two in Prague by default became a sightseeing trip.

Numerous traveller reviews on various websites recommended the city centre and nearby places within walking distance to spend an entire day at. The place was also home to lots of restaurants with very generous star ratings. If there was one place they needed to visit in Prague to get a sense of the culture, it was this. The city centre was instantly zeroed in on, and the art museums and botanical parks, one of them with a zoo, among various other places, were safely dropped. At the hotel reception, they got the manager to help them understand how to reach the heart of the city using public transport. A few geographical locations and points of interest were then circled on the public transport map they had got the day before from the airport. And with that they were good to go.

They could have gone to the tram stop where Amardeep and Ravin had got off the previous day, but instead they chose to walk another half a mile in the opposite direction to take the metro. Their logic – in the limited time they had to spend in Prague, they wanted to discover newer parts of the city. Besides, this time they didn't have any luggage with them, and the day looked pleasant enough to enjoy a long walk in each other's company in a brand-new city.

They walked in the shade of tall trees at the periphery of a huge park, the lawns of which were full of kids playing and their parents either reading a book or arranging a meal. Many of them had got their pets along.

On the wide footpaths bordering the public parks, they saw some high school boys practising stunts on their skateboards. A bunch of girls, in crop tops and shorts, walked by them. They witnessed how the boys acknowledged the girls, but then the next second got back on to their skateboards.

'Noticed that?' Amardeep asked.

'What?' Manpreet asked.

Amardeep raised his chin, pointing ahead.

'Those girls?' Harprit verified.

'No, the boys,' Amardeep answered.

'What about them?'

'Noticed how they reacted to the girls? Or didn't react?'

It took a couple of seconds for what he meant to sink in.

Harprit smiled and then said, '*Matlab ghoor nahi rahe they India waalon ki tarah*. Right (You mean they didn't ogle the girls like most men in India would)?'

'Exactly.'

For a couple of seconds, they walked in silence while their minds were busy reflecting upon the behaviour pattern of Indian men, including themselves.

Harprit finally broke the silence.

'It's an interesting topic you brought up, Raam ji, and I have some thoughts about it. I am sure having lived in the US for a while now, MP too will agree with me.'

'What thoughts?' asked Ravin.

'On why Indian men ogle women,' Harprit answered.

'All Indian men?' Manpreet questioned.

'Of course not, but a majority of them.'

'Do you really think so?'

'Let's see. Those among us who have never stared at women in public, please raise your hand,' Harprit asked.

Everyone heard his words, but kept silent. They continued to walk and even after a while, none of the four men raised their hand. And with that honest confession, a deep dive into the subject of the male gaze began.

'Got my point?' Harprit said. The rest of them acknowledged his words with their silence.

'Is it only Indian men?' Manpreet asked.

'Certainly not, and frankly I think this is about men from developed countries vs. men from developing countries. I said India because as Indians we are bound to understand scenarios back home way better than in other developing countries. No?'

'Correction – you aren't Indian any more, Mr British passport holder,' Ravin taunted. Others, including Harprit himself, chuckled.

'My bad. As a person of Indian origin who was born and brought up in India, and spent thirty years there, I do have—'

Amardeep cut him in the middle to say, 'Come on, he is pulling your leg. You don't have to justify yourself. And let's not digress.'

They got back to the point they had been discussing.

'So, we sum it up as: all men stare; Indian men stare more. What do you say? This is in the context of India vs. the developed world,' Manpreet summarized.

The other men nodded thoughtfully.

As they reached the stairs that would take them underground, Manpreet said, 'To your previous question, Happy, yes, I would have stared at women, but then the point is that I would not have made those women uncomfortable.'

'How do you know that?' Ravin immediately questioned.

It took him a few seconds to defend himself. 'From their body language.'

'Good point, MP,' Amardeep spoke.

'Guys, this topic in itself is very subjective and sensitive. I agree with you, MP, that you or for that matter any of us would not have wanted to make the women we look at uncomfortable. But the question is what if, unknowingly, we landed up doing just that? The question also is if on some occasions, women would have perceived our gaze as lustful even if it was appreciative in nature. You see, it is a grey area, which is why we are discussing it,' Ravin explained.

'Now we are making a lot of sense,' Harprit said as he pulled out his public transport pass from his wallet.

'So what are your thoughts on this, Happy?' asked Amardeep.

'On what?'

'On why Indian men ogle more than those from the developed world?'

'Because we are a sexually repressive society. You see, when you are starving, you turn into an animal. When you are satisfied, you are human.'

On both platforms, two underground metros stood, ready to depart any second. On noticing the trains on either side, the guys quickly checked the direction they were supposed to go in. Once this was confirmed, they ran and slipped inside the carriage before the doors shut.

The train wasn't crowded, yet they preferred to stand. They were anyway supposed to get down four stations later. Standing in close proximity to each other, they picked up the conversation from where they had left it before.

It was Manpreet who carried discussion forward.

'I agree with you, Happy. To add to it, I also believe it is the lack of sex education. The combination of these two leads to curiosity. I think the lack of these two increases the sexual tension to disproportionate levels and without any proper guidance to understand and channelize this energy, it leads to animal-like instincts.'

The others nodded thoughtfully.

'Why only Indian men then? If it's about belonging to a sexually repressive society, why don't Indian women display the same behaviour? I mean, why only one gender?' Amardeep asked. Even though he felt he knew the answer, it made a good counter to discuss.

'What do you think, Rinku veer?' Harprit asked Ravin.

'Because back home, we are also a patriarchal society. Women have been controlled and told that they can't cross so many lines, lines that men are allowed to,' Ravin said, looking at Amardeep. 'In addition, I think that our skewed gender ratio too has a role to play. The imbalance drives this animal-like instinct. Top it with the historical trend of objectification of women in Bollywood.'

'But things are gradually changing, right?' Manpreet pointed out.

'Yes, they are. Which is why even women check out men these days.' Ravin laughed, as did the others. It worked like a breather from the intense discussion they had indulged in. 'However, checking out and ogling are two different things and, of course, again subjective in nature.' He quickly made a standard disclaimer lest anybody got it wrong.

They got off the metro at their station and followed the exit signs. Outside, it was bright and sunny. Interestingly, and to their joy, the ground all around them was wet. It had drizzled while they had been underground. Sun and shower had begun playing hide-and-seek. However, in that moment, the sky above them looked spotless. In the aftermath of rain, the world around them shone. The air was clear and pleasant. At a distance from them, in the direction they were to take, they heard sounds of cheer and music. The place was bustling with people. As they walked ahead, they witnessed the Sunday farmers and flea market in all its glory. It welcomed them, like it had welcomed hundreds of people who had arrived before them. And soon they became part of it.

The local street food vendors, the hawkers and street performers at every nook and corner of the roads flooded with pedestrians were a treat to their eyes. They passed a band playing music and stuntmen performing stunts. The high tempo melody of the band lifted their mood. Then there were artists who had painted their bodies and stood still, like statues. People stopped to click selfies with them.

Infused with excitement, the air in the city centre of Prague also carried with it a mouth-watering aroma. It was emerging from a corner shop on the street. A crowd hovered around its tiny entrance. Some of them were stepping out with something peculiar in their hands. From a distance it looked like a big hollow croissant, but it wasn't. A closer look made it seem as if half a dozen donuts had been fused and given one cylindrical shape. Curiosity got the better of them and the boys halted to enquire what exactly that dish was. When asked, the folks eating them told them that the dish was called Trdelník.

It took them a while to get the name right and pronounce it properly. By then they had already made up their minds to try one each. To add to their delight, a swarm of bees was hovering around the shop, drawn by the sweetness of the Trdelník.

'Let's try it, boys,' Harprit said and walked closer to the shop, finding space amidst the crowd gathered there.

The guys awaited their turn and noticed that a few old women, who must have been at least in their sixties, were running the shop. With their aprons, gloves and chef's caps, each looked like a baker. When their turn to place their order came, Harprit asked the old lady serving him more about the dish.

Cutting through the hum of that place, she spoke loudly to explain. 'Well, son, Trdelník is a sweet pastry. As you see …' she said, pointing at the woman behind her, who was making another lot of them, '… it is made from rolled dough that is wrapped around a stick, then grilled and topped with a sugar and walnut mix.' She looked back at Harprit with a generous smile.

Harpit noticed how when put on fire, the white dough changed to a rich crimson brown.

'It looks gorgeous. So, this is the local delicacy?' he asked.

'A lot of people think that the Trdelník is a local Prague delicacy. However, it didn't originate here. It is a traditional Slovak cake and sweet pastry, originally from the Hungarian-speaking part of Transylvania, Romania. It is also part of the culinary heritage of other European countries like Hungary, Austria and, of course, the Czech Republic.'

Harprit genuinely appreciated the insights the old lady had offered him. He thanked her while paying, and took four Trdelník in four different brown paper bags from her.

'It is very popular among tourists as a sweet pastry here though. Hope you relish it and have a good stay in Czech,' the lady wished him and moved on to cater to the next customer in line.

Meanwhile, Manpreet had found them all an empty space to sit.

The boys sat and opened their paper bags to pull out the sweet pastry. The whiff of it was mouth-watering. Amardeep held his Trdelník close to his nose and inhaled its aroma. He closed his eyes when he did so. Their first bite into that sumptuous dessert felt incredible.

'Hmmm ... mmmmm,' the moans of appreciation echoed as they looked at each other. And with that, the discussion they had parked while getting themselves the Trdelník resumed again.

'To your earlier point, MP, we all must also agree that not every gaze is bad. And in this new world where women are rightfully claiming equal rights, they too want to stare,' Ravin said.

'Indeed, if the guy is hot, women too would want to look at him. And it may not mean anything beyond that,' seconded Amardeep.

'It is natural,' Harprit said before taking another bite.

'And then there are cases where women love the idea of being looked at. There is a sense of vanity in being a head-turner.'

'Hmm ... Oh yeah,' Amardeep wiped his lips with a tissue and went on. 'This is interesting. So there are situations where women too enjoy being stared at, but then that depends on the kind of guy who is checking her out. That will determine whether she enjoys the attention or not.'

'See, this is exactly the grey area we are talking about.'

'Hold on! So you guys agree that there is a possibility that staring at a woman may also be proof for her that she is attractive?'

'Absolutely.'

'Doesn't this make the whole thing complicated now?'

'It is complicated which is why we are discussing it, isn't it?'

'So what is the verdict then? When is it okay to stare at a woman, and when is it not?'

'Well, the onus is on men. I think the man should observe the woman's body language. She will drop hints. If she doesn't like it, she will convey it without even speaking.'

'So ultimately it is about her liking and not the man's? What if I play the man's advocate and demand – is it fair to the man?'

'I know what you mean. But I would say yes, it is fair, because the woman is the one who is being looked at. She isn't an object but a living being. You aren't supposed to keep staring at her unless she welcomes your gaze.'

'Point.'

'But yes, how we pick those hints is again subjective.'

'True. The problem is there is no dearth of men who are idiot enough not to get that. And then there are many who will knowingly ignore it for in their heads they are a superior gender.'

'In fact, if the man is smart enough, this staring thing can be used as a powerful tactic to woo women. You know what I mean, if used judiciously by men.'

'That's a whole other tangent now.'

'Guys, can we now please summarize this thesis and move on?' Harprit attempted to bring the long discussion to an end. 'We have to see the rest of the city centre as well,' he suggested, cleaning his hands with the paper napkin.

'Oh yes!' Manpreet looked at his watch. 'We should get going now.'

'So, here is the bullet point summary to what we discussed. Men check out women, men from the not-so-developed world do it more.'

'It is natural to look at someone who is attractive. This behaviour is gender-neutral. Women too love to stare. It's just that they don't make it as obvious as men do. What else?'

'There is a good stare and a bad stare and one should be able to differentiate between the two.'

'Anything else?'

'Also, be watchful of the person you are looking at. Follow her or his body language for cues on whether or not he or she is liking it,' Amardeep summed up the last point.

They had all risen from their seats and were about to step back on the road when Ravin turned to Amardeep.

'"He"? Raam ji, drop the he. Have you ever come across a man who would mind a woman ogling him?'

'No, but he may mind another man ogling him. No?'

'Oh, I see what you are talking about now.'

'Guys! Let's keep something for another day. Move your asses now!' shouted Harprit, who was ahead of all of them.

They all picked up pace. Ravin said one last thing before ending the discussion. 'Quite a thing. Four men discussing how women should be looked at. Guess what we have missed so far in this conversation?'

'A woman's point of view,' Manpreet answered, smiling ruefully.

15

Day 3, Prague

The day of their 'adventures' had finally arrived. Daydreams of this day had infused them with an excitement that had no parallel. Of course, the reunion was the very foundation of all their joys, but then the added adventures were the icing on the cake. However, the thing with adventures is that they have a propensity of turning into misadventures.

(Wondering why I am talking about misadventures? Well! You see, hardly anything so far had gone as per the original plan for our four boys on this so-called belated bachelor party trip. Through many twists and turns and a lot of ifs and buts, they had managed to reach where they had. In the wake of what I am going to tell you now, you will realize that everything so far had just been mini-crises. In fact, what follows from here on is why I chose to tell you this story in the first place. Just wait for night to fall and you will see what I am talking about. Till then, sit tight and enjoy this day of their reunion trip.)

This morning was a mirror image of the previous one. Toothbrushes to pots to loading breakfast plates, all crammed in the small window between quarter to ten and ten.

While they were eating breakfast, the hotel manager came to check on how their stay had been so far.

'Wonderful,' Manpreet said. Out of the blue, he asked her if she was aware of the most happening clubs in the city.

'Ah, clubs,' she repeated. Her eyes grew bigger. The black in them rolled. She took her own sweet time to think over the question and then asked, 'Is that for the four of you?'

'Yeah,' Manpreet nodded.

She gave them two options, and then added one more. Seemingly happy to be able to help her clients, she smiled at them. Ravin and Amardeep, with their mouths full of scrambled eggs, returned her smile.

'Which one would you recommend?' Manpreet asked her.

Amardeep's and Ravin's eyes met and they silently spoke to each other – *Are we clubbing tonight? I don't know, man, when was this planned?*

'Oh! I have heard they are all good,' she answered and was about to leave when Manpreet said, 'Oh, I thought you had been to them.'

Harprit looked at Manpreet and then at his other two friends. He wondered if the other two were also thinking what he was thinking.

'Oh no. I am straight. You guys have a good day,' she said, smiled and then left.

Her words didn't sink in immeditaely. By the time they did, she was already gone. Meanwhile, Ravin had googled the name of the last club the manager had mentioned.

'Oh shit,' he first screamed, then laughed and then turned the screen of his phone towards the others.

'The most happening gay club in town,' he read.

Amardeep immediately held his hand on his mouth, not shamefully but to prevent throwing up the scrambled eggs.

'Oh bhenchod,' Harprit murmured and held his forehead in his palm.

'What did we do to make her think this?' Amardeep spoke.

'*Bhai, jo ek doosre ke kandhe pe haath rakh kar chalte hain na* (The way we subconsciously place our arms on each other's shoulders while walking) ...' suggested Ravin and let the sentence hang.

Harprit complained churlishly, 'You guys anyway touch too much. The amount we hug is unnatural. See where it has got us now!'

Amardeep and Manpreet looked at each other and shook their heads in disbelief.

'Guess what?' Ravin asked. 'Almost ten years ago when I had first come to Europe to work, the natives felt Indians were more modern than them.' He chuckled.

'What do you mean?' Amardeep asked.

'In the sense of accepting the LGBT community.'

They waited for Ravin to continue, and he did.

'A majority of Indian men would hang out together and so was the case with Indian women.'

'Ohhhhhhhh!' uttered Amardeep.

'In fact, it was normal for two Indian men to rent out a flat to reduce expenses. They could sleep in the same room as well, the way we are doing now.'

'And this was unusual from the perspective of the native population?' Amardeep asked.

'Exactly, because they felt these two humans belonging to the same gender were romantically involved and hence they shared the same space.'

'And guess what? Indians, on the contrary, felt that the Europeans were modern. They lived in with their partners,' he chuckled.

Certainly, things back home weren't the same as they had been ten years ago. However, the assumption of the grass being greener in the other country, both for Europeans and Indians, was an interesting aspect to consider.

Once they finished eating their breakfast and were on their way to their rooms, Harprit chose to join them later. When Ravin asked where he was heading, he said, 'To correct the perception of Miss Manager.'

Long after finishing their lunch that afternoon, the boys were staring at their first interface with adventure. On the outskirts of the city, a silent space concealed within it one of the deadliest sounds living beings can hear on this planet – gunfire.

Eyes wide and hearts beating hard with anticipation, they entered the room full of guns. It was a scene right out of a Hollywood action movie. Four differently worded but emotionally identical reactions emerged from their mouths.

'Shit!'

'Fuck!'

'Oh bhenchod!'

'*Bhains ki poonch!*'

'Hmm ... that's new. That last one,' pointing his chin at Amardeep, the instructor at the firing range commented. Tall and well-built, he wore tall boots, denims and a jacket.

It took the other men in the room some time to interpret him. They laughed when they got the joke. Impulsively, Amardeep asked him, 'So did you understand the other words?'

He smiled and said, 'A lot of Indians come here.'

The guys smiled back at him and then shifted their gaze to the lethal beauties that lay right in front of them.

'So what does that last phrase mean?' The instructor was curious.

'Nothing abusive actually. It means the tail of a buffalo,' Ravin responded.

The instructor kept looking at Ravin , waiting for him to go on.

Ravin realized that the man needed more explanation. He said, 'It's useful if you want to express shock without being abusive, you know?'

The instructor smiled and shook hands with Ravin.

'Can we hold the guns?' Manpreet asked.

'Well, there is no way you can shoot them without doing that,' the instructor said and picked one of the many guns that lay in front of him.

'*Oye hoye hoye hoye! Yaar suno meri gall.* Guys, I say let's fire them all today. What do you say?' an overjoyed Harprit cried and without waiting for a response, went ahead to pick one up.

Immediately, Ravin looked at the instructor and whispered, 'Ignore him. I'll explain later.'

The guys looked at each other and went ahead to choose a weapon each.

Harprit ran his hand over the length of the AK-47 before lifting it. His fingers felt the cold metal of the gun. His eyes admired its splendour. He circled his forefinger first in the trigger guard and then the trigger.

Amardeep lifted another one and initially struggled with being comfortable in holding it right. He was a good learner though and soon he adjusted. He then mischievously pointed the gun at Ravin. The latter too had picked up a different weapon and reciprocated the move.

While preparing everything that was needed for their shooting spree, the instructor looked at both Ravin and Amardeep and said, 'Yeah, you can do that as much as you want till the time I give you bullets.' Ignoring his words, Amardeep and Ravin continued to indulge in their role play.

When the instructor was done, he announced, 'When you boys are ready for some real action, come out to the shooting lanes.' Then he left without waiting for them.

Manpreet, who had chosen a long sniper rifle for himself, looked at Harprit, who was still busy running his fingers on the Kalashnikov.

'*Bhai, foreplay khatam ho gaya ho to bandook chalaa lein* (If your foreplay is over, shall we shoot)?' he shouted at him.

Harprit chose to ignore him and continued appreciating the weapon. Moments later, he felt its weight in his arms. It was heavier than he had anticipated. He turned back to see Ravin and Amardeep holding a combat shotgun and a semi-automatic pistol in their hands, mimicking an action sequence. The two looked vaguely funny, especially because they were making fake gunshot sounds from their mouth.

Harprit didn't miss his chance to taunt them. 'If your Diwali kid fight is over, shall we step out for some grown-up action?'

His words caught everyone's attention.

Outside the room, four out of the six firing lanes were marked open. It wasn't a completely indoor activity, the way they had seen in some movies. It was a semi-indoor and semi-outdoor set-up. In the countryside wilderness, with trees surrounding them, the makeshift ground in front of them was divided into lanes. While they stood in the shed, their targets were out in the open, against the canvas of heavy wood log blocks stacked over each other, which made a pretty solid and tall wall. Holding their guns and standing in the woods, they felt as if they were on a real hunt. That in itself boosted their testosterone levels.

The sunlight swept across the shooting lanes and lit the entire line of sight for the boys to look at their targets. From underneath the dark shed, they had a crystal-clear view to the other end of the lane. Their targets hung at the end of the lane – a canvas paper with a series of concentric circles. Every circle carried a different number in sequence from one to ten. The smaller the circle, the higher the value of the number.

Based on the rifles the boys had chosen, the instructor brought and placed different boxes of bullets on different shooting stations. He then handed them headphones to cover their ears while taking the shots.

Manpreet's eyes immediately went to the array of dazzlingly chiselled golden bullets. He ran his fingers over them.

'Look at them. These beauties can take lives. How ironic,' he said softly to himself.

'Wait for me!' the instructor shouted from the other end when he saw Manpreet taking a bullet out of the box.

His next instruction made it very clear that they weren't supposed to touch the bullets or the gun till he told them to.

'Are we clear?' he screamed out loud.

With his one statement, he showed them who was the boss.

Fascinated, Manpreet could not wait for the instructor to let him feel the bullets again in his hands.

The instructor at the shooting range called them all to one place and took a brief class. He taught them all they needed to learn in order to safely fire the weapons they had picked up.

In the next fifteen minutes, they learned to load bullets in their guns, to take the recoil of the shotgun, to remember to avoid touching the barrel of the guns, more so the AK-47, since after use, it gets hot enough to burn your skin, to empty the leftover cartridge shell after firing the rifle before reloading a new one. The instructor also showed them the correct stance while shooting, and gave other general safety instructions.

And then one last time the instructor screamed, 'The barrel of your gun will only point in one direction, your target. Under no circumstance will it point in any other direction. Am I clear?'

'Crystal,' Amardeep answered. He had recalled some scenes from one of his favourite movies. With that he had started feeling the protagonist in his veins. His friends smiled at each other, witnessing the arrival of Tom Cruise in their midst.

The four friends took their positions in their respective lanes.

'Let's do this, guys!' Ravin said. All four of them looked like ecstatic kids in a candy store.

The others echoed Ravin's words and wore their headphones. All four of them were going to take shots in a sequence. The first in line was the shotgun. When it was fired, the loud noise of it shook them for a few seconds. In spite of their headphones, it felt as if they had heard a tank firing at a target. The hum that it generated hit their chest. They could hear their own heartbeat, which the noise-cancelling headphones amplified for them. The boys looked at each other. They then looked at the target and then screamed with joy. They couldn't clearly hear each other but the joy on their face said it all. Harprit had punched a hole in the canvas in the first lane.

After that, there was no looking back. Each one of them took turns shooting at his own target. They competed with each other. Mocked each other when they missed and boasted to themselves every time they punched a new hole.

The variety of guns brought in diversity to their experience. In a round-robin manner they tried all four weapons they had picked. For every new gun, there was a brand-new canvas target. For every loud noise of a shotgun fire, there was a sophisticated sound of the rifle shot. The unloading and reloading too was a lot of fun, more so of the sniper rifle. The ritual gave them the feeling of being in a combat operation. They learned how taking a shot with a sniper rifle looked a lot easier in movies, but maintaining the right distance between the eye and overhead binoculars, keeping the other eye shut for that entire duration and concentrating while taking aim was a real challenge. And Manpreet loved this weapon more than the others, for its bullets were the longest and most glamorous of all.

Twenty minutes later, they were all through with it. The rounds of bullets kept on their stations had all been fired. The instructor stepped closer to them. With a pulley run string, he fetched their targets. The four pieces of canvas, with circles within circles, came flying towards them from the other end of the lane. He pulled them out of the clips and handed them to the respective shooters.

The boys quickly counted their scores. The sum total of the four rounds established a tie between Ravin and Harprit for the winner's position. But Manpreet and Amardeep chose to look at their scores from a different perspective. Even though their sum total wasn't great, they had scored 10/10 in two different rounds and horribly horrible in the other two. Anyway, the good thing was that they had something to cheer about. They left the place with their spirits high and a thrill they were going to cherish for a while. They had captured the memories of their first shooting spree in numerous stills and videos. They couldn't wait to post it online, the moment they were back in their hotel and got on to the WiFi. What holiday is ever complete without telling others, who aren't holidaying, that you are holidaying?

16

Day 3, Prague

On their way back to the city in the evening, they had tea at a café next to a filling station. Instead of walking down to the bus stop where they had got down earlier, they chose to walk to the next one. The weather was nice. The evening sun was pleasant, and they had ample time on their hands before their next adventure.

Amardeep's eyes fell on a telecom ad displayed in a 24/7 retail store. 'Let's buy a SIM card.'

'Why?' Manpreet asked.

Buying a local SIM card had never been part of their plan earlier. Before arriving in Europe, they had promised themselves that they would stay away from phones as much as possible. That's why they hadn't availed of international roaming on their phones. Limited connectivity was a thrill they had wanted to enjoy.

'I think we need one, after all. It'll make it easier for us to find things while on the go,' he explained.

'I agree with Raam ji. I think we are going to need it on our day long-drive to Croatia as well,' Ravin added.

Harprit seconded that and it was a done deal.

Once the SIM was bought, installed and topped up with cash, Amardeep opened the map app on his phone and punched in their next destination.

'*Rinku bhai, wahaan jaane ke bajaye limo yahaan hi na bula lein* (Instead of us going there, shouldn't we call the limo here)?' Amardeep asked when he saw that it was going to take them about an hour to reach their destination.

The usual limousine strip tour in Prague was meant to see off customers at the airport. However, the boys had planned to leave for Croatia in their car the next day. Therefore, they had customized their luxury strip tour to suit their plan.

'*Dus, Rinku veer. Possible hai* (Tell, Rinku, if this is possible)?' Harprit asked, sipping his tea.

'Sorry guys, we can't do so,' Ravin responded.

Because Ravin had booked the striptease services, he had become the unspoken in-charge of it now. Excited, the rest of the gang looked to him to resolve their doubts. Needless to say, many of these questions were ridiculous.

'*Achha*, tell me this. Will the strip show continue even if the limo has a flat tyre?' Amardeep asked and everyone but Ravin laughed.

'Don't jinx it, yaar, or we may be the ones replacing that flat tyre with the spare one,' Harprit said.

'Dude, look on the positive side. We will get to be in the august company of those strippers for longer then,' Manpreet pointed out.

Harprit placed his hand on Manpreet's shoulder and said, 'Bhai, if we enjoy it, we will stretch it by paying for another hour. We don't need a flat tyre for that.'

The boys finished their tea and snacks, but there was still enough time left on their hands. In order to reach their destination, they had to pass by city centre.

Manpreet suggested they get down at the city centre and walk from there. He had to shop for a few souvenirs. He had missed doing that the day before. On the way, Amardeep too decided to buy some local souvenir for his wife. Harprit protested, saying that while they had some time, it was not enough for shopping. Besides, shopping always took longer than anticipated, like a doctor's waiting room. More so when you were in a place you were not familiar with. Harprit argued against the plan, but gave up when Amardeep reasoned that with a working SIM card now, they were better equipped to be on time than before.

Indians and punctuality have only the most minor overlap. Indians and procrastination have a big one. Business in the developed world runs the other way round, and that holds true for strip shows as well.

The boys reached the club half an hour late. Thanks to Amardeep's newly procured SIM card with data service, he had decided to consult his wife while shopping. All his friends paid for that mistake. Now, they realized that they had to buy stuff for their wives as well, lest Amardeep's wife posted photos of the things her husband had bought for her. Hence, the phone changed hands and the respective wives were contacted.

(Who makes gorgeous ladies waiting to strip for them wait in order to buy souvenirs for your wives?

Well, some Indian men.)

So there they were, on the pavement in a dark quiet neighbourhood, outside the closed door of a three-floor building.

The place looked less like a commercial outfit and more like a residential building, with some cafés around. There were very few pedestrians on the road. Occasionally, a few cars passed them on the road and broke the silence that otherwise reigned over the area.

It took them a while to find the exact place where they were supposed to report. Hesitantly, they pressed the bell at the main entrance door facing the road. In the speakerphone installed next to the bell they heard a ring. A voice from the other end said, 'Hello'. It was a woman.

Manpreet attempted to talk to her. He told her of their purpose. She replied in her native language.

Manpreet explained that they didn't understand her language, and the conversation continued in broken English.

'Can you open the door please?' Manpreet said.

'No.'

'What? But why?'

'Appointment? Here? You?'

'Yes, yes, I made a booking.'

'Booking? Bhaatt booking?'

'Booking in the name of Ravin.'

'Ray-veen?'

'That's my friend's name. He made a booking. In that name.'

'You bhaantt sex?'

'No. No. Strippers.'

'Bhaatt?'

'*Teri bhen ki,*' Amardeep exclaimed in frustration.

'Go. Aaway.'

The boys held their heads in dismay.

'LISTEN.' This time Ravin spoke into the speakerphone loudly and slowly.

'Yeah, yeah,' the lady responded.

'I MADE A BOOKING. ONE LIMOUSINE. FOUR PEOPLE.'

'Oh ... oh ... oh!' shouted the lady.

Hope flitted across the faces of the boys. It turned out to be short-lived though.

'LIMOUSINE!' she said.

'YES, LIMOUSINE.'

'YEAH, YEAH, YEAH, LIMOUSINE.'

'*Abey aagey bhi kuch bolegi* (Will you say anything more)?' That was Harprit.

'Shut up and let me talk.' Ravin pushed his friend away lest he lose her attention.

'Limousine time eight-thirty. Now time nine-twelve. We close. BYE!' she said, and disconnected the call.

Left with no other mode of communication, they went to take a look at the website on which they had booked this service. After all, they had paid 700 Czech korunas as a token payment to book their slot. It turned out they were more than half an hour late. As per their booking they were supposed to report half an hour before their drive time. In that duration they were supposed to have their welcome drinks, cherry pick the strippers of their choice and then pay the rest of the money.

'What? They would have paraded the strippers in front of us and we would have picked four for ourselves?' Amardeep wailed.

The three of them looked at Ravin.

'Oh, so now I am responsible for this mess?'

'We were supposed to be here by eight. You didn't tell us,' Amardeep said.

'Oh! As if we made it by eight-thirty, the time I had given? Come on, you don't have the right to complain.'

Nobody uttered a word for a few seconds. Then Harprit yelled at Amardeep. 'It's because of this guy. He had to shop. And call his wife.'

'Oh, I was done with my work in fifteen minutes if not ten. But then all of you wanted to call your wives too!'

The boys fought, but it was all in vain anyway. They were too late, and they weren't going to get their money back either.

'If the limo drive was supposed to kick start at eight-thirty and end by nine-thirty, then technically we still have some twenty minutes left. No? Which self-respecting Indian will let go of getting his money's worth? We should rightfully demand at least those many minutes,' Manpreet said.

'*Bhaagte chor ki langotti sahi* (Something is better than nothing),' Harprit murmured.

They wanted to meet the representative of the company organizing this, but the lady wouldn't let them in. They made two more calls and each time, in her broken English, the woman assured them that there was no way they could get their money back.

'What is this arrangement of not meeting and talking over speaker-phones?' Harprit asked.

'I think this is just the like the Uber model. They take bookings and you report on time. See, the website also states, if you are late you lose the booking and there will be no refunds,' Manpreet guessed.

In such a scenario, they chose to do what anybody would have done. They pleaded.

It didn't change anything and only led to further disappointment, frustration and anger. The third time they tried, she threatened to call the cops if the guys didn't leave the premises.

Finally, the boys did what naturally occurred to them. They hurled abuses into the microphone and ran away.

17

Day 3, Prague

The four men ran to the other end of the street and stopping to catch their breath, they sat on the pavement. They had missed the bus. No, not the bus, the limousine. Literally! That too, one with strippers in it. This was a sin not worthy of forgiveness.

'What the hell!' Pissed, Manpreet punched his fist into the wall in front of him.

The entire fun for that night had gone out of the window.

'Blame it on our lack of punctuality,' Harprit said to nobody in particular. He pulled out the lighter and lit a cigarette. He wasn't a smoker per se, but when in vacation mode, he liked a fag or two.

'*Ho gai KLPD*,' Amardeep murmured.

Hearing that college-time lingo after so many years cheered Harprit despite his agony.

He shifted his eyes from Amardeep to Manpreet. The frustration on his face appeared to fade away as a momentary smile, induced by nostalgia of their college time, made its way there.

'K-L-P-D, quite literally. No?' Manpreet said and burst into a loud laugh. His belly shook more than his shoulders.

He then looked at Ravin, who too was chuckling. The exactness of the metaphor made the four friends laugh in the face of their misfortune.

'Guys, what do we do now?' Amardeep said once they had all regained their composure.

Harprit opened his sling bag and pulled out a hip flask. He opened its lid and took a sip. The bitter taste of alcohol made his eyes water.

'When did you get this?' Ravin asked, stretching his arm towards him.

'The leftover from one of the bottles in the hotel. I had brought it along, just in case we needed it.'

'Looks like we need it after all, to swallow our misadventure now,' Amardeep said and waited for Ravin to have a sip and pass the flask on to him.

Amardeep then borrowed the cigarette from Harprit and took a puff. He passed it on to Manpreet, but the latter shook his head.

'*Aatta batta* ...' he said and again everyone laughed.

It was one of the Punjabi slangs popular from their college days. It was invented to make someone do a task against his wish. It implied that as and when those words were uttered, people hearing them were supposed to do what they were asked to do. Else, some horrible misfortune would fall upon them.

'I don't smoke,' Manpreet said.

'Don't make it sound like I do,' Amardeep retorted. 'None of us do. But this is a ritual. Come on.'

Nobody bothered to ask how a whim had become a ritual. They simply participated without much debate. It was their way of grieving the loss of a limo full of half-naked girls.

They coughed and puffed and drank. Reunions and rituals. Adventures and misadventures. They were willing to live them all as long as they were together.

'Your *aatta batta* worked, Raam ji,' Harprit congratulated him.

Ravin murmured those words and tried to recall the other creative slangs they had come across in their hostel. As the alcohol began to reduce their emotional pain, they moved into the crass and creative territories of their college days.

'Remember that one – *Gaand mein gooh nahi* ...' Manpreet began.

'... *aur chale hain sooar ko nyauta dene?*' Ravin finished.

'Don't invite a pig unless you have shit in your ass.' Harprit chuckled, translating it in English and further said, 'I once said that to a Brit in London.'

'There was this condom one as well, remember – *Abey phateley condom ke nateeje* (You are a result of a punctured condom).' All of them laughed.

Going over the filth from their engineering days made them nostalgic. Sitting on the footpath, they recalled all the slang they had picked up during that time. Most of it was from their hostel canteen vendor, who unfortunately used to call his teenage staff abusive names. Having picked up the words from him, those poor children would have put the hostel boys to shame had there been a spelling-bee style competition of abuses.

After reliving the good old days of cuss words, the men turned back to their gloomy present.

'*Bhai log, ab karna kya hai* (What do we do now)?' someone finally asked the difficult question.

This called for a serious discussion and some drunken brainstorming.

'*Kyu bhai Rinku, Prague sirf bandook chalaane aaye they kya hum* (Had we come only to fire some gunshots)?' somebody said.

'Will we have to go back without hunting and feeding ourselves?' someone else whined.

The sips of neat alcohol in the backdrop of anguish and frustration were now making them feel lighter than before.

'We anyway weren't going to feed ourselves,' Ravin said.

'All right man! Not hunting and feeding, but at least some luxurious window shopping,' came the alcohol-soaked words of wisdom.

The feeling was mutual. What was gone was gone. They wouldn't be able to fix the past hours, but they certainly could plan the future ones.

Minutes later, the boys came to the conclusion that they wouldn't let the night pass just like that, without them doing nothing. After overcoming all the turmoil, they hadn't come to Prague to drink booze on some dark pavement. There were enough places in India to do that, had they wanted.

'Just because we made a loss on a past investment, doesn't mean we aren't going to invest again,' Manpreet said.

'That was an expense, not an investment,' Ravin responded.

'*Bhai, maje laane wala expense investment hota hai* (The expense that leads to happiness is actually an investment),' Amardeep announced and pulled his phone out of his pocket.

The lazy ass that he was, he gave it to Ravin and asked him to search other available options in town.

'This place is full of strippers and limousines, Rinku. *Zaraa search to kar, bhai,*' (Search a bit bro) he said.

Manpreet and Harprit were busy smoking. By then the one lit cigarette had multiplied to two. Having done thorough research in the recent past, Ravin had a fair idea of where to look for things. He browsed and dialled a few numbers. They ran into the same trouble that they had run into the day before – advance booking.

The city was bustling with clients. Women were in demand. Business was on a roll. In such a tense atmosphere, getting what they wanted at such short notice was not only difficult but expensive as well.

Ravin finally found a cheap deal. It wasn't a car tour strip show but a strip club with private group chambers. First, the boys weren't happy about it. But in their current state, something that was available dirt-cheap demanded attention. And fortunately, the map showed the place to be a five-minute-walk away.

'Where are we? In some red-light area of Prague?' Harprit asked, looking at Ravin.

'I don't know, man.'

Minutes later, merry and tipsy, they stood in the reception of the dazzling club with red and blue lights. They looked at each other's faces, painted in the colourful lights. Just then, some really hot women clad in sexy fluorescent lingerie passed by, holding the hands of what appeared to be their male clients.

The boys looked at them and then at each other. Their twinkling eyes and mischievous smiles reflected their thoughts. They were all on the same page – the page of desire.

Two men at the reception understood their requirements and led them to a dimly lit room.

'Please be seated,' one of them said, and before leaving the room, he added, 'I will be sending the girls, so you can choose the ones you want. Five hundred korunas per girl.'

So they'd get to choose their girls here too. The boys couldn't be happier.

'Holy moly. Are you guys ready for this buffet?' Ravin said, rubbing his hands in excitement.

'I am starving,' Amardeep reciprocated, with equal enthusiasm.

'But what's the catch here? Why are we getting it this cheap?' Harprit thoughtfully asked amid the euphoria.

'Catch? Well! We aren't getting a limousine,' Manpreet said.

'Screw the limousine. Five hundred korunas per girl is way cheaper than our previous deal. What are we missing?' he pressed.

'Dude! You don't ask questions when you are getting something cheap,' Manpreet said.

Harprit was still not convinced. Ravin, from all his previous research done so far, knew what Harprit meant. Manpreet and Amardeep were too overwhelmed to even enter that debate.

A knock on the door interrupted their talks. In a jiffy, the boys sat up straight, as if they were the ones about to be paraded. Lack of experience makes itself effortlessly visible.

'May we come in?' a female voice uttered on behalf of everyone.

Unprepared on who should speak on their behalf, all the boys jumped to answer at the same time.

An eager 'yes' popped out of their mouths. For the sake of differentiating himself from the crowd, Manpreet quickly added a 'please' at the end, but the momentary pause before it made things more awkward.

They were embarrassed of naively showcasing their desperation. But soon shamelessness overtook it. After all, what business did embarrassment have in this place?

The tick-tock of the heels the ladies wore disrupted the calmness of the dimly lit room. A chill crawled up the guys. And then the bomb dropped.

'Rinku veer,' murmured Manpreet.

Even before Manpreet could finish, Ravin said, '*Tu wahi soch raha hai jo mein soch raha hoon* (Are you thinking what I am thinking)?'

'Ah ... yes' whispered Amardeep.

'I told you there has got to be a catch,' Harprit said unhappily.

Five women had paraded themselves into the room. They all now stood in front of the men, who they thought perhaps would be their clients for an hour or so. But then, on what grounds would the men have availed their erotic services, when there wasn't an iota of eroticism in what they were looking at.

Obese to very obese women, dressed up in flashy lingerie, stood in front of them, awaiting their decision. The men didn't know how to react to that. It wasn't what they had anticipated before arriving there or observed at the reception counter. They couldn't believe their eyes. A momentary silence descended upon the room.

Manpreet was man enough to ask if they could switch on the lights. In the wake of the recent tragedy, the dim light in the room, which was meant to enhance their mood, was instead spoiling it.

One of the ladies walked towards the wall behind her and switched on the lights. Their jaws dropped when the lights came on. Not only were the women grossly overweight, they were virtually on the threshold of qualifying for old age homes. Worse, as soon as the light was switched on, they all smiled looking at the men seated in front of them.

Adjusting their undergarments, a few of them posed for the men. Two of them waved kisses at them. One of them shifted her weight from one leg to the other and turned around to showcase every inch of her figure.

The guys looked at them in horror, like poultry chickens would look at the butcher.

In sheer disbelief, Amardeep murmured to Harprit, 'Five hundred korunas for this? I think *they* should pay us to watch them naked.'

Some shocks are massive. It takes more than a joke to overcome them.

'*Bhai, batti bujhwa de please* (Can we please turn the lights off)?' Harprit begged Manpreet. His voice was so low and tone so hopeless that it seemed like they were attending a funeral.

When the lights were finally dimmed, the boys ran out of the room, straight to the very pavement they had been standing on some time back.

'So it happened again,' Ravin said in muted voice.

'What?' Harprit asked.

'KLPD.'

(Remember what I had said earlier? That this was going to be day of misadventures? Well, it's not over yet.)

18

Day 3, Prague

Amardeep hit the edge of the wall with his foot in disgust.

Frustrated by the way the night was unfolding, Ravin shook his head.

'I think we should go with that VIP option. The one that was most expensive and had pretty strippers,' Manpreet said, hitting an empty can on the footpath.

'*Yaar suno meri gall!* I say we order the best. What do you say, Raam ji?' Harprit said in his signature style.

Amardeep fished out his phone and held it to his right ear.

'What are you doing?' Ravin asked him inquisitively.

'Calling the VIP club ...' he replied.

Startled at the lightning speed with which Amardeep had abided by Harprit's words, Ravin shifted his eyes to look at Harprit. The latter smiled and shrugged. They all wanted what Amardeep did. They wanted it badly enough that no one disputed availing of one of the most expensive services in town.

Amardeep quickly closed the deal. He didn't have to do much but say yes to everything that was pitched. Once bitten, twice shy, he double-checked the profile of the girls they were going to get. The voice on the other end of the line reassured him that as per the terms, they had to pay in cash to the girls only after they had seen them. One final 'okay' and the call was disconnected. Amardeep then sent their location to the last-dialled number.

He looked up at the faces and said, 'A limousine loaded with wine and women is arriving right here.'

'What? In how much time?' Ravin asked.

'Twenty minutes.'

'What is this? Pizza delivery?'

Meanwhile, the boys looked up the nearest available ATM. They had to withdraw a substantial amount. Even after pooling all the cash they had in their pockets, it didn't come to half of what was needed.

After they made the transaction, the balance left on their multicurrency cards caught their attention.

Amardeep asked Ravin, '*Bhai, dekhna zaraa. India wapis jaane ke paise bache hain* (Do we have enough money left to go back to India)?'

The funny part was he was serious.

Their Croatia accommodation was already paid for. The return flights too were pre-booked. Their major spending henceforth was going to be on the rented car they were going to get the next morning and on food till they were in Europe.

Ravin nodded in response and they walked away from the ATM.

Amardeep's phone rang. This was the first time there was an incoming call on his local SIM. It felt strangely good to receive it. The purpose of Amardeep's investment was being fulfilled.

'Hello,' he said.

'Is that Mr Mar-Deep?'

'Not Mar. Amar. Amardeep.'

'All right, Mr Mar-Deep, I am Bruno.'

Amardeep covered his phone with one hand and turned to his friends, '*Bhai, kisi kuttey wale naam ke insaan ka phone hai* (Some guy with a dog-like name is on the call).'

'Yes, Bruno. And my name is Amardeep. A-mar-deep,' he said, getting back to the call.

Bruno didn't give a damn about the name. He repeated the line he had rehearsed and delivered for half a decade. 'A heaven full of angels will descend upon your house in the next ten minutes.'

Upon hearing those words, Amardeep let go of the pronunciation of his name. This time, his otherwise slow brain decoded things at lightning speed. It was the limousine driver.

'Guys, it's our limo driver,' he delightedly updated the others.

(What can I say, dear reader? There are men who are once bitten, twice shy. Then there are those who are ... well, idiots. They get excited at every opportunity, and forget about the previous disaster. Some call this behaviour never giving up hope.)

'Oh yeah, yeah.' Suddenly Amardeep's accent changed to match the driver's. Then recollecting Bruno's words, he clarified, 'Well, we are not in a house. This heaven of angels will have to descend on the road itself.'

'Hahaha!' Bruno's laugh was deafening. For a moment, Amardeep moved the phone away from his ear.

'All right, Mr Mar-deep. I have the location on map. I am bringing you the angels,' he said, and disconnected.

The limo arrived before time. At the sight of it, four hearts pumped harder than ever before. Finally, it was happening!

The driver's door opened. Bruno stepped out. He was an African with braided hair, very tall – a few inches over six feet and so well built he looked as if he should have been in the WWE ring instead of behind the wheel.

Bruno first confirmed whether he had brought the vehicle to the correct clients. Amardeep quickly acknowledged him before Bruno could mispronounce his name in front of his friends.

Once he confirmed their identities, Bruno smiled, showing white teeth in a dark face. He then winked and opened the back door of the car, giving the boys a glimpse of the world he had brought along with him.

Amardeep was the first in line. A heaven full of angels had indeed arrived. The driver's words echoed in his head as he looked inside the vehicle. Three heads behind him turned here and there, eyes wide open and mouths agape.

The boys bent down to take a good look at the sight inside. Four stunning ladies in lingerie waved them hello and blew kisses at them. Never ever in their lives so far had they received such a warm welcome.

The boys all waved back at them.

'Come in, boys,' one of the ladies said.

Amardeep immediately obliged. Concealing the excitement in their hearts, others followed him in.

Swathed in the dim blue-white light, the atmosphere inside the car was scintillating. The air smelled of the fruity cologne that the strippers wore. With a bar installed at one end and an LCD broadcasting soft porn at the other, the mood inside the limo was set just right. In between the two ends and facing each other, two long chestnut brown leather seats ran parallel along the length of the vehicle.

Overcoming their initial inhibitions, the boys looked at the women, who weren't even an arm's length away from them now. Clad in sexy bikinis, they possessed bodies that commanded a man's devotion.

Spellbound, the guys admired the sight. They wanted to forget everything and sink deeper into the ecstatic state they were in. In the laps of God's four most beautiful creations, the next hour looked very promising.

The fun began when one of the women slipped her ass close to Amardeep. She playfully ran her finger on the back of his hand and asked him where he was from.

The woman sitting next to Manpreet rested one hand on his lap before she possessively looked into his eyes and asked his name.

Harprit behaved as if he was the smarter one. Even before the stripper by his side could connect with him, he extended his hand for a handshake. 'I am Happy. How about you?'

'How interesting. I'm happy too,' she replied mischievously while taking his hand in hers.

Harprit laughed at that and waited for her to introduce herself.

'I am Gabriella from Ukraine,' she said with a smile.

'What do you do?' he asked her.

Three male heads turned to look at Harprit and wanted to disown him. Harprit bit his tongue for making such a stupid mistake, blaming his bubbling hormones. However, their jaws dropped when they heard her answer.

'I am doing my master's in economics,' she said, moving the gum in her mouth from left to right.

In the next couple of minutes that passed, the men learned a lot about the women they were with. These women were doing what they were doing out of sheer choice. It was a lot of easy money for them. And they had zero inhibitions in their minds. At the same time, they were studying, because they knew that the night business would eventually come to an end sooner than other businesses, as they grew older and their bodies aged. A decade from now, they would earn lesser money than what they were earning now. Younger girls would replace them, like they had replaced the older ones.

And on that insightful note, they came straight to the point.

'So you guys are ready for fun?'

'Absolutely!' Manpreet shouted and smiled.

'Oh really? But we were told that you guys didn't want too much fun.'

'No, we want all the fun.' Without getting her point, Amardeep quickly set the agenda straight.

Harprit looked at him and with his gaze made him understand what he had failed to realize on his own.

Meanwhile, Gabriella added, 'Then why do you guys just want to witness the show and not indulge in action?'

The boys had understood by then. The strippers were trying to make more money by offering things beyond the strip show, which the boys were certainly not looking for.

Amardeep, who had turned wiser than he had been fifteen seconds back, turned his head from Harprit to Ravin. He nodded as if he was the one who had caught on to the conspiracy. Just then the gorgeous hand of the lady sitting next to him cupped his chin and turned his face towards her.

'You don't want boom-boom?' she said while her hands made a gesture they understood well.

The men instantly burst into laughter, listening to this homemade synonym for sex.

The strippers looked kind of offended.

'Come on! I thought you guys were men enough,' Gabriella tried to provoke them.

This time Amadeep spoke on their behalf, safeguarding their pride. 'Well, ladies, with all due respect, let's just say we are in Prague to become boys again. We will be men enough once we go back to India.'

Manpreet felt like enveloping his ex-roommate in a tight embrace and holding him that way for a while.

Gabriella understood she wouldn't have her way. 'Well then, boys, show us the money and let this show begin.'

It is a business wherein hundred per cent of the payment is secured in advance. It felt awkward to hand over the cash even before availing of the services. They had anyway lost 700 korunas some three hours back.

'Can we pay afterwards?' Ravin asked.

'Sweet Jesus!' one of the ladies sighed.

High on their libidos, the men felt that invoking Jesus in that atmosphere was unnecessary and disrespectful.

'*Yaar, ye to nakhre dikha rahi hai. Apni koi izzat hai ke nahi* (Dude, she is throwing tantrums. Do we have any self-respect or not)?' Harprit said.

'*Haan, hum baddi izzat wale kaam karne aaye hain* (As if we are here to do something worthy of self-respect),' Ravin showed them the mirror.

'Let's give the cash, *na,* and get started,' Manpreet said, making a puppy face.

So they did.

As soon as the money was secured, Gabriella tapped twice on the partition dividing the driver's and the passengers' compartments. That was a signal for the driver, and the glittering alloy wheels finally rolled on the tarmac. With that rolled the good time for the boys.

The bar was opened. Wine glasses and two bottles of white wine were brought out from the freezer. Drinks were poured. The party had finally started. The party, which the guys had paid for and hosted for themselves.

The men were anyway somewhat drunk from before, and more so now on the visual treat in front of them. Yet, they delightedly accepted the glasses. After all, they had paid for them.

'Cheers!' Eight wine glasses went up in the air.

'Are we paying for their alcohol as well?' Manpreet asked Amardeep.

The latter elbowed him and asked him to shut up, but Manpreet kept looking at his friend for an explanation.

Finally Amardeep responded. 'Don't overthink now. We have already paid the money.'

Once you pay for something in advance, to derive pleasure from whatever you've paid for becomes your responsibility as well.

Chitchats got cosier over wine from Bordeaux. The women had the men's full attention. What else would they focus upon? As minutes passed, the guys stopped talking among themselves and turned to the women they were facing. The only issue was that of the language barrier. Only Gabriella was well versed in English. Others somehow managed in broken sentences and words.

However, this brought in the fun of using gestures and signs. It became the last resort for the guys when the easier English synonyms failed to make sense to the ladies. As part of the dumb charade they played, they often broke into laughter. The fun over their inability to make the other person understand what they meant broke the ice between them.

The ladies were very comfortable with touching their male clients as part of their interaction – something the men enjoyed. Someone placed her hand over somebody's hand while explaining something, while someone else tapped somebody else's shoulder while breaking into a laugh. By the time their wine glasses had emptied, the men too had begun to reciprocate the touch.

Intermittently, the men checked on each other to see what the others were up to. They smiled when they looked at each other. On rare occasions, they glanced at the LED screen wherein a boudoir photo shoot was in progress. When they looked back into the eyes of the woman in front of them, they smiled again.

The second round of wine was only meant for the guys, for the women were ready to do what they were supposed to do.

And then it all began.

At the click of the remote, the music in the car altered. The visuals on the LED changed to something that closely resembled the opening title and credits sequence of James Bond movies. Just that the one they were gazing at was way more erotic and intimate than that.

The fire and ice theme on the flat screen against the backdrop of seductive music lifted the mood. The ladies shifted and took different spots in the spacious vehicle. They did so in order to create space for themselves.

Certainly, they were experienced and knew their job quite well.

Then at once, on the first drop of the music beat, four gorgeous feminine bodies began to sway, all in sync. It was a sight to see. They caught the men by surprise.

Occasionally, a pair of mascara-tinted eyelashes came dangerously close to those of the men. And then in a split second pulled away from them. Every time the women did so, they left behind their sweet scent in the air the men inhaled. The physical distance the strippers created between their respective clients and themselves turned out to be hotter than their proximity to them for it promised a seductive return. The *tease* had begun; the *strip* was yet to.

The touch progressed from fingers to palms, from the forearms to the shoulders. Clutching the back of the men's necks in their palms, they squatted on the deck of the limousine.

'Oh boy!' uttered Manpreet, quite ecstatic.

Each woman used her man as a pole to dance against. That wasn't even the sexiest part – it was the way they looked into their man's eyes.

Adjusting their body weight on their squatted legs, the strippers moved their hand from the nape of the men's necks on to their faces. They rubbed their lips with their thumb and then the next second again pulled away from the guys, leaving them wanting more.

The boys began to space-travel. Their bodies felt lighter. Gravity was fast approaching zero.

At one point, the women held their hands on the chest of their men. Then all of a sudden, they pushed them back, making their backs rest against the leather of the seats. That's when they again distanced themselves from them. It was a signal for the men to relax and watch. And so they did.

This time those fingers ran on their own bodies; on to places of their man's interest. They began from the toe and after covering the entire seductive terrain, came to rest on their cleavages. Their teeth bit their lower lips and forefingers slipped inside their bras. They made multiple moves to pull the cups down. Every attempt revealed a little more than the last.

The men eyed the distance between the girls and them. They tried to lean forward, but were immediately pushed back. The strippers slid their bra straps down their shoulders. It was going to happen any time now.

The women unhooked their bras but held the edges. They paused for a quick second and then matching the rhythm of the music, at the drop of a loud beat, they let their bras fall on the deck of the limo. Just when this happened, they arched their backs and simultaneously rolled their hips in the air.

The strippers seductively played with their bodies. They held their breasts, rubbed them, squeezed them, pulled them, and lifted them only to release them with a bounce, which again was coordinated with the sudden drop of the music beat. Their bodies were sexy and even sexier were their facial expressions. Dangerously erotic!

The men wanted more. Their every attempt to touch the women's bodies was expertly thwarted. At times the ladies pushed them back, at times they grabbed their hands and crossed them against their own chests. Then they gave a peck on their cheeks and immediately distanced themselves again. At no point did they let the men touch their bodies. They were extremely good at theatrics. Their eyes, while being seductive, were also authoritative. They silently conveyed to the men that while they were the clients, the real people in charge of the situation were the strippers.

Moving their focus from top to bottom, they pulled the men closer. The men found that their one thigh was squeezed in between the two of the ladies. They rubbed their naked thighs against their covered one. And damn, the men felt good.

The background score changed and so did the visuals on the flat LED screen. The women seamlessly shifted their posture and began giving lap dances to the men, who sat back, relaxed and enjoyed. Cunning as the strippers were, even now they didn't let the men touch them even once, and yet at the same time kept asking them in a seductive voice, 'Is it good enough for you?' They had perfected some lines in English; it was part of their professional communication.

The hypocrisy in the act was playful. The guys didn't mind it though. They kept acknowledging them with polite 'yeah's.

Then once again, the women got up from their laps and got down on the deck of the car. They turned around and faced away from their clients. Cautiously creating enough vertical space for them, they arched their backs, giving a clear glimpse of their butt. They spanked their own butt and yet again asked their men. 'Is this okay for you?'

'More than okay,' Harprit responded enthusiastically. Other men smiled at that.

The strippers indulged in playing with their panties. They had all the time in the world to pull them down. They made the men wait for it. When they were done teasing them enough, they finally began to roll them down, but not all the way.

The girls took their sweet time before they sat down next to the men again. Then the next moment, over the edge of the seat, they stretched their legs in the air. And their hands rolled their panties down the length of their legs. They were left wearing nothing but their heels.

They got up, fully naked. Turning their backs towards the men, they arched their backs, their torso ran parallel to the roof of the car while their legs held firm on the deck. The stretched their bodies. Giving the men a full view of their voluptuous asses, they finally spread their legs apart and shook their booty in sync with the music. They bent down further and looked at them through the inverse V their legs had made.

As the music came to an end, they squatted, stylishly raised back their hips, turned towards their men, crawled up their legs and then sat in their lap.

They gave the men a peck on each cheek and thanked them for availing of their services. The music on their playlist died a natural death. The men applauded the wonderful show the women had put up.

'You guys liked it?' Gabriella asked.

'Loved it,' Ravin answered.

'Well, thank you sir,' she said. 'How about a wine break before we continue?' she suggested.

Manpreet's eyes twinkled the second he realized all the fun wasn't over yet. He silently looked into Ravin's eyes, who murmured back, '*Bhai, ek ghante ki baat hui hai. Abhi bees minute bache hain* (We were promised one hour of fun, bro. There are twenty more minutes to go).'

It indeed was the case. After pouring more wine in their glasses, Gabriella pulled out a strip of tablets from her bag. She took out four pills from it.

'Who wants these?' she screamed and waited for the men to get excited.

However, the men looked at the pills like a Chihuahua would look at a group of street dogs.

'What is this thing?' Manpreet asked.

'Mood relaxers,' one of the strippers said.

Worried if it was some conspiracy to drug them and run away with money that none of them anyway had, the men balked.

'Thank you, we are already ... you know ... pretty much relaxed,' Harprit said.

'Chill guys,' Gabriella said, reading their minds and dropping one pill in every wine glass. She then offered the same to the girls and said, 'She was pulling your leg. It's meant to be a precaution against a hangover. We need them in our business, you know. But you can try them.'

The boys sighed in relief as soon as they watched the girls sipping their wine.

'I will have one,' Ravin dared to say.

The girls sipped some more. And then the other men too came on board.

Not everyone can make you take party drug in the name of hangover pill. It needs a confidence of a different kind. Gabriella had it.

The music began again. The girls switched their attention from one man to another. The choreography was different this time. The idea was to ensure that every girl would have catered to every guy before the show came to an end.

Good times sped by and the strip party too came to an end. The boys were on cloud nine. They were in no mood to leave the company they were in. It was the pill in them at work.

The driver was punctual. He pulled over at the said destination right on time. The strippers finally wrapped up their cosmic act, but not before they had dropped a very luring bait in front of the sharks, who they knew were hungry for more.

After wearing their lingerie, two of the women took centre stage between the seats, unannounced. Without any delay, they began kissing each other. The men hadn't seen this coming. The unforeseen sight of two women passionately kissing each other while holding each other's naked bodies was a thing of immense and unexplained joy.

With their eyes wide and mouths open, the boys watched them with bated breath. The triple influence of alcohol, the pill and the kiss had them hypnotized.

So far, they had been able to defend their don't-drop-your-pants pact. It had been massively challenging, and yet they had stood their ground. They were proud of themselves.

They had said no to Gabriella before, when she had asked them if they wanted to go beyond the striptease. Now she looked at them and asked, 'Would you enjoy watching the girls make out?'

And this is where it all went wrong.

19

Day 3, Prague

What she offered, the way she offered it, against the backdrop of what her co-workers were already offering, made for a very convincing pitch.

The boys looked at each other. They felt ecstatic; just the way Ecstasy, the party drug they had taken, was supposed to make them feel.

'*Oye hoye hoye hoye! Yaar suno meri gall!* Guys, I say let's do this. What do you say?' Harprit said.

This time, perhaps for the first time, Harprit's excitement wasn't immediately countered.

'Why not?' Ravin added.

'We don't have cash at the moment,' Manpreet said.

The men looked at the strippers. The strippers looked back at the men. A temporary silence ensued. Manpreet finally broke it by saying, 'We will withdraw it afterwards. Works for you?'

Gabriella gave it a quick thought and wickedly nodded a 'yes'.

The men were back to being happy.

Then all of a sudden, the Gladiator in Amardeep awakened. Nobody saw it coming.

'My name is Maximus Decimus Meridius.'

The girls were at first taken aback. The boys looked at him. He didn't give a shit and continued, 'Commander of the armies of the North and a loyal servant to the true emperor.'

'What the fuck!' Ravin said and held his forehead in his palm.

Manpreet giggled and said, 'Holy shit man!'

The girls needed a few seconds to adjust with what they were witnessing.

Amardeep meanwhile continued, 'And tonight, I want my men to show the loyalty over the pact we have signed with our blood.' He actually meant the don't-drop-your-pants pact. Getting carried away with emotions, he had unnecessarily amplified it with blood and whatnot.

'*Bhenchod hame nahi karna. Sirf dekhna hai* (You asshole, we aren't supposed to do anything, only watch),' Harprit consoled him.

'This is madness!' Gabriella said.

'This is Sparta!' Amardeep rebutted.

The pill in his blood made him switch gears effortlessly between Leonidas and Maximus. He wasn't too sure who he was, but he didn't care much. As long as four naked women stood before him, he was prepared to be any warrior from any corner of Europe.

'Looks like he's bought his own story about his royal bloodline,' Manpreet said, laughing.

Unlike Indian folks' substantial appetite for drama, Gabriella couldn't tolerate much of it. She had a business to do. She hit the final nail in the coffin.

'As repeat clients, we will charge you half of the amount we have charged you before.'

That calmed Amardeep down. However, they all remained high. The seasoned strippers were immune to just one dose, but for the men, it was a completely new experience.

The mood was cheerful and relaxed, and no one wanted to take a break to do the maths and figure out if they could spend more of the leftover balance on their international currency card. All they remembered to verify was that this new opportunity didn't require them to drop their pants.

'Watching gorgeous naked women make out with each other is a better proposition than only seeing gorgeous naked women,' Ravin said.

The catch?

Well, his statement would have been true had they not already done the latter. But then Gabriella had played her cards right with that half of the cost condition. The men, with their decision centre now residing in their pants, and under the heady influence of drugs and alcohol, nodded their heads easily in agreement.

'This rate is only for half an hour. Tell us when to stop.' Gabriella smiled and then knocked twice on the partition screen between them and the driver. The car began to roll yet again and with that the kisses between the two women in the centre turned wetter.

As time passed by, they watched the two girls teasing and playing with each other – kissing, licking, biting. They heard them moan louder with each passing minute. They looked at them sucking and fingering each other as they changed their postures and did the same thing again in a wilder manner. Then they heard them cry out with desire and acknowledgements of fulfilment. The men enjoyed it all.

When it was the turn of the other pair of girls, one of whom was Gabriella herself, the women took a different route. They began it with a wrestling match. Who would pin down the other in order to reach the opposite end of the limo. Again, this was something new for the boys. In no time the semi-naked women began jostling with each other on the deck of the car.

It was a scene straight out of a wrestling match. The other two strippers were assigned to either team. They stood on standby as if this was a tag team championship match. The men were first awarded the role of referees. However, they soon turned into cheerleaders instead, shouting and screaming and egging the girls on.

In the heat of the competitive spirit, the girls shouted for the men to step into the arena and help them pin down their opponent. The men willingly and happily obliged. It wasn't about lust any more. This had turned into an unexpected match they wanted to win.

Soon, it was a mixed doubles of wrestling. It didn't take much time before another mixed doubles kick-started at the other end of the car.

Time flew by. The half hour Gabriella had referred to earlier had turned into two. It was the men's responsibility to call it a day. Gabriella had told them so. The limo kept rolling down the streets. By the time good sense prevailed, it had already been two and a half hours. This was over and above the first one hour when they had watched the girls strip.

'Fuck!' Ravin screamed when he realized what the time was.

It took him a while to make his friends understand the same.

They were all high.

Manpreet heard Ravin. He took a moment to settle down. He thought of something and then did the maths of how much they owed the strippers. He couldn't say anything but echoed what Ravin had said. "Fuck.'

'You boys want to fuck us?' Gabriella immediately asked, sensing the possibility of another business opportunity.

'*Chup karja yaar* (Shut up),' Manpreet said, coming out of his trance.

Thankfully they were all fully clothed. Ravin thought to himself.

Amardeep didn't care. He was still busy being happy.

Harprit freaked out in his own way.

'We are bankrupt,' he screamed.

That caught Amardeep's attention.

He looked at the worried faces of his friends and raised his eyebrows. He shifted his ass on the seat and got closer to Ravin and Manpreet on the other end. The women wondered what the men were up to. Abruptly, they ended their slugfest and looked at the guys.

Cutting to the chase, Ravin asked the women, 'How much do we owe you?'

'Hmmm ...' Gabriella adjusted her hair and glanced at the time on her cellphone. 'Nine thousand korunas.'

Their fear had been realized.

They emptied their international-currency card and withdrew all the cash from the ATM and even then, were short of 4,500 Czech korunas. The limo waited in front of the ATM. The guys talked among themselves, trying to think of an excuse. When Bruno, the driver, couldn't wait any longer, he stepped out and walked to the guys. His tone had changed.

'Come on guys, hurry up.'

'Yeah yeah.' Manpreet nodded and then stammered a bit before adding, 'Can we make part of the payment now and the rest in a few days?'

Bruno stepped back and took a good look at the four of them. He slightly lifted the right side of his tuxedo to show them what he had with him. A mouser.

'Oh shit.' The boys balked.

'Sorry, man, but you will have to pay the full amount.'

Ravin swallowed down the lump of saliva at the back of his throat. He tried to explain the situation they were in but Bruno was adamant. Understanding was not his forte. Showing off the gun was. Amardeep pitched in. He asked if they could talk to the women inside the limo.

Reluctantly, the driver walked back and opened the back door of the vehicle. The girls looked at them in anticipation. Amardeep was the first to speak.

'Madam,' he said.

Seriously? Harprit thought to himself.

The boys felt Amardeep was about to beg them. At first they felt sick, but then they swallowed their pride. As long as they didn't have to do it, they were okay if their friend begged on their behalf.

Who among them had thought that on the other side of wine, pills and naked women in a limousine, life was going to be so brutal? Here they were, in the middle of asking four strippers to let them go without paying in full for their services.

It didn't cut any ice. Gabriella explained it wasn't her decision. To make things worse, she added that it was in the hands of their boss, who was a local mafia.

'Mafia?' Ravin repeated that word.

'Yeah. Even if Bruno let's you walk free, they won't. They will find you and make you pay,' she said and added, 'with interest.'

There was mercy in her eyes, but her words were loaded with threat.

Every attempt to renegotiate the payment terms was closed. Bruno continued to flash his gun. He and his unseen boss had prematurely killed their ultimate plan to run away without paying.

Fifteen minutes later, the boys were inside the limo. They were cooperating and the strippers ideating. Their mutual goal was to find out ways to internationally credit money in the strip club's bank account – in real time.

International banking finance and the foreign exchange market were discussed. Bruno stood outside, smoking his cigarette. He was least interested in being a part of the delegation discussing international trade inside his limousine. The atmosphere inside his car had changed altogether.

'How about Internet banking?' Gabriella asked.

'It doesn't support international transfer,' Ravin answered.

'Credit cards?'

'Needs OTP on SMS. None of us are on roaming.'

One after the other, they ran through their options.

'A loan from your friends back home?'

'We are each other's friends.'

'You don't have more friends?'

'No one who would loan us money at this time of the night,' Amardeep said.

She thought more and then said, 'Call your family.'

'Are you kidding me?'

Bruno had finished his cigarette. He opened the door of the vehicle and looked at the people inside. He seemed angry, very angry. His anger made something that was not supposed to happen, happen.

Moments later, with Bruno's revolver pointing at his forehead, using the very phone on which he had called the strippers, Amardeep made a call to his wife.

It was dawn in India. His wife was in deep sleep. He had no option but to wake her up. Several rings later, she picked up the call. On hearing her husband's voice, at that hour of the day, she got worried.

On behalf of all the men, Amardeep swallowed his shame and told her that he was fine and that he needed her to make an online transaction of money on her card.

'But why?' she asked.

'Some issue with our international-currency card and I can't access my credit card due to OTP. So I need yours.'

'Okay, wait.'

Four losers, four strippers and one Bruno on the other end waited in anticipation. Meanwhile, Gabriella opened the payment gateway link on her phone.

'What's the amount?' asked Amardeep's wife coming out of her sleep on the other end of the call. She had got her credit card in her lap.

Hesitantly Amardeep answered, 'Hmm ... around ... thirty ... thirty-five thousand.'

Amardeep cleverly saved the cash they boys had withdrawn and made his wife transact the full amount. They needed the cash for the rest of the trip.

'What are you buying?'

The men looked at each other. Amardeep bit his tongue and managed to say, 'Renting out a limousine for the four of us.'

'Wow! Quite a luxury!'

He dodged the possibility of any further questions. 'Baby, tell me the card number?'

'Yeah ... yeah okay, hold.'

She slowly dictated the numbers, the expiry date and the CVV to Amardeep. He slowly dictated them to Gabriella. Finally, they waited for his wife to give them the OTP and voila! it was done.

About fifty seconds later, he said to his wife, 'Thank you so much, baby. It's done. Please go back to sleep now.'

The call was disconnected. The boys breathed a sigh of relief.

They were finally off the hook.

Back in Hyderabad, there arrived a delayed acknowledgement message on the phone. It read:

DEAR CUSTOMER, TRANSACTION OF CZECH KORUNA 9000.00 USING CREDIT CARD XX3011 DONE AT VIPSEXCLUB HAS BEEN SUCCESSFUL.

The owner of the phone was already asleep by then. The tremors had been felt. The earthquake was yet to come.

20

Goodbye, Prague

After a stressful night, Ravin and Harprit stood at the reception of the hotel. None of the boys had got any sleep the night before. Their bags were packed and the hotel checkout was in progress. The two awaited the arrival of Manpreet and Amardeep, who had gone to pick up the car they had rented to drive down to Croatia.

Once the two arrived at the hotel, the boys placed their luggage in the boot of the sedan. Manpreet had remained behind the wheel ever since they had rented the car. He was the default driver, for he was the only one who was comfortable with left-hand driving.

'One of you two can take over once we are out of the city and on the freeway,' Manpreet said, looking at Harprit and Ravin in the back seat.

Amardeep, who was sitting shotgun, immediately asked, 'Why only those two? We added four names to the drivers' list while renting this car.'

An hour back, in the office of the car-rental company, while filling up the form, Manpreet had put only three names on the drivers' list. He had left Amardeep out because the latter didn't have a valid international driving licence. Manpreet and Harprit had brought their US and UK driving licences with them. As per traffic rules in Europe, drivers with US and UK driving licences don't need any separate document to drive a four-wheeler. Ravin's Indian driving licence was not enough for the same purpose. He had therefore gotten himself an international driving permit before leaving India. However, Amardeep had been too lazy to get one made.

Next to the driver's name on the form, the rental company had also asked for the driver's valid driving licence number. Knowing Amardeep didn't have one, Manpreet had left out his name. Noticing this, Amardeep had argued with Manpreet. He too wanted to drive. So what if he didn't have a valid document? He insisted Manpreet write his name as well, but the latter had overruled him.

Later, on the pretext of reading the form, Amardeep had taken it from Manpreet's hands. He had then grabbed a pen and added his name to the drivers' list. Manpreet had asked him not to do so, but when his friend didn't stop, he gave up trying. Trying to play smart, Amardeep had taken out his passport from his pocket. He had been about to write his passport number in the section meant for his driving licence number when the person behind the desk had objected.

'That's your passport, sir. I need your driving licence number.'

Sheepishly, Amardeep had looked at Manpreet.

'*Karaa li beizzati* (Done embarrassing yourself)?' Manpreet had asked drily.

'Oh, I am sorry,' Amardeep had said to the representative.

He had then opened his wallet and pulled out the only glossy card in there. It was his PAN card. He had flashed it from a distance far enough for the representative to not really be able to read it clearly.

'Go ahead,' the rep had nodded.

'Do you need a photocopy of this?' Amardeep had asked.

'No, sir. Just mention the identity number. If only the cops ask, then you will need to show them your original licence.'

Amardeep had looked back at Manpreet and winked.

'Because a PAN card isn't a driving licence,' Manpreet responded to Amardeep's protest, turning on the ignition. He then told the others what Amardeep had done back in the car-rental office.

Harprit and Ravin shared a laugh at Amardeep's shrewdness. The vehicle pulled out of the parking slot. The map on the phone was opened. The destination was punched in – Dubrovnik. It was a twelve-hour drive, cutting across two countries. Manpreet looked at the time on his watch. It was ten in the morning. There was no way they were going to make it before midnight.

The boys were looking forward to this long drive. It was another kind of adventure they had been waiting for. More so after the previous night's episode, which had turned into such a disaster.

But the past was the past. There was nothing much they could do about their misadventure, apart from laugh about it. Which they did.

Manpreet floored the accelerator as soon as he was out of the city. The car picked up speed on the freeway. The beautiful city of Prague was drifting away from them.

'What the hell did we do last night?' Ravin asked, breaking the momentary silence in the car.

'Exercised our God-given right to stupidity,' Harprit quipped.

They laughed at themselves. Amardeep turned back and high-fived Harprit. The car now sped past the countryside farms. The open grassland on their either side was neatly manicured. Herds of cattle were left out in the open to graze. The view was scenic. The weather was sanguine.

Ravin paired his phone with the car's Bluetooth. Earlier, he had downloaded all the 1990s' songs they used to listen to in their hostel. A lot of them were Punjabi. It took them back in time, to the days when they were more carefree than they were now; to the nights when they had tapped their feet to uncountable bhangra beats.

The volume was turned up. Every subsequent song which blasted through the car speakers brought with it applause along with nostalgic joy. Memories bubbled up in their heads. The car raced ahead while they swept back to their past.

'Happy veer, in which year did you get your hair cut?' recalling something, Manpreet shouted over the loud music.

Once upon a time, all four friends had kept their hair unshorn. Eventually two of them had made different choices for themselves.

'First year itself,' Ravin answered on Harprit's behalf.

'And you, Rinku veer, got yours cut long after college, right?' Amardeep asked Ravin. The latter nodded.

'Was it your dad or mom who didn't talk to you for ages after that?' Manpreet asked, his eyes focused on the road ahead.

'Mom. For a year,' Harprit responded.

'What about you, Rinku?' Amardeep asked.

'Dad. For a year,' Ravin replied.

Manpreet turned down the volume on the stereo to continue the discussion. He had an idea which way the conversation was going to go, but then that's the best part about being with best friends. They don't judge you and you can talk freely.

'Any of you regretted doing that?' he asked without looking at anyone.

A moment of silence passed as Harprit and Ravin thought about the question.

'I don't think so,' Harprit said thoughtfully.

They waited for Ravin to answer.

When he had finished thinking, he said, 'No, but I am sad about it hurting my parents.'

Harprit jumped in to second that as soon as he heard Ravin. 'Oh yeah, that part even I would agree.'

'But not sad enough to go back in time and change your decision?' Amardeep asked and waited for their responses. Both of them agreed with Amardeep.

'You know, that's one big reason why I didn't take that path,' Manpreet shared, not so as to show that he was better than them, but for the sake of a heart-to-heart conversation with his friends.

'You wanted to?' Ravin asked.

'Well, at some point the thought did cross my mind. But it wasn't that big an urge and I let it pass for various reasons.'

'Reasons like?' Harprit questioned.

'As I said, parents, religion, identity,' he clarified.

Amardeep's case was completely different from the rest of the boys. His parents had never objected to his choice of life. It was Amardeep who had made the choice of not doing so. He loved his hair, which was long and thick and would be the envy of many girls.

When asked why he didn't opt for the other choice, his answer was pretty simple – getting used to a new look would be a task for him. Amardeep abhorred change. Not doing something that he would do otherwise was also a learning curve for him.

Meanwhile, Ravin and Harprit wished they could have exchanged their parents with Amardeep's, for he was clearly not going to make use of that opportunity.

'What eventually made your respective parents speak to you?' Manpreet asked.

'*Putra-prem* (The love for their child),' Harprit said without even a moment's thought.

Manpreet briefly looked at Ravin, who replied in one word, 'Ditto.'

Half a minute passed. Taking a cue from what they had been discussing, Harprit gave words to the thoughts doing the rounds in his mind.

'Why do our parents want us to live the way they want us to live?'

Amardeep looked back at Harprit and giggled, nodding his head.

'*Nahi, Rinku veer* (What do you say, Rinku veer)?' Harprit further asked Ravin, who too was smiling. Ravin's tongue touched his upper incisors. His eyes shifted from Amardeep to Harprit. And then he said, 'Because they tend to believe they know better than us.'

'But why?'

'Because they have spent more time on this planet than us.'

'And do you think that's right?'

Amardeep intervened. 'Right and wrong are subjective. Depends from whose perspective you look at it from. They brought us into this world. They have raised us in a certain way. It—'

Manpreet cut him off and pitched in. 'Maybe the problem is that they don't know when they should stop raising us. They don't get that, beyond a point, it is our lives that they are interfering in. That we are responsible and accountable for our lives and therefore have the right to live our way doesn't sink in.'

'Exactly,' Amardeep said and continued to speak. 'We have come from them. We are a piece of their hearts. And parents find it extremely difficult to see a part of them deviating from their way of life.'

'But isn't there wisdom in understanding that even if your children are a piece of your heart, their minds are independent? That they will have their own wishes and want to make their own choices? And therefore, just because you brought them into this world doesn't mean they will live in this world by your standards. In fact, to expect that children should live as per their parents' choices in itself is incorrect. It compromises the very fundamental aspect of freedom,' Ravin said. He continued after a pause. 'And talking of religion. I respect all religions, while I am more of an atheist than a religious person. Why should I inherit the idea of being religious or not from my parents? Why does not following religion hurt the sentiments of our religious parents? I mean, shouldn't religion be a choice *I* make? In fact, on logical grounds, I can also ask why my parents don't adopt my idea of religion?'

There were too many whys in what Ravin had said. While others in the car were in the middle of processing them all, he added one more.

'Why can my dad say that my clean-shaven look bothers him, but I can't say that his bearded look bothers me?'

On that last one, everyone burst into laughter.

'O *bete* (Oh boy)!' Manpreet exclaimed.

Harprit clapped and said, 'MP, let's stop the car and buy him a medal first.'

In the heat of the argument, Ravin had ended up asking a difficult question, which in the company of orthodox men would have been held inappropriate and discouraged.

'*Tu ulti Ganga bahaane ki baat kar raha hai, bhai* (You are trying to turn the tide),' Amardeep chuckled.

'*But sawaal to jaayaz hai na mera*?' (But isn't my question valid?)

Amardeep chose to address his friend's concern. 'It surely is. But then a response to your last question would be, who changed the status quo? He didn't. You did. So, fingers will be pointed at you.'

Ravin immediately responded, 'Well, then the right question should be, who *got* to establish the status quo in the first place? Him, not me. And why?'

'Because, he came into this world before you?' Harprit answered, laughing.

The debate, while being a rational one, was entertaining as well. Everyone had their more-than-two cents to offer.

Ravin continued, 'Well, I grew up his way and now I want to establish my status quo, which can be different from his. You see, I am not trying to force my status quo upon him, but he very strongly expected me to follow his. Just because you bring your children into this world doesn't mean you get to control their lives forever.'

'*Shaant, gadaadhaari bheem, shaant* (Relax buddy)!' Manpreet said, realizing that Ravin was getting worked up.

His words helped Ravin realize that there was no need to be agitated. After all, it was a friendly debate in which nobody was proving anybody wrong. If anything, it was more of a candid conversation. Ravin calmed down and sat back.

'But Rinku veer, as far as I know, your father never shouted at you because of this choice you made?'

'No, he didn't. Never. But he didn't talk to me and the fact that my decision to live my life my way made him this sad, hurt me.'

'Come on, dude. Your dad has been a good man. Give the old man the benefit of the social conditioning he has lived through. You made your choice. He made his choice of not talking to you. And then eventually, he changed his stand and accepted you with your change. In his circle, due to your actions, even though it wasn't your fault or his, he would have taken so many questions on his chin. It would have brought turmoil in his life as well. But be happy because eventually, you are living life your way.'

Nobody said anything for a few seconds. In that thoughtful silence, Ravin nodded to himself. He only wished that his dad and he hadn't gone through one long year of not talking to each other.

'Be happy. Unlike us, at least you are getting to live with your parents,' Manpreet said.

Ravin raised his eyebrows. 'And what stops you all from doing that too?'

'I live in the US. My parents don't want to come and live with me. Even if they want to, they can't come and live there forever. It's the same case with Happy,' Manpreet responded.

'See now, that's exactly the case in my house as well. They don't want to come and live with me in the US or UK. So I live in Gurgaon.'

Amardeep, whose parents didn't want to leave Bareilly where they had lived almost their entire lives and join him in Hyderabad, asked, 'But they didn't stop you from going and settling down abroad either. Did they?'

'No, they didn't. Just that in my case my parents are dependent on me. And therefore, for their sake, to stay back in India is a choice I made. Or one that I had to make,' Ravin said.

'You are a good son. You know that, right?' Harprit looked into Ravin's eyes and said.

'I am not,' he responded.

Harprit waited for him to explain.

'I love having my parents around. But then the truth also is that there are days I want to run away from looking after them. A knee-replacement surgery, cataract operation, weeks together of daily physiotherapy pick-ups and drops, countless visits to the hospitals for mom's multiple ailments, and then a father who lost his leg in his sixties and has to learn to walk on prosthetics. It's a lot. I've made around two hundred visits to the hospital and prosthetic centre for him. I am fortunate I don't have a nine-to-five office job and could do this for him. But then I will confess that on many occasions, shamelessly and selfishly so, I have wanted to run away from all this, to a place where I can have some peace.'

When he finished, he felt Harprit's hand on his shoulder. 'But you didn't run away. And that makes you a good son.'

'Exactly.' Manpreet expressed his agreement.

A couple of moments of silence passed.

'In their old age, parents tend to become kids. And what I now do is parenting my old parents,' Ravin said softly.

'That's how the circle of life is, my friend. Unless gone too soon and way ahead of our times, we all will live through this,' Manpreet said.

'They took care of us when we needed it. It is time we care for them,' Amardeep agreed.

'Yes. But you know why I think I am not a good son? It's because, in my head, I question this understanding as well,' Ravin confessed.

'What understanding?' Harprit asked.

'Parents take care of their kids because they brought them into this world. Kids can't look after themselves. Hence, it becomes the responsibility of those who had them to look after them now that they have brought them into this world.'

'I see where you are heading,' Manpreet said.

Ravin continued. 'However, in the case of this kid, he never had the choice. Decades later, his parents will age and by default become his or her responsibility. How unfair!'

Everyone giggled at the way Ravin put that point.

'I know it's not possible, but I so wish that there had been a way that my parents could have taken my approval. Like they and I could have negotiated and reached an agreement on my choice of religion, being looked after in my childhood and looking after them in their old age, you know … like a contract for everything. And only after my consent would they have been allowed to have unprotected sex to produce me …'

The car rang with laughter as Ravin continued, 'Yeah I mean, I would have also asked them how much they earn, where we'd go on vacation after I was born, etc. You know! Life would have been so much easier then. No?'

'You mean you wish you had a choice about being born,' Amardeep summed it up.

'Absolutely.'

The car sped down south on the highway. There was little traffic. Soon they were going to leave the Czech Republic and enter Austria.

'Rinku veer, your perspective on this is indeed interesting. However, I can offer you another way to look at it,' Harprit said.

Everyone waited for him to enlighten them.

'What if your soul had agreed upon a contract? With God! And you were born to your parents only after you approved it. But now, in this birth, you don't have any memory of giving your approval before birth.'

'Come on, dude. A contract is meant to exist for the entire span of the business. I mean a system with evidence should exist,' Ravin retorted, laughing.

'Business?' Amardeep chuckled.

'Of being each other's parent and child.'

Manpreet chuckled.

Meanwhile, Harprit continued. 'Think of it this way. That your parents have the right to have a baby. It's not in their hands whether it will be your soul or somebody else's that will land up in the body of the baby they produce. I am sure if they too had a choice, like you want one, they would have preferred a Sachin Tendulkar.'

Ravin looked at Harprit with disgust. He tried hard to think of a response, but failed. And then all he ended up saying was, 'I make a good son.'

'This is what we told you when, moments back, you said you aren't one,' Manpreet took another dig at him.

'Stop the car,' Ravin shouted.

'What? You don't want to come with us any more?' Harprit jokingly asked.

Annoyed, Ravin responded, 'No I have to pee.'

The serious discussion, after seeing a variety of thought-provoking insights, ran into humorous lanes. And yet it was all worth it. Nobody stopped the car for Ravin.

'Well, jokes apart, guys, here is my question,' Harprit said. 'What will we do when our grown-up children come to us with the questions Rinku veer is raising at the moment? Will we become like our parents are now?'

Amardeep added, 'And if we truly turn out to be different and a lot more liberal, then the question is – wouldn't our parents have thought exactly this way when they were dealing with their parents?'

Manpreet said, 'Who knows if we are going to check ourselves into old-age homes like they do in America?'

'Speaking like an American?' Ravin chuckled.

'Well, that's what I see happening around me in the US,' he responded.

'So, is the Western way of life the solution? Once you become an adult, leave your parents to live your life by your choice?' Amardeep asked.

'Western way?' Ravin interjected. 'Guys, in case you haven't noticed it yet, all three of you have been living away from your parents anyway.'

'Come on, Rinku veer, we stepped out because of work, looking for growth. Westerners move out of their parents' house otherwise as well. Even if their jobs are in the very city their parents live in,' Harprit said.

Amardeep pitched in to second Ravin. 'Well, a good number of Indians, just like Americans or Europeans, are moving out of their parents' houses. In a way he is right. The reasons may be different, but the point he is making is they both move out because of their respective needs. If you look at this not through the lens of intent but impact, the gap between our lifestyle and that of Westerners is fast reducing.'

The others nodded at his words.

Meanwhile, Harprit tried to get back to Amardeep's previous point. 'But Raam ji, maybe our parents are more liberal than their parents were. Maybe we will be more liberal than our parents are. And yet our children may feel about us the way we feel about our parents.'

'Maybe, the generation gap is a constant,' Ravin concluded, looking out of the window for the exit. They needed to stop soon. He had to pee and was finding it difficult to hold it any longer.

21

Hello, Austria

Early in the afternoon, Manpreet pulled up the vehicle to one of the freeway services. Bryan Adams, whose turn on the car audio had finally come, was put on pause for a while. Before him MLTR, the Backstreet Boys and Boyzone had already entertained them, in that sequence.

Manpreet pulled out the keys from the neck of the steering wheel. Four doors of the vehicle opened, and the boys stepped out. Under the cloudy sky of northern Austria, they took their sweet time stretching their backs and legs. They had been in the car for nearly four hours now.

Behind the gas station, the services bay had a variety of eating options, along with a 24/7 retail outlet and pharmacy. After using the restroom and freshening up, the boys decided to eat, and Amardeep chose the Mexican fast-food restaurant for everyone. It looked great from outside and its menu too was tempting.

However, when they pulled open the door, they saw that the place was empty, which made them wonder if they'd picked wisely.

Cheerful-looking waiters from behind the counter greeted them with enthusiasm. That warm welcome momentarily eased their doubts. The boys looked at each other and then shrugged. 'Let's order?' Amardeep suggested.

Moments later, cherry-picking their favourite veggies, sauces and meat, they ordered themselves a wrap each, along with sodas. The Mexican wrap had the distinctive black rice along with the familiar red kidney beans as its main ingredient. From underneath a dining table next to a glass wall, Harprit pulled out four fibre chairs. They all sat with their respective trays.

'Hmm ... not bad,' Ravin said after he had taken a bite of his wrap.

'Yeah, it's quite good,' Harprit agreed.

Outside the glass wall, the sky was gradually changing. The sun, which had been out in full force back in Prague, was nowhere to be seen in the Austrian sky. Clouds had sailed in from the south and decorated the canvas of what had been, till only some time back, a clear sky. As the boys ate and talked, some people walked into the restaurant.

The creak of the door being pulled open broke the calm of the place. All eyes turned in the direction of the newcomers, and immediately, they commanded the boys' undivided attention.

No, it wasn't a group of hot, blonde women, or even cute kids in colourful attire. The latest diners were four men, two bald and two white-haired. Under the layers of clothes, their feeble bodies moved slowly. Three of them were using walking sticks, the fourth a walker.

'How are you guys feeling today?' shouted the woman from behind the service counter.

'Like I should propose to you today,' the old man using the walker said in English.

The woman smiled. It appeared as if she was used to it.

The boys enjoyed listening to the conversation, which was finally in a language they could understand.

'Hey, you tried your luck last time. It's my turn,' another old man said to his friend, cackling.

'Come on, Mr Oak! You are so handsome. You deserve better,' the woman teased.

'Oh Cecelia, stop underestimating yourself,' Mr Oak responded.

The boys, their wraps forgotten as they took in the amusing scene, realized that these four men were frequent customers at the joint.

'She won't tell you,' another old man in the group stopped walking, raised his walking stick to point to Cecelia, and said, 'but she admires me more than you, Oak.'

Mr Oak looked at Cecelia and raised his eyebrows, 'He said the same thing to that Sandra working in the bar at the end of this road.'

Cecelia smiled and walked out from behind the counter. She went up to the four men, seated them in their booth, and gave them all a peck on their cheeks.

'You guys must stop drinking,' she said sternly, clearly familiar enough with them to be comfortable with lecturing them.

'He made us!' Mr Oak jutted his chin towards his friend seated across from him.

Cecelia shifted her interrogating eyes to the man.

'Mr Bank!' she said, shaking her head.

Mr Bank hurried to explain himself. 'What? I only had two mocktails. Oak and Benjamin had three pegs of whisky each,' he said defensively.

Silently, Cecelia shifted her disapproving gaze back to Mr Oak, who suddenly looked engrossed in the menu in front of him. Cecelia waited for him to finish his theatrics. Finally, Mr Oak looked up and confessed.

'Ah ... they were small.'

'What?'

'The pegs,' he said, making a puppy face, and Cecelia couldn't hold back her smile.

'If any of you want me to consider your romantic proposals, you better bring that down to one small peg. All right?'

The men looked properly contrite and nodded, though their eyes were twinkling with mischief.

'Anything for you, Cecelia!' Mr Benjamin declared.

'All right then, on that note, should I get you boys your usual?' she asked.

Four voices in unison said a loud yes, and once Cecelia left, began chatting amongst each other.

Looking at them, from the other side of the restaurant, Harprit said, 'That's us, forty years from now.'

Amardeep nodded. 'I was about to say that.'

It was evident that, looking at the old men, all four younger men felt the same.

'If we all survive till then,' Ravin said thoughtfully and took a bite of his wrap, shifting his eyes back to the sky, which was now completely enveloped with clouds.

His words left the others to ponder on what he was hinting at.

'Do you mean ... if any of us ...' Manpreet began, and then paused for a couple of seconds before continuing, 'you know ... dies?' He paused again, and then said, 'Well, we all have to die one day, but I mean, when one of us dies, do we still carry on with our reunions?'

Ever since they had ideated about their future reunion plans on that railway platform in Hyderabad, they had never given a thought to this.

'Rinku veer?' Harprit said, pulling Ravin's attention from the outside sky. 'If I die, will you guys go on having these reunions without me?' he asked.

'If there is a limousine full of strippers involved, then why not?' Ravin replied, grinning with his mouth full of food.

Manpreet laughed out loud and high-fived Ravin.

When they settled down, Amardeep said, 'On a serious note, irrespective of which one of us goes first, we should keep this reunion tradition going.'

He then took a deep breath and sat back, thinking of something.

'What happened, Raam ji?' Manpreet raised his eyebrows.

'I kind of feel sad for the last one left among us.'

To Amardeep, this was a deep and painful thought, more tragic than the idea of death itself. To be left alone, when the other three weren't there any more, was unthinkable. A difficult silence enveloped the table. For a few seconds, they sat frozen, their food untouched. Their eyes shifted from one to the other.

In their subconscious minds they knew they would die one day, but never had they thought about who would be the last one to die. What would he go through? Would he look at their pictures and reminisce about the laughter, the fights, the mischief, the celebrations and their reunions?

An emotional moment that they hadn't anticipated descended upon the table, and the men sat with dark thoughts. But then suddenly, Manpreet broke the heavy mood by making a profound statement. He looked into Amardeep's eyes and said, '*Wo tu hi hoga bhenchod. Chal ab khaa* (That would be you, asshole. Now eat),' he quipped.

And with that, like always, they dismissed their worries of the future with laughter. It wasn't time to think of death and loneliness. This was their reunion, and they were here to celebrate what they had, not worry about what they wouldn't have one day.

'Why are we talking about all this? Look at them. As I said, that's us forty years from now. When we reach that table some day, we can talk about death then.'

On that note, Ravin quoted lines by his favourite Punjabi singer, Sartaj – '*Filhaal hawaawan rumk diyaan, jad jhakkar challu vekhaange* (For the time being the breeze is waft, when the storm comes, we'll see).'

With that, they put the subject of death on the back burner, finished their meal and left to take their journey forward down south.

It had begun to drizzle and the boys ran to the car. Manpreet tossed the key in the air towards Ravin and asked him to take the wheel while he himself took the navigator's seat. He had to assist Ravin with left-hand driving.

Ravin spent a couple of minutes getting acquainted with the controls. Once he could differentiate between the wiper and the indicators, he slowly drove the car out on the slip road.

Instead of dumping an overload of information on him, Manpreet only had one instruction for his friend. 'Maintain a one-foot distance between that lane divider on your left and this car. Now drive,' he said the second they got on the highway tarmac.

Adhering to the directive, Ravin pressed the accelerator. A traffic rule devotee back home, he felt like he was committing a crime by driving on the wrong side of the road. In the first few minutes, he continuously had to tell himself in his head that it was the right thing to do. Till he got familiar with it, every other activity inside the car was put on hold. It included not letting Bryan Adams sing and not letting Harprit and Amardeep talk over the sound of the moving wipers, something that was already irritating him.

In about ten minutes though, Ravin had begun to feel much more comfortable.

It turned out that Manpreet was an excellent tutor. He could notice Ravin's confidence when the latter pushed the accelerator paddle further and the needle on the speedometer went north. More instructions came from Manpreet as and when they were needed – things like what to keep in mind while overtaking in left-hand driving on a freeway in a developed country.

With the turn of the volume knob, Bryan Adams's voice burst forth. And with that, everyone was free to talk again. Gradually, the rain too picked up momentum. In the rear-view mirror, Ravin saw the fast rolling tyres of his car splashing rainwater away from it.

For the next couple of hours, the rain kept playing hide-and-seek with them. It kept them company on some long stretches on their route and left them to themselves on others. Then there were tracts where the sun had the audacity to peek at them from behind the clouds. Under a playful sky, Austria looked breathtakingly gorgeous. It certainly was one of the most beautiful countries in central Europe. After a dash of rain, the lush green hills looked even more spectacular than they already were. The air outside was refreshing. To drive through the countryside with hills in the background and houses nested in them was a spectacular experience they were going to remember for a long time.

'This place is beautiful. Where exactly are we?' Harprit asked.

'This entire country is beautiful. We are very close to Vienna,' Amardeep updated them while looking at the map on his phone. They were travelling from north to south in the eastern region of Austria.

Hearing that, Manpreet immediately asked, '*O teri!* Happy veer, are we going to pass through Vienna?'

'Indeed. But the sad part is we won't enter the capital city but continue on the freeway,' Ravin announced.

'Why, yaar? Let's stop by for an hour and see this beautiful city,' Harprit suggested.

'We are already forty-five minutes late to Dubrovnik, as per this,' Amardeep said, flashing his phone, which had the GPS map opened on it.

'So we are now reaching by quarter-to-one in the night?' Ravin asked.

'Yes, sir.'

'Sorry, buddy. In this intermittent rain, there is a possibility of further delay. By the time night falls, we will be very tired of sitting in this car,' Amardeep said.

It made sense not to stop in Vienna. Besides, the sun had already begun its descent in the west. With a heavy heart, they decided instead to make do by pulling over on the outskirts of Vienna for a short break.

A short break later, when they were ready to drive again, an adamant Amardeep grabbed the car keys from Ravin and ran to get into the driver's seat. By the time the rest of the boys made it to the car, he had already turned the ignition on.

'I am not letting you drive. You don't have a valid licence,' Ravin said, looking down at his friend with a stern expression on his face.

Amardeep remained inflexible.

Manpreet and Harprit were neutral about the matter. However, on Ravin's numerous denials, they took his side and asked Amardeep to let it go.

'He is right. Let's not take an unnecessary risk,' Harprit said.

Amardeep surrendered, but on one condition. 'If I am not going to drive, I would like to drink while being driven in this awesome weather.'

'Help yourself,' Ravin offered.

'I will also need company,' Amardeep demanded.

Harprit looked at Manpreet and asked, 'MP veer?'

Manpreet instantly agreed. Harprit didn't waste a second to swap his seat with Amardeep. The latter took the seat behind in the company of Manpreet.

'There's a half-empty bottle of scotch in Rinku's bag and some chips and peanuts in mine,' Manpreet said, rolling down the window on his side.

Amardeep walked out and opened the boot space, asking, 'And do we have glasses?'

'I don't think so. We made no plans to drink during this drive,' Ravin shouted from the navigator's seat.

'Raam ji, do one thing. Check this store for disposable glasses.' Harprit pointed at the retail outlet behind them.

'Good idea.' Amardeep clicked his fingers and ran towards the store.

'Thank God he agreed,' Ravin murmured in a tone loud enough to be heard by his friends inside the car.

Five minutes later, they watched their friend come back, holding a few tall, colourful paper glasses and a big bottle of chilled water.

'Why is he getting a water bottle when we have plenty with us?' Ravin wondered.

Once back, Amardeep made Manpreet hold everything before getting into the car from the other side.

'You got these glasses from ...' Manpreet hadn't even finished when Amardeep answered.

'This burger joint,' he said, pointing to the name printed on the paper glasses. 'The retail store didn't have disposable glasses. I got a water bottle instead from the store. For our drink.'

'Smart! So that we don't need ice, which we don't have,' Manpreet said and opened the bottle of Scotch. The two boys in the back seat poured themselves a drink each. Once they said 'cheers', Harprit pressed the accelerator.

They reached Graz around eight in the evening. This was going to be their final stopover in Austria before entering Slovenia, the last country they were to cross before entering Croatia.

That they would eat dinner in Graz was pre-decided. Somewhere between Vienna and Graz, the rain had subsided and then eventually vanished. Manpreet and

Amardeep were drunk. The two had not only finished the half bottle of Scotch, but also opened a new one. Ravin and Harprit remained sober, while their friends in the back seat practically transported themselves to a different zone in their haze of drunkenness.

The world around them was getting dark with every passing minute. The boys wanted a good meal and a break to stretch their legs. The fuel tank was also grumbling for a refill. Ravin picked out one of the upcoming services with good ratings and reviews. Seven miles down the freeway, they took the exit leading to it.

Unexpectedly, at the filling station, there was a long queue of vehicles waiting their turn. They waited to fill the fuel tank while their drunken friends rushed to the restroom to empty their bladders. Harprit and Ravin joined the tail of the queue. They wanted to finish one task while the other two ordered dinner for everyone.

Night was finally descending upon them. They still had to cross two countries before they could finally crash in their beds, and the boys were looking forward to a good night's rest.

(But then, if everything went as planned, how would the trip be a memorable one? Oh! You thought their misadventures were over the night before? Well! Wait and watch.)

Half an hour later, after they had hurriedly finished their dinner, Amardeep stepped out alone from the food joint. His phone was inside the car; Ravin had been using it for navigation and had left it in the holder of the gearbox unit.

Amardeep unlocked the vehicle and stepped inside from the driver's side. Drunk and unable to locate the switch to turn on the inside light, he plugged in the key and turned on the ignition.

The vehicle came to life. Along with the light inside the car, the headlights came alive. He immediately traced his phone, shut down the engine, stepped out and locked the vehicle.

Quite as Mr Murphy would have predicted, at that very moment an Austrian police car patrolling the area pulled over at the station to refuel its tank. In next two seconds, the window on the driver side of the vehicle rolled down.

All the two cops seated in the police car noticed was a man who had turned off the ignition of his car, got out and walked towards the eating joint with the unmistakable gait of a completely inebriated person.

22

Goodbye, Austria

With their bellies full, the four friends returned to their car. It was Ravin's turn to drive a good length of their remaining route. Harprit settled down in the navigator seat and Manpreet and Amardeep sank into the back seat, amid the mess of spilled snacks and used liquor glasses.

'*Chalo bhaiyon*. Good night,' Amardeep announced. 'Wake me up when we reach,' he added as he stretched back and rested his head on the headrest.

Ravin was about to start the engine when there was a knock on the window on Amardeep's side.

Rubbing his eyes open, Amardeep braved the bright light of the torch being shone at him through the glass.

'What the hell,' he murmured to himself and pushed the button to roll down the window on his side.

'Sir, can I see your ID and a valid driving licence, please?' a uniformed policeman asked Amardeep.

'Kyun be (What for)?' Amardeep shot back in his inebriated state, not knowing who the person standing outside their car was.

'Cops,' Harprit worriedly whispered to his friend, warning him.

'O teri (Oh boy)!' Manpreet mumbled and jumped to pull Amardeep by his shoulder, trying to stop him from saying anything that could get them into trouble.

Thankfully, Amardeep hadn't said anything in English so far, though the cop could clearly make out that the Hindi words uttered by the man weren't complimentary.

'Officer—' Ravin was about to say something but was stopped right then and there.

'Hold on, sir. I am talking to your friend at the moment.'

'But Officer, if you could just hear me—'

'I said hold on, sir.' The man turned to Amardeep and asked, 'Are these your friends?'

For some reason, the question made Amardeep uncomfortable. He braved the torchlight to look straight into the eyes of the cop. When he finally opened his mouth to speak, those golden words of brotherhood rolled out through his liquor-soiled throat in an American accent.

'I don't have friends. I *gaat* family.'

'Teri bhen di (Oh shit),' Harprit muttered and slapped his forehead.

'Amardeep!' Ravin called his name, trying to stop him from going any further.

Outside the car, the cop was taken aback. He looked at his colleague, who was in the driver's seat in the police vehicle.

'Hey Anthony!' he shouted. 'What was the name of the character that bald guy played in that movie with those fast cars you like a lot?'

'Why, what happened?' Anthony shouted back at him.

'Just tell me, man.' The first cop chuckled.

'Hmm ... yeah ... Don!'

The next second, Amardeep's head popped out of the window. It turned in the direction of the police car.

'Not Don. DOM! Dominic Toretto,' he shouted.

'Did you hear that?' the first cop shouted to the one in the car.

The other three friends inside were petrified. The two cops burst into laughter, and it was a mean one.

Manpreet pulled his friend back inside the car, '*Saaleya chup ho ja* (Please shut up),' he begged.

'What? Aren't you my brother, MP? You are my family, man,' Amardeep went on a different tangent.

'Yes. And that's our uncle standing outside,' Ravin murmured.

However, Amardeep wasn't done yet. He turned back and gave another one in Dom's words.

'The most important thing in life will always be ... the people in this car. Right here, right now.'

The cop said three words in response. 'Enough. Come out.'

Sixty seconds later, Amardeep's family of four stood in one line, ten feet away from their car.

The second policeman had stepped out of his vehicle and joined the scene. Looking at Ravin and pointing his chin at Amardeep, he said, 'I need to see his driving licence.'

'Oh, he doesn't have one,' answered Ravin.

'Here,' Amardeep said. He had pulled out his PAN card from his wallet.

'*Bhai andar rakh ise* (Keep it back).' Manpreet quickly tried to conceal it.

'Stop,' the cop warned Manpreet. 'Show me,' he said and took the card from Amardeep.

'What's this?' he asked the boys when he couldn't make out what it was.

'That's an Indian identity card for taxation purposes,' Harprit answered.

'Where's his driving licence?' he repeated, handing the PAN card back to Manpreet.

'He doesn't have one,' Ravin reiterated.

All this while, none of them were sure why the police were questioning only Amardeep in the first place. It was Harprit who finally asked them the right question. He made sure he did so without further inviting the wrath of the cops.

'Sir, with your permission, may I know the reason why you are questioning our friend?' he asked them hesitantly.

The second policeman stepped closer. Instead of answering the question, he rather raised his chin and took a deep breath. 'Who all are drunk here?' he asked.

'Both of us,' Manpreet acknowledged, gesturing to himself and Amardeep.

'Were you driving this car too?' the first cop asked Manpreet.

'I was, but not after I got drunk.'

'And when did your friend drive?' he asked, pointing his baton at Amardeep.

Manpreet looked at Amardeep and then back at both the cops. 'Oh, he hasn't driven the car at all.'

'Oh, really?' the first policeman asked. After all, he had seen Amardeep step out of the driver's seat after shutting the engine.

On that note, the policemen demanded every little detail of their drive from Prague to Graz. The paperwork with the car-rental company, their international driving licences, their passports, the route that they had followed. The men knew that the cops would be tracing their car's CCTV footage on the cameras installed all along the freeway.

And they did exactly that. They called up every toll gate–handling department on their route to trace in their database the images of their car. The RFID toll sticker, meant to auto-deduct the toll whenever the vehicle passed by a toll gate, became the key to looking up the time-stamp of when they crossed the respective tolls.

To pull up the images of that time period and check the vehicle number on screen was a cakewalk after that.

It took them thirty-five minutes to complete the entire exercise. In the images that were forwarded to their mobile phones, the cops couldn't see Amardeep in the driver's seat. That pissed them off even more. Trying hard to find evidence, they then traced the CCTV footage of the service station they were at. That was going to be the best shot, for they had seen Amardeep stepping out of the driver's seat at this station.

However, they failed miserably again. It wasn't him in the driver's seat when the car had entered the gas station.

'Thank God,' Manpreet said, looking at Ravin, for the latter had got into a heated debate with Amardeep and hadn't let him drive. Harprit too looked thankfully at Ravin. All this time, the boys had been standing while the cops were busy making calls. By now, Amardeep's senses too had somewhat emerged from the boozy haze.

When the cops found nothing against them, they finally took their passports and went to their vehicle, while the boys waited, growing more and more impatient. They were already running late, and now the cops had unnecessarily delayed them further by over forty-five minutes.

The cops checked up on the men's passports and Schengen visas; first with a magnifying glass and then by making some calls to the immigration department. They didn't want to leave any stone unturned. They seemed desperate to find something against them. And that they kept failing made them angrier.

'What do they want? A bribe?' Ravin whispered to Harprit. In his mind, he was drawing parallels with the cops in India.

Harprit closed his eyes for a second and then said wearily, 'It's our skin colour.'

'What?'

'What we are experiencing now is plain old racism.'

'Really?'

'I have lived in the UK for seven years now. I know what this is.'

Ravin's blood began to boil as he waited for the cops to return. About fifteen minutes later, one of the policemen rolled down the window of their car and called out.

Harprit stepped forward.

'Here,' the policeman said, handing back all four passports.

Harprit looked into his eyes and saw anger and defeat in them. He smiled back and asked, 'Is there anything else we can do for you, *Officer*?'

'No,' the man said shortly. Then he rolled up his window and drove away.

23

No Man's Land

Dead tired and sleep deprived, the boys had crossed the length of Slovenia and were now about to reach the Slovenia–Croatia border. Manpreet and Amardeep had long been asleep. For a change, the music in the car was on low volume. Peace was much desired by the two companions who were awake.

It had rained intermittently through the night. The fluorescent reflector signboards and the lights of the vehicles passing by broke the monotony of the dark night. The moon was nowhere to be seen, nor were any stars visible. The sky remained cloudy and threatened more showers.

It was ten minutes past one in the night when Ravin awakened Manpreet and Amardeep. They had arrived at the border checkpost of Slovenia. The security person asked for their passports, and the boys handed them over.

After their recent experience of having their passports thoroughly scanned by the Austrian police, the four wondered if there were further adventures in store for them.

However, it all went smoothly. The security person asked them where they were heading, and that was it. He stamped something on their passports and handed them back.

'Goodbye,' he said.

'Goodbye,' Harprit responded and drove on.

After only thirty seconds of driving, the four friends were surprised to see another security checkpost awaiting them.

'In my dream, we had crossed a similar checkpost,' Manpreet said, rubbing his sleepy eyes, wondering if they were caught in some twilight zone.

'This one too is in your dream,' Ravin said. Only Harprit understood the joke. The other two were too dazed to get it.

Harprit rolled down his window, and a security officer said something to him in a language none of them understood.

'Do you speak English?' Harprit asked him.

He only said one word, 'Passports.'

'I feel like this too has already happened,' Manpreet murmured.

Harprit turned back and ask Manpreet, 'And what do you think we do now?'

'Give him our passports,' Manpreet said in all innocence. Harprit and Ravin looked at each other and laughed.

'Here, officer,' Harprit said, passing on the four passports to the man.

Unlike at the previous checkpost, the guy here spent considerably more time in scanning their documents. He flipped a lot of pages. It appeared he was looking for something but couldn't find it. He kept the burgundy passport aside and thoroughly checked the remaining three navy-blue ones.

'What the fuck has happened now?' Amardeep murmured in the car. All eyes were on the security officer.

The man looked at them and asked something, but the four couldn't understand it.

He kept repeating himself, but in vain.

Amardeep rolled down his window. 'English?' he shouted, loud and clear.

Shaking his head, the security person responded in English, 'No English.'

Amardeep gave him another option. 'Punjabi?'

Everyone else inside the car burst into laughter. The security person, who didn't understand, frowned and looked visibly irritated. After taking all four passports into his custody, he walked out of his booth and towards another one.

'Where the hell is he going now?' Ravin worriedly said.

The man soon walked back to their car and went up to Ravin's window, accompanied by another security person. Smartly dressed in his uniform and with gelled hair, the new guy looked like he had just arrived for his late-night shift, and was clearly the first man's senior.

'Sir, where are you heading?' he asked.

The boys thanked their stars for the man's English.

'Dubrovnik,' Ravin replied.

'All of you?'

'Yeah. All of us.'

'But I can allow only one of you … hmm … Mr Haar … prit … Singh,' he read the name haltingly.

'What? But why?'

'I don't see your visas on your passports.'

'*Saale ne pee rakhi hai* (He must be drunk),' Amardeep said, getting to the root of the officer's unintelligent behaviour.

Harprit glared at his friend.

'Sorry,' Amardeep quickly said and fell silent.

'You must have missed it. Let me show you,' Ravin said, taking his passport from the security person's hands. He flipped the pages and, arriving at the one he was looking for, passed it back to the man. 'Here it is.'

'But this is a Schengen visa.'

'Yes, this is a Schengen visa.'

'But Croatia isn't a Schengen country.'

'What! What do you mean Croatia isn't a Schengen country?'

'I thought you understood English.'

'I do … but …' Ravin left his sentence incomplete.

Agape, he looked back at his friends.

Three pairs of eyes were on him, waiting for an explanation. After all, he was in charge of the entire trip. He was supposed to know what the officer was talking about. And he was supposed to have known it long back.

'Guys …' he said, fumbled and stopped.

They had driven for fourteen hours by then. They had booked one of the most expensive stays in Dubrovnik. Their return flight was booked from that city.

Like vultures, his three friends kept looking at him; waiting for him to speak up.

Some silences are more explosive than noise.

In that brief period of self-reflection, Ravin attempted a new excuse. 'Who among us, on call, had said that Croatia is a Schengen country?'

Harprit let a loud breath out.

'Nobody,' he said. His eyes were glued to Ravin's face, lit under the lamp post.

'Oh ... I thought ...' Ravin said, then shifted his eyes to the back seat. 'Would you have guessed Croatia to be a non-Schengen country?'

There was no response for the next five seconds, just steady eye contact. And then one of them finally spoke. It was a one-word statement.

'Teri bhen di saaleya!'

And then the abuses came, loud and fast.

Meanwhile, a mini pressure cooker of defensiveness began bubbling within Ravin. 'So that's it? All of it is my fault?' he asked, indignant.

'You planned this trip,' Manpreet pointed out.

'Yes, I did, because nobody else was willing to,' he rebutted.

'So you took the responsibility. And you failed,' Harprit accused.

'And you failed us!' Amardeep said.

'I *failed* you all?' Ravin slowly repeated Amardeep's words.

In that very moment, something changed.

Tiredness and the prolonged journey had already scaled up their irritation levels. And running into a new hassle, that too of a kind that would likely change the rest of their trip completely, was frustrating beyond measure.

Fiercely looking at Amardeep, the pressure cooker inside Ravin finally exploded.

'*Bhai, tu toh kuch bol hi mat. Saalaa sab se baddi responsibility to tu hai. Licence hai tere paas? Nahi. Currency card hai? Nahi. Flight and hotel tickets book ki tuney? Nahi. Tere chakkar mein saale mera visa late hua.* And look at you. You are the one who is being driven, getting drunk and sleeping. I just saved you from the cops back in Austria when you were trying your stupid stunt to drive a car on a fucking PAN card. Are you responsible enough to even manage your own underwear? No (You don't utter a single word. You yourself are a huge responsibility. Do you even have your driving licence? No. Do you even carry your currency card? No. Did you search or book flight or hotel tickets for that matter? My own visa got delayed because of you)!'

He then looked at Harprit and countered, 'I didn't fail everyone, Happy. British citizens are allowed. So you can pass through.'

'How intelligent! And what am I supposed to do there alone, without you guys?' Harprit said. 'In case you are forgetting, we are on a reunion trip and having a reunion with yourself is a bit pointless,' he added.

(Dear readers, this is where I woke up. Yes, I need to sleep too, don't I? And it was quite late. Perhaps I should have stayed alert, because after ages, for the first time I felt like I was under threat. These four have always argued, always bickered, but never had things turned so ugly between them. Was it just the result of a long, tiring, troubling day? Perhaps. But I needed to watch my back!)

The security person, who had been watching this exchange, now tapped on their window. 'Folks, can you move your car and park it in that bay and come with me?' He pointed his finger at an open space.

'Why?' Ravin asked him.

'Look behind you.'

Behind their car was a long queue of vehicles waiting their turn to enter Croatia. And they had been blocking their way for a while now.

'Okay,' Ravin said, and did as the man had asked.

Adjacent to the border checkpost lanes was a security forces office. The boys were asked to bring their entire luggage along with them and put it on the conveyor belt for an X-ray scan. In the distance they saw a few shabby-looking men in torn and patchy attire. They all stood in a queue.

The boys proceeded with the formalities. One after the other, they placed their bags on the X-ray belt and walked through an adjacent metal detector.

Moments later, the guard at the X-ray station raised an alarm. He spoke in the native language, so the boys couldn't understand any of it. A few heads in the queue of shabby-looking men turned in their direction. The senior security person rushed to the X-ray station. He looked at the screen first and then broadcasted in English. 'Excuse me, whose bag is this?'

'Mine,' Manpreet confidently said.

'*Hun ki syaapaa pai gaya* (What the hell has happened now)?' Ravin murmured to himself.

Manpreet was called and made to open the bag. Looking at the screen image, the two security persons made him pull out half a dozen clothes and searched the pockets. In the denims Manpreet had worn the day before, they finally found what they were looking for – one long rifle cartridge.

'What the ...' Harprit stopped short of finishing his sentence.

'Is this yours?' the officer asked.

'Yes ... I mean no ... I mean yes,' Manpreet stammered.

'So it's a yes?' he double-checked.

'It's in my bag. But it's not mine.'

'Hmm ... I see. So, it's in your bag and you put it in there and yet you say it's not yours?'

'I mean ...' Manpreet stumbled on his words.

'What's a live cartridge doing in your bag?' the officer asked sternly.

'It's a souvenir,' he answered innocently.

Behind Manpreet, his friends watched, worried.

'I took it from the shooting range we visited,' he explained.

'You mean you stole it,' Ravin, who felt it was time to give it back to the others, confronted him. He did it purposely in public.

'I didn't steal it! I took it and nobody noticed it. And I forgot to talk about it to you guys.'

'Fancy words for stealing!' Ravin retorted.

Harprit, yet again, let out a deep breath. This time he too lost his cool. 'Shut up, both of you.' He could see that washing their dirty linen in front of the security forces was not going to help their case.

Meanwhile, a sniffer dog was called and clean tissue papers were rubbed on their belongings to trace any samples of explosive in their bags. Two security guards had been asked to check every inch of the bags. To the security officers, these men could have been anybody. Even terrorists!

One of the guards raised an alarm again. He walked up to his senior and showed him something, which looked like a strip of tablets.

'Voila!' the senior officer said in French. 'Which one of you had this?'

'What is this?' Harprit asked, seeing it was his bag the other guard held in his hand.

'Nice try,' the officer said, looking right into his eyes.

'I seriously don't know what this is.'

'This is ecstasy. A banned party drug.' He flashed the half-empty strip in front of them.

And then at once, horror struck their already weary hearts as they all recalled how the strippers had offered them a pill each with alcohol. Again, three heads looked at one.

'Holy shit!' said Ravin.

'Oh fuck.' Amardeep sighed.

'You stole it?' Manpreet wasted no time in settling the score.

When you are wrong, the best defence is going on the offensive.

'What the hell!' the officer yelled and held his forehead. He was having trouble keeping up with the drama unfolding in front of his eyes.

'Are you guys even together? Because if you are, you need to stop fighting. Do you even realize that each one of you is fighting with the only people you know in this no man's land?'

His words broke into the fog of anger that had taken over the friends. They turned to him.

'What?'

'What do you mean?'

'What do you mean by *no man's land*?'

'Here!' he said and flipped the pages of one of their navy-blue passports. He arrived on the page with their Schengen visa and flashed it to everyone. 'Do you see these two stamps?'

They nodded in unison.

Putting his finger on an older stamp he said, 'This stamp signifies the date and port of your entry in the Schengen zone. It also tells you your mode of entry, which is by air. You guys took a flight.'

'That's right,' one of them acknowledged.

'And this,' he said, shifting his finger to the fresh ink stamp on the same page, 'tells you your date and port of your exit from Schengen zone. In case you are not aware by now, about fifteen minutes back, at the Slovenian border checkpost, you exited the Schengen area. Your one-time tourist visa has expired. Do you understand that?'

'OH SHIT.'

'Fuck!'

The officer finally noticed the horror on their faces and continued enlightening them. 'This stretch of a hundred metres between the Slovenian and Croatian borders is no man's land. You have exited Slovenia. Your visa has expired, and they won't take you back. Croatia won't accept you as you don't have the valid visa yet. You are stuck in no man's land.'

'*Marwaa li humne apni* (We got screwed) ...' Ravin said in horror, his eyes still glued to his passport on the table.

'So, I want you to stop behaving like kids and understand the gravity of this situation. And with that party drug and live cartridge, you all are in deep shit, fellas.'

'What do we do now, sir?' Amardeep asked.

'For now, go and stand in that queue,' the officer said, in no mood to entertain them any further. He pointed to the line in which the untidy-looking men were standing.

Like school-kids thrown out of their class, the four quietly walked to the queue with their heads bowed.

'What's this line meant for?' Ravin asked the guy who stood in front of him.

In his dirty denims, broken sneakers and long-unkempt beard, the man reeked. It had probably been days since he had bathed.

'Welcome to the club. We are going to be strip-searched.'

So there they were, in the august company of gentlemen who, they learned, had been caught smuggling drugs across the border.

It was difficult to process all the damage, more so with next to no sleep. For the sake of paraphrasing, Amardeep summed up their situation, so that there wasn't any confusion left and they were all on the same horribly unlucky page.

'We have been thrown out of the country we held a valid visa for, which by means of our actions has now expired. We want to enter a country for which we don't have a visa. Instead we have one bullet for an assault rifle and a banned party drug in our possession. We are now in no man's land, which means if anything happens to us, no one will give a shit about us. And soon we are going to be butt-naked in front of these strange men.'

Then, as if all hell had not broken loose already, it was time for the grand finale of this miserable day that was going nowhere. Amardeep's phone with the European SIM card in it rang. Startled, he took the call. It was his wife on the other end.

'You made me pay that money to a *brothel*?' her voice came screaming down the line.

24

Naked in No Man's Land

To be stripped in public is humiliating. The only comforting part, perhaps, is if you aren't alone in such a situation, in which case the humiliation gets equally divided among the group.

The four friends, like the drug peddlers, had to brave the embarrassment. They were no longer bachelors in a college hostel. In an attempt to overcome their shame, they looked up to those drug peddlers and derived strength from them.

Life is so strange. Every now and then it offers you crazy role models that you would have otherwise abhorred. Those guys took no time in dropping everything they wore. They looked so comfortable in their skin, as if they were going to take a bath in some invisible, private bathrooms.

The four desis first looked at those men and then at each other. Standing topless, they swallowed the spit in the back of their throat and then moved their hands to the elastics of their underwear. In no time, four more Adams joined the clan, in the forest of the no man's land between the borders of Slovenia and Croatia.

The immediate first challenge, after becoming naked in public, is to decide where to keep your hands. There are no pant pockets to put them in. To cross them over your chest would make you look stupid – what's the point of covering your chest when everything beneath it remains uncovered. And you also don't want to hold both sides of your hips, for that would only ensure that you are opening up a viewing gallery to display your embarrassed jewels.

The first few seconds for the boys began with making use of their hands to cover their respective manhoods. They stood just like soccer players in the line of defence to a free kick would. And then, when seconds eventually turned into minutes, the most important lesson in life sank in – let it go.

(There is a crucial difference between understanding something and accepting it, isn't there? Understanding only makes you ... well ... understand it. Accepting makes you act upon that understanding. When they accepted their fate, they let their hands hang freely.)

The boys kept their line of sight at face level and ensured that they didn't look down and be scarred for life. In all their glory, they joined the queue of the drug peddlers. On one command of the security officer, they were all made to turn and face the wall on their left.

(How living beings, going through a common disaster together, tend to connect with each other. Tragedies often

bring along with them opportunities to get over differences, irrespective of how big they are. In other words, I was going to be saved, after all!)

As minutes passed by and the four heated heads cooled down, each one of them accepted the situation they all were in and began to adjust. Ignoring who'd said what and putting aside their one too many tiffs in the past half an hour, they grew patient and began talking in a tone they had been familiar with for ages. Manpreet was the first to speak as they stared at the wall in front of them.

'Look at the irony. Twenty-four hours back, we were watching women strip for us. And now we ...' He left the sentence incomplete, for no more words were needed to connect the dots.

The sombre mood broke, and the boys struggled to control their laughter. It was a sight to behold: four grown men standing naked, talking and giggling as they faced the wall.

'Karma finds a way,' Ravin quoted.

'Quite a belated bachelor party, guys. I will never forget this,' Harprit said.

'None of us will,' Amardeep added.

With everyone participating in the banter, the bonhomie among the four had been successfully restored. Individually, none of them felt sorry, but they chose to forgive each other.

'Oh shit!' Ravin said and looked at everybody before saying what was on his mind. 'Guess what? We ended up breaking our don't-drop-your-pants pact,' he said, and immediately another wave of laughter ran through the group and the drug peddlers looked on, amused.

The next second Manpreet confessed his fear. 'I have heard stories of cops stripping the male prisoners in their custody and raping them. This when human rights are supposed to be upheld in prisons; they aren't in no man's land.'

'*Shubh-shubh bol, bhai* (Say only good things, man),' Harprit said. 'We will soon have to pull out our butt-cheeks,' Harprit said.

'Shit! Why?' an alarmed Amardeep asked.

'Cavity search. Why else have we been stripped, unless the security guards have another agenda?' Harprit said dismally.

Two guards appeared, and everyone fell silent. It didn't take much time for the officers to inspect them. Thankfully, Manpreet's fears didn't come true and their cavities search went smoothly. The boys didn't waste a second more, grabbing their underwear as soon as they were told to dress up. Meanwhile, all their belongings and the vehicle they were travelling in were thoroughly checked.

That was one problem solved, but many more were still looming on their heads. The bullet was the biggest and most lethal one. It had to be resolved first. The officer agreed to believe Manpreet's story, provided he could prove it.

'Yes, we can!' Amardeep quickly jumped in.

He pulled out his phone and opened the photo gallery. In it were the pictures and videos of them shooting.

'Officer! See these,' he said and then pointed to the time-stamp on them.

'And here is more proof,' Ravin said, showing everyone the email of the booking he had made at the shooting range.

In light of this evidence, it was crystal clear that the bullet in Manpreet's belongings was only a careless adventurous act and nothing more. The security officer had already seized the cartridge in a zipped polybag and after some reluctance, decided not to pursue further action against Manpreet.

In lieu of letting them off the hook, he addressed his own interest as well. The ecstasy pills never made it to the list of items seized in the security records. Instead, the leftover strip of the party drug went straight into the officer's pocket.

His wink was their command. None of the boys had any issue with letting him have his fun. Those pills anyway were a liability and they were only too happy to bargain a legitimate escape, from the patch of land between two borders, to a world where human rights were valued.

That meant they were now three problems down, and two remained. The challenge of how to either enter Croatia or get back to the Schengen region was the next one on their plate. To get into Croatia would cost them another day of the trip, if only they could get an instant visa. And that was a big if.

'You can try applying for one in the morning. However, chances are you won't be able to enter the country till tomorrow evening.'

Given the number of days left in their trip and in light of the advice given by the security officer, with heavy heart's they dropped the idea of going to Dubrovnik.

'But what to do if we want to go back to Slovenia?' Harprit asked the next logical question.

'You annul the exit on your Schengen visa,' the officer replied.

'Annul? What does that mean?' Amardeep asked.

'Due procedure has to be followed. As you haven't entered any other country yet, there is a procedure wherein the previous country allows you back in and nullifies your exit. We will issue you documents that will state that we don't accept you in our country and that you request the previous country to undo your exit, as it was a mistake you made. Besides, even though your Schengen visa grants only one-time entry, the date on it allows you to stay for another three days.'

'Oh yes, that's when our return tickets are booked for,' Ravin quickly pointed out.

'What are we now? Refugees seeking temporary asylum?' Amardeep asked.

'*Bhai chup kar ja* (Please shut up),' Manpreet begged him and then immediately looked at the officer. 'And you are sure it is the best way out for us?'

'If you do not want to remain stranded here for another day, it is the only way out for you guys.'

'But will it work? This whole annulling the exit thing? Will Slovenia take us back?' Ravin double-checked.

'Oh yes. Think of it as instead of crossing the border by road, you were going to take a flight back to India from any of the Schengen countries. And that after immigration exit and before taking off, you fell sick or due to any other reason you couldn't fly out of the Schengen zone. In that case you can step out of the airport and enter the city after annulling your exit. Only thing is your visa shouldn't have expired,' the officer patiently explained.

Thirty minutes later, after all the paperwork was done, they arrived at the Slovenia border. This time from the other side.

Harprit handed them their passports, along with a brand-new set of documents made for them by the Croatia border force.

On the back seat Manpreet joked, 'What a quick *ghar waapasi*!'

Against their expectations, their return in Slovenia was as simple as their exit had been. Only this time the officer smiled and asked them another question.

'Change of plans?'

'Yes sir.'

And with that, he stamped a NULL on the EXIT he had stamped before.

'Welcome back,' he said with a smile, which found its reciprocation on four faces.

25

Back in Schengen

It was 3.30 a.m. Dawn was fast approaching. A very long day was not yet over for the four friends, and there still remained one problem that needed their immediate attention.

It was time for Amardeep to call his wife and explain the situation. Well, not only explain, but also pacify her. Earlier, he had had to disconnect the call in the middle of her shouting at him. Standing naked in the august company of other naked men, he had only had time to promise her that it wasn't what she was thinking. It was now time to play with fire and at least attempt to not get burned along the way.

A council of equally nervous advisers was called upon and everyone helped Amardeep with what he could say and how he could say it. He muttered a little prayer before he made the call.

His opening statement was '*Rinku, Happy aur MP bhi saath mein gaye they* (The four of us had gone together).'

(If you can't rise yourself, pull others down with you. What's the fun in being flushed down the toilet bowl alone? Well played, Amardeep!)

The other three men looked at each other in disappointment. Amardeep's eyes clearly said – we are together in this shit.

The car was parked 200 metres inside the Slovenian border. They had all thought it better to close this last thing before driving ahead.

'Are you kidding me?' Amardeep said on the phone.

The three listened as he defended himself.

'No, darling. Of course it wasn't a brothel.'

'How can you even think of it, baby?'

'Why on earth would I go to a brothel?'

'What do you mean – why wouldn't I?'

'Achha, baby, please calm down first and listen to me. It was a strip club. Not a brothel.'

'Yeah.'

'No, they weren't prostitutes. They were just strippers,' he said, while his eyes shifted from Manpreet to Ravin and then to Harprit.

'Just strippers,' Harprit echoed his words.

Ravin slapped his shoulder to shut him up, lest Amardeep's wife hear.

'No, I wasn't alone for even a second,' Amardeep said.

He made it sound as if they had attended a public show.

'No, baby, it wasn't a closed room,' he said, smartly tiptoeing around the actual facts.

Of course, it wasn't some shitty closed room. It was a lavish limousine. But he didn't need to reveal that part.

'Yaar, it was a high-end arrangement with bouncer and guns. You know? Very protected! Very professional! No loose business.' The boys grinned. Now Amardeep sounded like a very convincing salesperson trying to sell the strip club's services to his wife.

About ten full minutes of conversation later, things appeared to mellow down.

'In fact, the next year when we go to Amsterdam together, we must visit the red light district there. I've heard it is the number one tourist attraction there.'

The other three friends were zapped, listening to that part of his conversation. It sounded as odd as inviting your parents to see your hidden stash of porn. They looked at each other, verifying if what they were hearing was true.

'What is this guy doing?' Harprit whispered in disbelief.

'Turning the tide,' Ravin whispered back.

In their hearts the three said a little prayer, praising the Almighty and then were all ears again.

'Are you still mad at me, shona babu?' Amardeep's voice was soft and pleading.

He then went on to tell her about the other mess they had gotten into and how only moments back they had managed to extricate themselves from it. He summarized everything in a few minutes and gathered enough empathy for himself.

Ten minutes later, they all heard Amardeep saying, 'I love you too, baby.'

'Yes, I will see my sweetest heart in three days.'

Three collective sighs of relief filled the car.

Amardeep disconnected the call, lifted his forearms in the air and then sang out loud. *Dhinaa-Dhin-Dhaa ...*

As he imitated that famous Anil Kapur step, his head and shoulders moved in opposite directions, in sync with the beats.

Ravin too joined in. *Dhinaa-Dhin-Dhaa ...*

And then everyone pitched in.

'*Ram-pam-pam*

Ram-pam-pam

Ram-pa-pa-pa-pam-pam ...'

Their tiredness waning, their heads and torsos swayed in the car for straight thirty seconds. When the celebrations were over, they pulled out some leftover snacks from their bags. They were hungry. All they wanted now, and badly so, was to stretch their legs and sleep like dogs. With Croatia thrown out of their plan, they promptly had to look for a hotel in Slovenia.

Amardeep's European SIM card again came in handy. At 3.30 a.m., they searched for hotels in Slovenia that would allow them an instant check-in. The sad part was that there were none available, not until the next day. They made several cold calls as well, to see if there was a dim possibility of finding something.

No luck. Zilch.

'What? An entire country has run out of space?' Manpreet exclaimed as he hung up on another unsuccessful call.

'It's peak season and short notice,' Harprit reasoned.

'What do we do now?' Amardeep asked.

'Shall we go back to Austria? It's not like we made plans to spend the remaining days in Slovenia anyway,' Ravin suggested.

They all were on the same page when it came to picking a proxy for Croatia. However, they were running on no sleep, and another long drive in the wee hours of the morning wasn't feasible. They had been in the car for fifteen hours now.

'Who can drive?' Ravin asked.

Nobody answered.

Moments later, Harprit suggested, 'Guys, I don't think it is even safe for us to drive any more. We have had a really long day. What we now need is some sleep. I think we should take a nap in the car itself.'

Everyone nodded in agreement.

'Cool. Then let's look for the next exit for services?' Amardeep asked.

'Let's do that,' Harprit agreed.

The wheels of the car began rolling again. The vehicle picked up speed. After a long break, it had begun to rain again. However, this time it really was a challenge to look through and beyond the fiercely moving wipers. For the next ten miles, they didn't find an exit. Things were getting more and more difficult every minute.

Thankfully, some of the fast moving big trucks, which had overtaken them a couple of minutes before, were slowing down ahead of them. Harprit followed them as they took a slight detour from the freeway.

Beyond the shoulder on the highway, they suddenly discovered a huge space where some eight to ten trucks were parked. As Harprit slowed down the car, the guys took a good look at the place. Amid the rain hitting the ground, they noticed long and big slots carved on the ground.

'This is a truck parking,' Ravin deduced.

'We should pull over here,' Amardeep suggested.

'Yeah. We should,' Harprit agreed and found them a spot next to a truck in the corner. It was a safe place to be.

'All right guys, let's see if we can get some sleep now,' Harprit said, switching off the ignition. Outside, the rain had turned the weather cold. They had a sip of water each, adjusted their limbs to make themselves as comfortable as they could in the limited space and closed their eyes.

An hour passed and then another. The rain had stopped. A few more trucks had pulled up and parked in the lot.

Meanwhile, the guys in the car kept tossing and turning. Sleep came to them, but only in interrupted snatches. And then, eventually, it didn't come at all.

'Rinku veer?' Amardeep said softly in a hoarse voice.

'Hmmm ...' Ravin yawned as he responded.

'Were you able to sleep?'

'Barely, yaar. You?'

'Not much.'

They stretched their arms, rubbed their eyes and looked out of the window. Fog had enveloped them. It clung to the windows.

Ravin rubbed the surface of the glass. It felt cold to touch. The temperature outside had dropped. Body heat, deep breaths, yawns and occasional farts had kept the car warm inside.

It took them a while to realize it was already dawn.

Awakened by their voices, Harprit murmured, 'What time is it?'

Amardeep checked his phone. 'Ten past five,' he said.

Harprit cleared his nose and woke up Manpreet by pulling his shoulder.

'Manpreet Singh. Were they your farts?'

'Which ones?' Manpreet mumbled.

'There, that's a confirmation,' Harprit said, while drinking whatever water was left in the bottle.

Manpreet tried to make sense of what was being said, but he was still not fully awake. He looked at Amardeep and Ravin, who only smiled back and were too lazy to explain anything.

'*Challiye hun, mitron* (Shall we drive, guys)?' Harprit asked.

Ravin didn't answer but opened his door. He stepped out of the car. The crisp, cool air outside felt refreshing. He took a deep breath and then stretched his back and hamstrings.

'Guys!' he shouted. 'There are washrooms here,' he announced.

A couple of minutes later, they were splashing tap water on their faces. The toothbrushes and face wash, which they had fished out from their bags, lay on the washbasin counters.

'What's this place?' Amardeep asked, wiping the water off his face.

'Looks like a parking lot for trucks. One which lets the drivers take a nap in the night, freshen up in the morning and get back on the road,' Ravin said, taking a good look at his surroundings.

A little while later, they were back in the car. This time, the windowpanes were rolled down. The fresh morning breeze hit their faces and lifted their mood. Manpreet had taken the driver's seat.

'Raam ji, how long will it take us?' Harprit asked wanting to know when they would reach Vienna.

'The map says around two hours,' Amardeep responded, looking at the screen of his phone. He then got back to the other important task of booking them a hotel in Vienna.

They stopped for a brief while at the next available services on their route. Ravin had expressed his urge to have some tea. It was a must for him; more so in the morning. Nobody minded stopping for this either. They had ample time on their hands till they found themselves a shelter in Vienna.

As he drained his cup of tea, Amardeep announced, 'No hotel available for immediate check-in. All check-ins are at two in the afternoon. I am trying to book one where I can get an early check-in, by noon at least. Works?'

'Beggars can't be choosers,' Harprit said.

'Go ahead,' Manpreet agreed.

Amardeep got busy and moments later he said triumphantly, 'Booked.'

'Guys, we can't remain in this car any longer,' Ravin said as they all walked down to it.

'Yes, I badly need a place to lie down,' Manpreet said.

'What do we do till noon?' Amardeep asked.

'I think I know a place,' Harprit said, grabbing everyone's attention.

'What place?' Amardeep asked, curious.

Harprit merely said, 'Give me your phone, Raam ji.'

As they took their seats inside the car, Harprit looked up something on his phone.

'You all know this place. This is a place where you will find shelter when all other doors are shut. Often, this is the last resort for many,' he said to them, his eyes on the screen.

One after the other, Manpreet and Ravin started understanding what Harprit was referring to. But they waited for him to finish.

'We will go to this place where we once used to go when we didn't have money left in our pockets. It was our getaway from the mundane hostel life. It was our go-to place to eat when we wanted a change from the hostel food. In fact, even before we met each other in hostels, we would have bumped into each other at this place.'

Manpreet and Ravin, who had connected the dots in their respective heads, smiled at each other when they realized Harprit was referring to the home of God.

'Gurdwara?' Manpreet asked, delighted.

Harprit turned the mobile phone towards them. The map on it showed their new destination – Gurdwara Sahib in Vienna.

The joy on their faces was unparalleled.

At around seven-thirty in the morning, with empty stomachs, weary bodies and immense gratitude in their hearts, the four friends stepped inside the gurdwara complex.

The boys covered their heads with handkerchiefs. They felt proud that they belonged to a community which believed in service to mankind; which had built gurdwaras in almost every part of the world. Tired and sleepless, they had failed to find any options to rest in this developed nation. A city full of hotels had failed to give them rooms in the early hours. And now this gurdwara, which connected them to their roots, had become their last resort.

It was an overwhelming feeling to realize this. Never in the past had they felt the way they were feeling in that moment, standing inside that gurdwara. It felt like a home far away from home. They felt at peace. And with all such feelings of gratefulness flooding their hearts, for once they chose not to talk and spoil that moment, deciding instead to live in it and connect with the supreme power. They kept calm as they would always do when they stepped inside the sanctum sanctorum of the holy place.

They bowed before the sacred Guru Granth Sahib and then sat for a while on the carpeted floor covered with white sheets. There was nobody around them in that hall at that moment. The burning incense sticks filled the room with a pleasant and comforting sandalwood smell. Unlike a Sunday when a lot of people turn up at the gurdwara, it was a weekday. The morning prayers and services had gotten over some time back.

On a slab, they found a big steel bowl. In it there was *kadda prashaad*, not hot but lukewarm. Seeing it brought a big smile on all four faces. Ravin did the honours of first serving his friends. They were all hungry. After finishing the first round, like kids, they were ready for another round. There was enough of it left in the bowl.

'Where do we rest now?' Amardeep asked Ravin once they were seated.

'Let's first find out if we can get anything to eat here,' suggested Ravin.

'Where?'

'*Langar hall labh de haan* (Let's find where is the community kitchen hall here).'

Even before they could have begun their search, they bumped into someone, who from his attire appeared to be the *granthi singh* (the priest). When they asked him about the langar hall, he told them that langar was served only on Sundays. However, there was some leftover dal and vegetable from the night before. It was made for the gurdwara staff, the granthi singh explained.

'*Bus kaafi hai saade lai* (That would be enough for us),' said Harprit with folded hands.

The granthi singh also asked them to look for bread and milk in the refrigerator. And that, should they wish to make themselves some tea, where exactly to look for the tea dust and sugar. Excited, the boys couldn't wait to get to the langar hall and cook themselves a meal.

The kitchen was very spacious. At one end were three burners, two big and one small, meant to cook meals for about two hundred people in one go. Next to it was a huge makeshift washbasin. In it there were a couple of used utensils, which were supposed to be washed. There also was a rack with a stack of fresh utensils. The supplies, like flour, lentils etc. lay in jute bags underneath it. The place smelled like an Indian kitchen. The boys felt at home. At the other end of the kitchen was the refrigerator.

Manpreet opened it and found milk, bread and even butter. Along with it they found some Indian sweets and fruits, which they learned, had been brought to the gurdwara as prashaad.

'Waheguru ... Waheguru,' they chanted and proceeded to make some tea.

Amardeep took the bread and got busy heating the slices on the pan. Ravin washed the utensils needed to make tea. Harprit began heating the leftover dal. And for no reason Manpreet, chose to supervise the task. One could never take the project manager out of him.

After how the past twenty-four hours had turned out for them, they had immense fun in everything they did in the kitchen. From lighting the burner to dousing the flame, lest the tea which had come to a boil spilled over, they cherished every moment of being in the gurdwara kitchen. It was a different feeling altogether, one of overcoming a series of challenges. The boys had overcome all the obstacles and now they were together and safe, making themselves a meal. It felt like a sacred celebration of their brotherhood in the presence of fire, food and the divine.

Although Manpreet had championed the art of monitoring everything and successfully evaded any real work, none of the other three let him get away that easily. They had plans for him. Once the meal was ready, they unanimously handed the task of cleaning the place to Manpreet. He couldn't refuse that. After all, he had to do something in the house of God.

Seconds later, they all watched their supervisor friend holding a mop and wiping the floor. When he struggled with it, they offered him a helping hand. Together they washed the utensils they had used and the ones which had been in the sink since before they arrived. They wiped the floor and the kitchen slab and left it tidy.

They were about to sit in the langar hall with their plates when they saw a family of three arrive and sit down. The family thought the guys were making langar for everyone, since that's the norm in the gurdwara – you cook for everyone.

When the elderly lady in the family asked them if the boys could serve them something to eat, the boys realized that they had only prepared a meal for the four of them. However, on second thought, they were delighted. It was their chance to serve someone.

'*Hanji, bilkul* (Of course),' Harprit said.

They looked at each other and went back to the kitchen. The food and tea made for four was then divided into seven equal shares. They served the family first, before sitting down to eat. In addition, they also brought them the sweets and fruits from the refrigerator.

In that very moment they knew they would never forget the meal they were having then. It felt fulfilling in every way, like nothing else they had eaten since they arrived in Prague.

Twenty minutes after having the food, the four of them lay down on the mattress on the floor of the veranda outside the main hall. Finally, with soft cushions under their heads, they got to stretch their legs and rest their aching backs.

In the past forty-eight hours, they had had experiences with strippers, guns, party drugs, and the cops of more than one country. From no man's land to not finding shelter in man's land, they had had enough. They finally felt at peace.

In that peaceful silence, looking at the ceiling, Amardeep said those final words before they all fell into a deep sleep. '*Aisa lag raha hai, jaise Prague wale saare paap dhul gaye hamaare* (Feels like all our sins in Prague have been washed away).'

They all turned their heads to look at each other. The twinkle in their sleep-deprived eyes was that of agreement. They slept in the lap of God for a long, long time.

26

Hotel in Vienna

The one good thing they had done while planning their trip was getting a car on rent. It had come in very handy, more so when their plans had changed.

A little after midday and finally feeling fresh after a long sleep, the boys got back to their car. They first spent some time in cleaning the mess they had made in it the day before. The empty bottles, the disposable glasses, the wrappers and littered snacks – all of it was trashed. The side pockets in the doors were emptied and the bags were neatly arranged in the boot. Once the car stopped resembling a nuclear waste dump and was tidy, the boys reconnected the Bluetooth to the car's audio system. Punjabi songs, once again, made it to the playlist.

It took them nearly half an hour to get to the hotel and park their car in the basement parking.

They checked in and went up to their rooms, which were nice, cosy and comfortable. Harprit jumped on one of the beds as soon as he entered the room.

'Rinku veer, go and take a bath. I will go once you are back.'

Manpreet and Amardeep, after dropping their bags in the other room, had come to join Harprit and Ravin. Manpreet took the other bed and asked Amardeep to take a bath as well. Amardeep chose to ignore him and instead parked his butt on the couch.

Ravin looked at the three of them in disappointment. 'I thought we were going out for lunch.'

'We still are,' Harprit said and then added, 'but you are going to get us late if you don't take a shower right now.'

The other two laughed shamelessly, high-fiving each other.

The mommy in the group folded his arms across his chest and looked hard at his friends. 'I am the only one standing, while all of you have chosen to crash.'

Nobody responded to him. Instead, they got busy connecting their phones to the hotel WiFi.

'Fine. I anyway need to take a shower.' Ravin said and opened his luggage to take out a fresh pair of clothes.

Ten minutes later, when he walked out of the washroom, drying his wet hair with a towel, he summoned Amardeep. The latter was standing by the window. The curtains were drawn apart and he was looking out.

'You haven't gone yet to take a bath? What the hell are you doing?'

Without looking back at him, Amardeep announced. 'Enjoying watching the waves break on the Croatian seashore.'

There was a moment of pin-drop silence, and then came a blast of laughter. Amardeep turned back. Manpreet and Harprit were rolling in bed, laughing.

In the eye of sarcasm was Ravin. He wanted to hold back his laugh, but he couldn't. At the same time he was angry, for his friends were taking a dig at him. He walked fast to Amardeep and playfully punched his belly.

'Aaooch!' Amardeep screamed trying to defend himself against the second punch.

'Pour us some wine, Rinku veer, as we soak in the infinity pool, from where we look at the land end and the beginning of the Adriatic Sea,' Manpreet said, echoing what Ravin had said to make them all visualize the Croatian dream, something he had failed to execute.

Ravin turned back and candidly confessed in front of everyone. 'Guys! I made a terrible mistake. I own it and I am extremely sorry about it.'

'Chill, dude! Yesterday was full of adventure and thrill. I don't regret any of it.' Harprit laughed, getting up from bed. He perhaps was finally ready to take his shower.

'I second that,' Amardeep echoed him.

That's when Manpreet pitched in and said, 'Guess what? Maybe when we go back to our homes, this is the story we are going to tell our families. Maybe not being able to go to Croatia has been more adventurous than making it there?'

Standing right there in the middle of the room, Ravin looked at his friends smiling. None of them had any regrets. He finally felt the tight knot of guilt in his chest loosen.

Over the next half-hour, they all freshened up and got ready to step out. Amardeep's phone came in handy and they found the nearest restaurant with good ratings. A lunch and a coffee later, they decided to walk down to the city centre of Vienna.

It was Harprit's idea to walk. The weather was very pleasant. '*Oye hoye hoye hoye! Yaar suno meri gall!*' he exclaimed, gazing at the sky above them. 'Guys, I say let's ditch the car. Let's walk and explore this beautiful city. What do you say?'

Having spent almost twenty-four hours in the car just the previous day, the others readily agreed to Harprit's proposal. So, they walked for about forty minutes. The best part – they passed by a good number of landmark and historical places on their way. A car drive wouldn't have been that much fun, especially when the weather was so nice. They stopped by wherever they wanted to, for as long as they wanted.

They followed the map and marched towards the heart of the city. On their way, they passed by some of the marvellous architecture of the city. Numerous historical statues, some complete with horses and chariots, stood tall, amplifying the splendid beauty of the city. They were everywhere – at the grand entrance of some historical buildings, at the roundabouts overlooking the traffic signals, in those open vast parks. To their eyes that was a perfect amalgamation of the old Europe and the new.

On their way, they passed by Museumsquartier in Wien. They learned that it was one of the largest cultural quarters in the world. It combined institutions of different fields of art, restaurants, cafés and shops in an area of over 6,40,000 square feet. It was a mixture of baroque buildings and modern architecture.

They decided not to visit it. To see historical artefacts and learn about the culture of bygone eras wasn't on their agenda. They passed by it and came across an amphitheatre. The place looked refreshing, and had a vibe. They stopped by to click a few selfies. At times, they asked someone else to click a photograph of all of them in one frame. Ravin made a few candid videos of his friends walking down the streets of Vienna.

Next, they came across a gorgeous park, called the Burggarten. From the write-up at the entrance, they learnt that this place had once been a palace garden next to the imperial palace of the Habsburg monarchs. Now it was a pleasant public park with a number of statues and an elegant palm house.

The statue that fascinated them the most was that of Mozart. Quite tall and built entirely in white stone, it was installed on an impressive platform.

The boys gazed at it longer than they had at anything else so far on their walk. For some unknown reason, Manpreet decided to imitate 'Mozart's' pose. Harprit pulled out his phone and captured both Mozart and Mozart in disguise in one frame.

'*Eh gaane gaanda si ga, na* (He used to sing songs, right)?' Harprit asked innocently, trying to recall where he had heard that name.

Others broke into a laugh at how, with his words, Harprit had reduced the towering legacy of Mozart.

'*Naale bhangre vi paonda si* (And dance as well),' Ravin added sarcastically.

Harprit got an idea and looked at Amardeep. The latter apprised him that Mozart was a composer, one of the best the world had seen.

'Legendary!' added Manpreet coming out of his pose.

'Composer as in music composer?' Harprit rechecked.

'Yes.' Ravin nodded.

'So he played some instruments?'

'Keyboard and violin, I guess,' Amardeep said.

'Oh! So he was a background musician. Who used to sing then? I mean the lead?' Clearly, Harprit's curiosities weren't over yet.

Manpreet held his forehead in frustration.

'Dude.' He addressed Harprit. 'He wasn't a background musician. He was *the* musician, who would compose the entire symphony. The orchestra would play it on his command. There wasn't a lead singer. He was the lead. In fact, there were seldom any songs or a singer. You've seen those Western classical music bands, where there is one person who stands in the centre and leads the entire symphony with their hand gestures.'

'Oh yeah, yeah, yeah …' Harprit nodded. He spent thirty more seconds thinking, and then spoke again, 'So you mean he didn't even play the keyboard or violin. Just stood there, shaking his hands in the air, displacing mosquitoes.'

The boys looked at Harprit and chose to ignore him. They walked inside the park, while their friend shouted after them, '*Is ka ek German bhai bhi toh tha na. Beethoven. Nai* (Wasn't there a German guy of his kind as well? Beethoven. No)?'

None of the three looked back. They now knew that their friend was just messing with them. Arsehole!

Inside the park, the three took the only available bench. Harprit arrived moments later. There was no space left for him, and his friends didn't bother to make any. So, the poor chap lay on the ground. Manpreet observed Harprit's posture and commented on it.

'Why do you look like a dead frog?'

The others chuckled. Harprit laughed too. He was too lazy to stretch his legs.

The four friends relaxed and kept talking. Some time passed. They remained there for a while, observing their surroundings, the people walking around with their pets and their kids.

Vienna had never been on their list. A day before, they had wanted to explore it, but had had to rush for they were already running late. And here they were, with time in abundance to explore the city, so much that they could afford to laze around in a park.

When darkness began to fall, they pulled themselves up. The city centre was next door. They found themselves the correct exit and then landed right in the middle of the busiest spot of the capital city. Surrounded by thousands of tourists and the local population, it was a sight to behold, more so in the evening light. They kept roaming around the city and had their dinner very late in the night. The idea was to live that night for as long as possible. The next day they had plans to get up late, chill in the hotel swimming pool, get a relaxing massage and drive back to Prague in the evening.

27

Prague Airport

The wheels of their rented car came to their final halt. It was around one-thirty at night. They were in the parking lot at the airport in Prague. It was one of the few drop locations the car-rental company had offered them. As per their previous itinerary, they were supposed to take a connecting flight from Dubrovnik to Prague. After the accidental detour from the Croatia border the boys had cancelled that part of the air ticket, which had meant a small refund.

'So, this is it, boys,' Ravin said, shutting the boot of the car. He had pulled out the last piece of luggage from the boot space.

'Yeah man! This is it,' Harprit said, tapping his hand on the closed boot. It was his way of bidding goodbye to the car. It had been their companion for a large part of their trip.

Ravin thought about how the car had witnessed so much of the trip. It had seen the four friends walk down memory lane and recall their hostel life while it played the 1990s' music for them. It had heard them laugh over each other and then fight with each other as well. It had observed them getting drunk in it and then from a distance it had caught them naked. It had beheld their friendship. And now they were supposed to leave it behind. A part of his emotional brain wondered if the car too was going to miss them. If the feelings between them and the car were mutual.

(Humans! At times they just overdo it.)

Amardeep kept looking at the vehicle. Manpreet put an arm over his friend's shoulders and asked, 'You feel like crying?'

'No.'

'Then?'

'I am trying to recall what happened to that bottle of alcohol. I didn't find it in the back seat.'

'Idiot!' Manpreet murmured, pulling his hand off Amardeep's shoulder. He then walked down to Ravin. Together they bitched about Amardeep's lack of emotions.

'He won't understand. He didn't get to drive it,' Ravin said.

Thirty seconds later, Amardeep shouted, 'Now, if you guys have read your eulogy to this car, then can we move our asses?'

The boys exhaled a deep breath and left the spot. They handed over the key at the 24/7 office of the car rental at the airport parking lot. After inspection, the guy at the car rental digitally removed Manpreet's credit card the agency had held to be charged in case of damages. He signed the papers, after which they all marched out of that office.

There was ample time left for their flights. Around five hours before the first one would depart. Ravin had strategically planned their flights. They were all to fly out between 6.30 a.m. and 8.00 a.m.

It was Manpreet who was to leave first. Harprit would be the last one to fly out.

After checking in their luggage and securing their boarding passes, the four roamed here and there in the duty-free section, carrying their cabin luggage. They had no plans to buy anything, but spent their time window shopping, trying sunglasses and admiring their not-so-good-looking faces time and again in the mirror. Unfortunately, all that they had wanted to buy for their wives back home had already been purchased days back. Besides, they didn't even have the luxury of cash to spend. A while later, when they were bored and tired of playing hide-and-seek with mirrors and sunglasses, they decided on a place to sit down and relax.

The decision of where to sit was based on empty reclining lounge chairs. The airport wasn't crowded at that time of the day. Yet they didn't find four empty recliners next to each other. Their best chance was the row where there were three empty recliners next to each other. On spotting them, they walked fast to take them.

Harprit arrived last. The other three had secured their thrones. He stood there contemplating something.

On the seat next to Ravin's was a blonde. Wearing an eye mask, she was taking a nap. Surprising his friends, Harprit tapped her shoulder.

'O *bete!* Manpreet murmured to Amardeep as they watched their friend's audacity. The two turned to see what their friend was up to.

The lady, who must have been their age, hurriedly got up. She immediately pulled down her mask. She looked threatened.

'See, he has that sort of impression on sleeping women,' Amardeep whispered in Manpreet's ear.

Meanwhile, Ravin was only bothered about himself. He knew what his friend was up to. He screamed in Hindi, '*Tujhe meri khushi kyun bardaasht hogi* (Yeah, why would you ever tolerate my happiness)?'

Ignoring him, Harprit politely asked the lady, 'I am so sorry to wake you up. Would you mind taking that recliner?' He said, pointing to empty one in the row opposite them.

Irritated to be woken up this way by an unknown man, she first looked at the empty recliner and then at Harprit.

Ravin immediately jumped to grab the opportunity.

'How insensitive of you! Where is your chivalry?' he rudely said to Harprit and then looked at the lady who by now had come to realize there wasn't one unknown man, but a bouquet of four unknown ones that she had to deal with. She knew what she was supposed to do for the sake of her sleep.

Without a word, she got up and dragged her rucksack to the empty recliner. She pulled her mask down and went back to sleep.

'*Aa ki kitaa tu* (What have you done)?' shouted Manpreet from the far end. Though in his heart he was glad that Ravin didn't have the advantage of being next to the blonde.

'I want to spend the final few hours of our belated bachelor party with my brothers,' Harprit announced while stretching his legs on the recliner.

When they had all settled down in their comfortable seats, finally next to each other, they thought they would talk through the last few hours of night till dawn.

Earlier in the night, on their way to the airport, they had discussed how emotional each one of them was feeling as their trip drew to a close. They realized how precious these last hours were. They wanted to take a long moment to relive this entire week gone by; to reflect upon everything that had happened, a lot of which was crazy enough to be remembered for a lifetime.

However, three and a half minutes after burrowing into their recliners, all of them were snoring in deep sleep.

'*Bhai, aaj jagraata hai* (It's going to be a sleepless night),' Harprit had announced a while back when they were driving to the airport. Together they had imagined a perfect end for the reunion trip. They had also envisaged how when the sun rose, they would hug each other tight for one last time before saying goodbye. And then, through different gates, they would take off in the same sky but fly in different directions.

And here they were, sleeping like dogs.

(It's difficult to improve on perfection. The four were perfectly engineered to bring crisis upon themselves Every time! Look back at their journey. How catastrophic had it been! Right from the very beginning, from the time of applying for visas. It could all have been simple and seamlessly done, had they been mindful. But no, that's too much to ask. You must be wondering why all of a sudden I am telling you all this, now that the trip is over. Well, it's not over yet. Our friends have one last heart attack in store for them before they depart.)

The boarding time on Manpreet's boarding pass, in his pocket, read 5.45 a.m. It was 6.20 a.m. when the rebellious pressure in Ravin's bladder woke him up. Rubbing his eyes, he looked for the nearest restroom and walked down to it. He was midway relieving himself, when the pressure fizzled out. Up above on the wall in front of him were tiny glass windows that gave him a glimpse of the sky. It was lit. The sky was lit!

He couldn't pee any more.

He looked down. No not there, at his wristwatch. It was 6.23 a.m.

For a second, he froze. He tried to recall if, when he had got up from his chair moments back, the recliners around him had been occupied.

His first thought was that they had all left him behind. *No! It can't be,* he thought to himself. *Has Manpreet left?* He couldn't recall him bidding goodbye either. *No!* He had seen his fat ass after getting up.

'OH MY GOD!' he screamed at the wall in front of him. And then, zipping his pants back up, he ran back to his friends. Washing his hands could wait.

'*Uth saale, teri flight udd rahi hai* (Get up you moron, your flight is taking off).' He slapped Manpreet's back and then woke up everyone with his scream.

Other passengers who weren't supposed to get up, also got up because of Ravin's shouting. They jumped out of their seats, suspecting some terrorist activity. One of them was the lady in the row in front of them, whom they had woken up some four hours back.

She pulled up her eye mask, looked at them, cursed them heartily and went back to sleep.

The rug was swept from under Manpreet's feet.

He opened his eyes to the world with a start and a loud one-word greeting. 'HAIN?'

He looked at his watch. Jumping up, he held his cabin trolley bag and ran. It didn't matter in which direction – he just ran.

(You see! That is what happens when your body is ready but the mind isn't.)

His reaction time was so quick that Ravin couldn't interpret if all that Manpreet did happened in sequence or simultaneously.

Through his half-opened eyes, Harprit looked at his friend sprinting away. Pointing at him, he asked Ravin, '*Shit aai hai* (Is he running to shit)?'

'No. That can wait,' Ravin said, flashing his watch in front of Harprit's face.

'*O teri!*' screamed Amardeep behind Ravin's back. He did all that Manpreet had done moments before, minus the run. He was smart to wait for Ravin to find out which direction to take. His majesty would never do that himself.

Even though Harprit was the last one to fly out, his heart had sunk in horror, for he could understand the repercussions of Manpreet missing his flight. He was still in his seat, while Ravin and Amardep stood facing him.

'Oh no!' he cried, this time looking at something behind Ravin and Amardeep.

Behind the two of them was Manpreet. He was now running in the opposite direction, and coming towards them. Harprit had never seen Manpreet run this fast. His trolley bag behind him was barely able to match his speed. Half the time it remained in the air.

If that guy reaches escape velocity, he would take off any time – the crazy thought crossed Harprit's mind. *If he takes off, will he shit in the air over everyone?* For some reason, ever since he had woken up, he hadn't been able to think anything beyond shit. He realized that he might need to run down to the restroom and relieve himself. But then, how could he, when they were all running against time?

'What the hell are you all waiting for?' Manpreet shouted from the fast-reducing distance between them.

Ravin immediately turned back and yelled, 'Why the hell are you back?'

'I am not back, you idiot. My gate is on the other side.' He ran past them as he said those words.

'Superb!' Amardeep said sarcastically.

'Really?' Manpreet managed to shout at him over the now fast-increasing distance between them. 'If I miss my flight, I won't let anyone take theirs,' he threatened and vanished around the corner.

'Shit!'

'Fuck!'

'NO!'

Three pairs of eyes looked at each other. In the next moment, holding their bags, they ran behind their friend.

Holy shit! They had not anticipated such a tragic end to their reunion, despite all the near-tragedies they had already suffered.

'Rinku veer, my gate is in the opposite direction,' Harprit shouted while running on Ravin's left.

'If that arsehole misses his flight, it won't matter any more where your gate is,' Amardeep yelled, trying to overtake Ravin from the right.

'But why?' Harprit asked, taking the lead.

'Because we came together, and we will go together,' Ravin screamed.

'That's not done!' Harprit shouted louder. 'The agreement we had was limited to if one of us couldn't make it to the trip, others won't make it either. That's it.'

'Oh yes!' Amardeep seconded while picking up pace. 'Thank God we had never talked anything about the journey back home.'

'Good point, guys. We will use it if he misses the flight,' Ravin said as he navigated his way through the crowd ahead of him.

'Which most likely he *is* going to miss,' Amardeep added.

Right in that moment, while running through the airport to support their friend, they had also conspired and found a way to leave him alone, should need be.

(Honestly, I felt embarrassed in that moment. They weren't just betraying him, but me as well. However, there was no time to ruminate on that. Instead, I chose to pay attention to the ongoing crisis.)

Ravin's words gave Harprit an incentive to slow down and finally say those golden words. 'Guys, I have to shit.'

'No! Hold your shit tight and run. We are almost there,' Ravin screamed, letting the world around them know of Harprit's condition.

Harprit squeezed his butt and ran like a penguin.

They could see Manpreet. He stood in front of the gate, holding one hand to his forehead. He was the only one talking to the airline representatives. The entire array of seats were taken up by passengers.

The boys slowed down, catching their breaths.

'Looks like he has missed it,' Ravin said.

'Huh! Even the passengers for the next flight are all here. We are that late.' Harprit agreed.

Amardeep bent over. His hands grasped his knees as he breathed in and out fast. His eyes caught the flight LED display. It read two words. New York. He immediately shifted his eyes to Manpreet, and noticed a smile on his face.

He looked back at the LED. On it the departure time read 8.15 a.m.

'The flight is delayed,' Manpreet announced, showing all his teeth.

'What? Oh thank God!' Ravin said and high-fived Manpreet.

'Phew! Such a narrow escape,' Amardeep said, clapping Manpreet's shoulder.

'Yeah man! I can't believe this,' Manpreet said and then added, 'I am glad you guys rushed for me.'

'Rushed for you? Come on, man! We would have missed our flights for you,' Amardeep said.

Ravin and Harprit first looked at Amardeep and then at each other.

Bastard, Harprit said in his head. Ravin thought something similar in his.

Putting his arm around Manpreet's shoulders, Ravin said, 'MP veer, we would have been together in this shit as well.'

On that note, before any lethal gasses were released amidst unsuspecting passengers, Harprit excused himself for a much-needed bio break.

Amardeep looked into Ravin's eyes. His eyes secretly spoke to him. *Such an opportunist you are.*

Ravin reciprocated his friend's smile and looked back at him. His eyes silently conveyed his response. *If I am an opportunist, then you are looking into a mirror.*

In that moment, they both had the same thought in their minds – had they been in Manpreet's shoes, the rest of them would have made the same decision.

'Now check your own boarding time and gate,' Manpreet said to Ravin and Amardeep, lest they ended up missing their flight. Both of them were to take the same plane back to Delhi.

'Boarding begins in fifteen minutes,' Ravin said after looking at his boarding pass. 'Five gates ahead is where we need to report,' he added.

Twenty minutes later, the four of them stood at the gate from where the airplane to Delhi via Vienna was to depart.

The four huddled together in a circle, their arms on each other's shoulders. It was time. They knew.

(In that very moment, I couldn't keep myself from travelling two decades back in time and see them making that circle at the railway station. From that railway station in their lives to this international airport and from those trunks to these fancy trolley bags, so much had changed in their lives. However, what had remained constant between them was me – their friendship.

Of course, on occasions they behaved like arseholes. Like they had done half an hour back. At times they had fought over petty issues. At times, they'd played tricks on each other.

However, dear reader, my presence doesn't mean not having differences. It means coming back to each other despite those differences.

So there I was, looking at the four of them holding me tight before they let go of each other. I am glad they kept me alive and that I got an opportunity to tell you this story – the story of one hell of a reunion, which they had named their belated bachelor party.)

Epilogue

One year, three months later

One Sunday afternoon, on the flat panel TV screen, there is a Hindi movie on. The heroine in it has made up her mind. She is not going to cancel her honeymoon trip to Europe. This in spite of the fact that moments back her wedding was called off by the very man she was supposed to marry. What follows on screen is a lot more than a mere solo honeymoon trip. It's a journey of self-discovery for the heroine in which she experiences the joy of breaking free, cherishing life and living it on her own terms.

'Baby!' the husband says while taking a bite of the chapatti from his plate. They are having their lunch in bed.

'Bolo,' the wife says, without taking her eyes off the screen.

'Didn't we watch this movie together in the theatre?'

'Hmm ... we did,' she says.

The wife is interested in the movie. The husband is interested in something else.

'And didn't you say then that you wanted to go on a solo trip after watching it?'

She turns her head to look at the husband. Now that he has her attention he waits for her to answer, but she doesn't.

'Why are you asking?' she asks instead.

He serves himself some dal without looking at her and says nonchalantly, 'Arre, you wanted to go, but never went na. That's why!'

The wife waits for him to look at her. He doesn't.

'You think I should go?' she asks.

At that, he instantly looks up at her. Hope shines in his eyes.

'Well ...' he says and takes a long pause before adding, 'I think you should.' And then quickly goes on, 'I mean, it's your call. Only if it makes you happy. You know.'

He smiles a bit and keeps looking at her face.

'Yeah, because then you will get to go on another all boys' trip?'

The smile on his face fades away.

Acknowledgements

My sincere thanks to the following people, without whom this story would not have taken the shape of a book:

My brothers Harprit, Manpreet and Amardeep, for letting me go against your will and write this book, solely as per my interest. For welcoming your character assassinations at my hands. For allowing me to use you, misuse you and finally abuse you. I owe you! (Not my royalties though.) I owe you so much for standing by me, rock solid through the ups and downs of my life.

Ananth Padmanabhan, my friend and the CEO of HarperCollins India, for making me visualize this story as a book and finally getting me on board to turn it into one. Ananth, I remember how casually I had told you about this trip over a meal and how persistent you were that I write this book. Well, here it is.

Richa S. Mukherjee, a debut author I published at my publishing venture, Black Ink, and who is now my friend and a fellow author. Thank you for being the very first reader of this book, and for helping me enhance the humour in it. Richa, you did all this while you were writing your next book. It means a lot to me.

My editor, Swati Daftuar, for wonderfully cleaning the mess I had made of the manuscript. For always being patient with me and improving my work. Swati, this is my first book with you. I hope that I will make you proud when this goes out in the market. Fingers crossed!

Diya Kar, my publisher at HarperCollins India – even though I missed you during the journey of writing this book, thank you for instilling confidence in me after reading the first sample chapters. It made for a great start. I hope to see you soon after the book comes out in the market.

Akriti Tyagi and Aman Arora in marketing and Rahul Dixit in sales, for being by my side while ideating the strategy and executing the plan. I hope that very soon, we will look back and realize that we did the right things.

Bonita Vaz-Shimray, for wonderfully packaging my creative work in her creative wrapper.

And last but not the least, Rupali Tyagi, for helping me give that classic finishing touch to this book.

Behind the Scenes

1:35
4G
40
Yaar Anmuley
Happy, MP, Raam Ji, You
Raam Ji
Soon mere veer 1:26 AM
Alright listen guys 1:26 AM
I met this publisher friend of mine over drinks 1:27 AM
I was telling him how we messed up our trip at Croatia border 1:27 AM
MP
YOU 1:27 AM
What? 1:27 AM
MP
Not we. YOU. You messed it up 1:27 AM
Raam Ji
sahi bola 1:28 AM
Happy
Well done MP veer 1:28 AM
Will u guys listen now? 1:28 AM

1:36
4G
40
Yaar Anmuley
Happy, MP, Raam Ji, You
MP
Ok say 1:28 AM
He thinks our Eurotrip should be a book 1:29 AM
Happy
Really? 1:29 AM
What do u guys think? 1:29 AM
Raam Ji
I think it's great 1:29 AM
MP
That's cool man 1:30 AM
What do u think Happy veer? 1:30 AM
Happy
Interesting. What did you say? 1:30 AM
Yet to get back to him. I thought to check with u guys how u feel bout it first 1:30 AM

Three months later

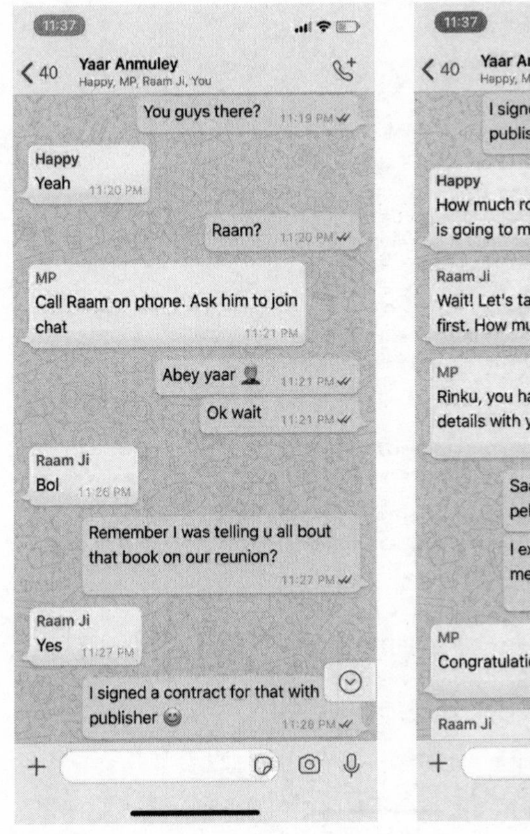

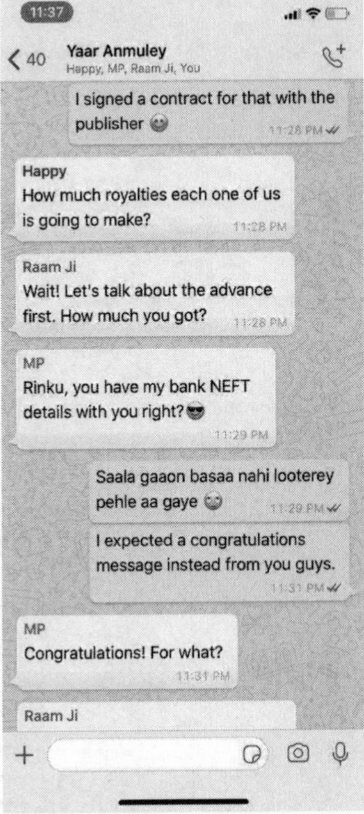

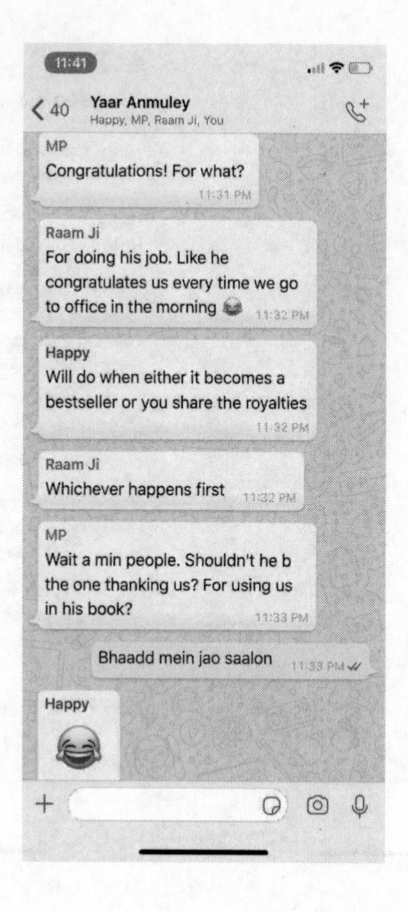
11:41
Yaar Anmuley
Happy, MP, Raam Ji, You
MP
Congratulations! For what?
11:31 PM
Raam Ji
For doing his job. Like he congratulates us every time we go to office in the morning 😂
11:32 PM
Happy
Will do when either it becomes a bestseller or you share the royalties
11:32 PM
Raam Ji
Whichever happens first
11:32 PM
MP
Wait a min people. Shouldn't he b the one thanking us? For using us in his book?
11:33 PM
Bhaadd mein jao saalon
11:33 PM
Happy
😂

Six months later

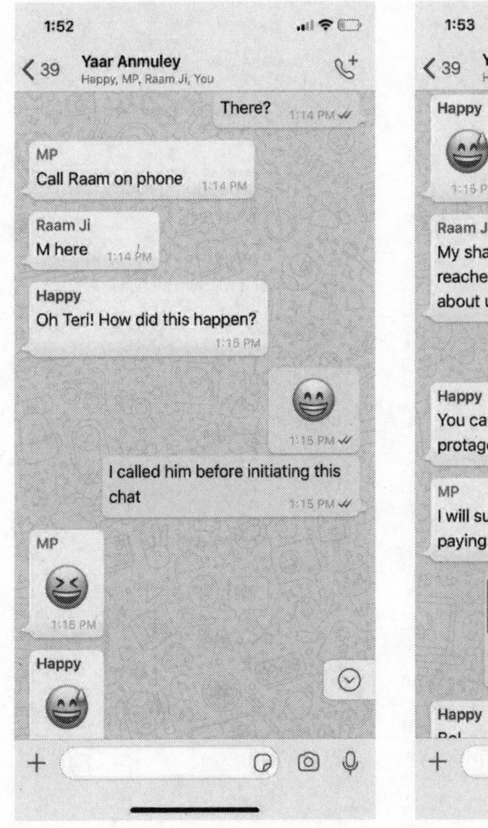

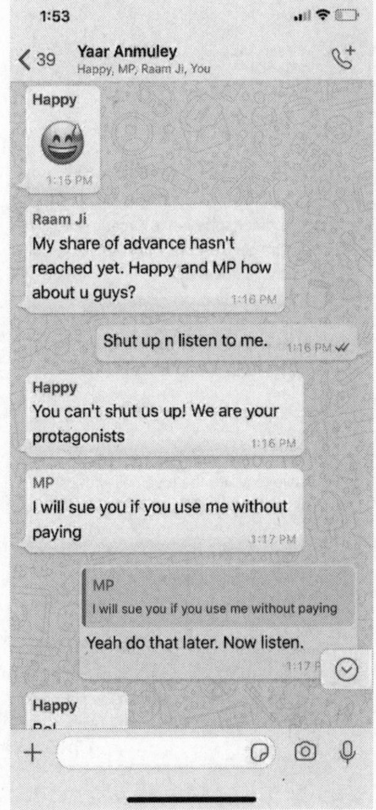

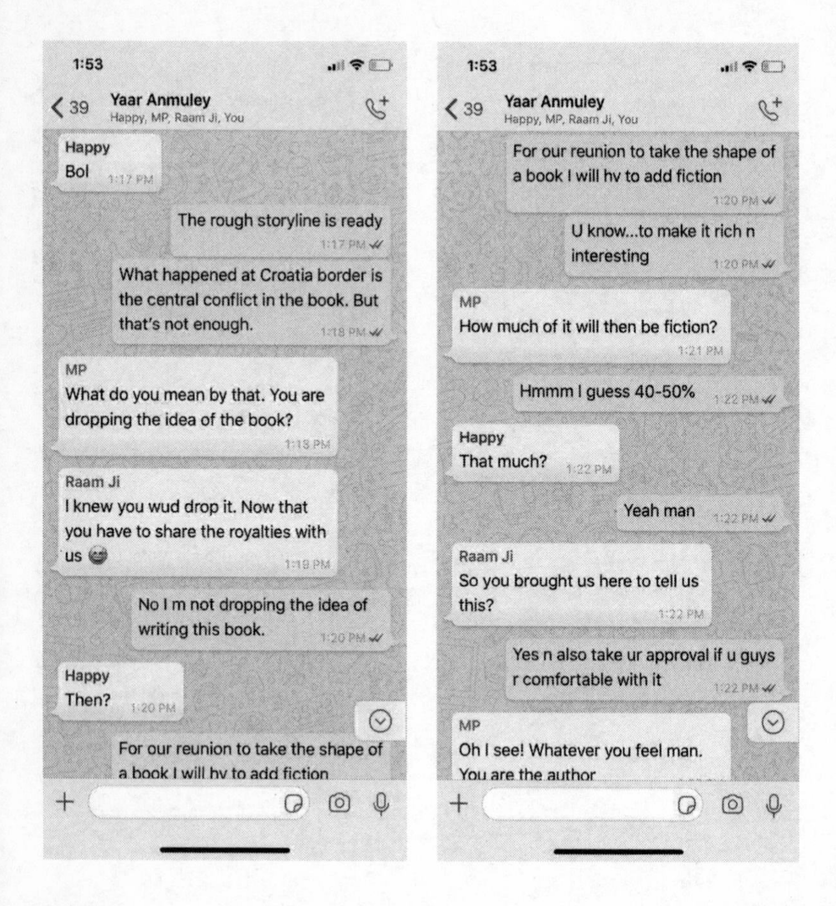
1:53
39
Yaar Anmuley
Happy, MP, Raam Ji, You
Happy
Bol 1:17 PM
The rough storyline is ready 1:17 PM
What happened at Croatia border is the central conflict in the book. But that's not enough. 1:18 PM
MP
What do you mean by that. You are dropping the idea of the book? 1:18 PM
Raam Ji
I knew you wud drop it. Now that you have to share the royalties with us 1:19 PM
No I m not dropping the idea of writing this book. 1:20 PM
Happy
Then? 1:20 PM
For our reunion to take the shape of a book I will hv to add fiction
1:53
39
Yaar Anmuley
Happy, MP, Raam Ji, You
For our reunion to take the shape of a book I will hv to add fiction 1:20 PM
U know...to make it rich n interesting 1:20 PM
MP
How much of it will then be fiction? 1:21 PM
Hmmm I guess 40-50% 1:22 PM
Happy
That much? 1:22 PM
Yeah man 1:22 PM
Raam Ji
So you brought us here to tell us this? 1:22 PM
Yes n also take ur approval if u guys r comfortable with it 1:22 PM
MP
Oh I see! Whatever you feel man. You are the author

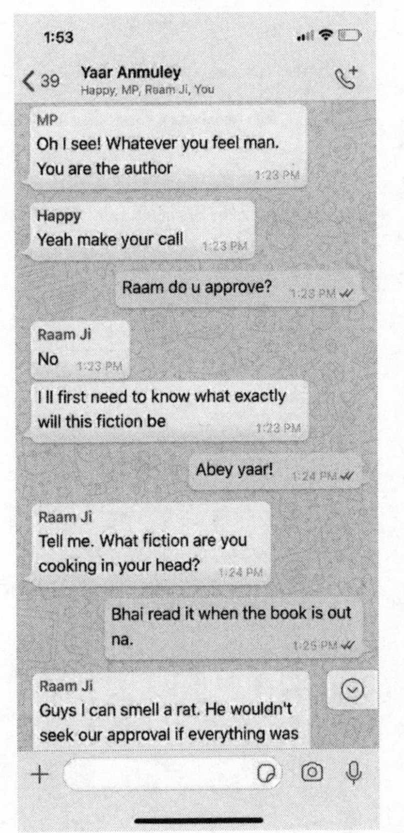
1:53
39
Yaar Anmuley
Happy, MP, Raam Ji, You
MP
Oh I see! Whatever you feel man. You are the author
1:23 PM
Happy
Yeah make your call
1:23 PM
Raam do u approve?
1:23 PM
Raam Ji
No
1:23 PM
I ll first need to know what exactly will this fiction be
1:23 PM
Abey yaar!
1:24 PM
Raam Ji
Tell me. What fiction are you cooking in your head?
1:24 PM
Bhai read it when the book is out na.
1:25 PM
Raam Ji
Guys I can smell a rat. He wouldn't seek our approval if everything was

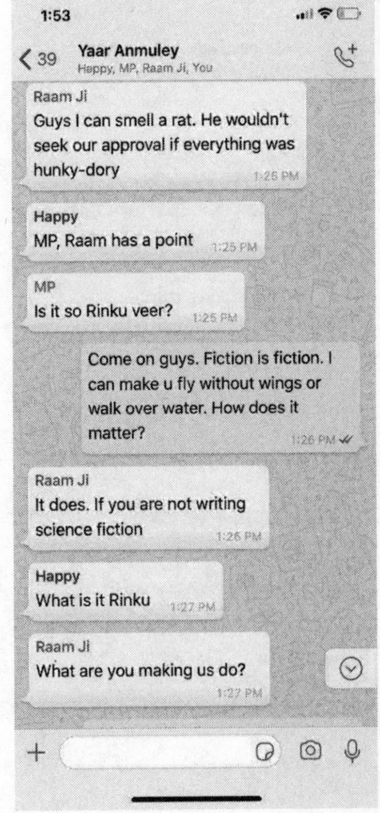
1:53
39
Yaar Anmuley
Happy, MP, Raam Ji, You
Raam Ji
Guys I can smell a rat. He wouldn't seek our approval if everything was hunky-dory
1:25 PM
Happy
MP, Raam has a point
1:25 PM
MP
Is it so Rinku veer?
1:25 PM
Come on guys. Fiction is fiction. I can make u fly without wings or walk over water. How does it matter?
1:26 PM
Raam Ji
It does. If you are not writing science fiction
1:26 PM
Happy
What is it Rinku
1:27 PM
Raam Ji
What are you making us do?
1:27 PM

1:54

< 39 **Yaar Anmuley**
Happy, MP, Raam Ji, You

Raam Ji
What are you making us do? 1:27 PM

Alright I will tell u. But u hv to listen to me with an open mind. Ok? 1:29 PM

Raam Ji
See guys! I told you 1:29 PM

Happy
Let him speak first Raam 1:29 PM

One of us shoots someone. 1:29 PM

MP
What? 1:29 PM

WHAT? 😳 1:30 PM

And that someone dies. 1:30 PM

Happy
Dies? 1:30 PM

Yeah because he shoots him at

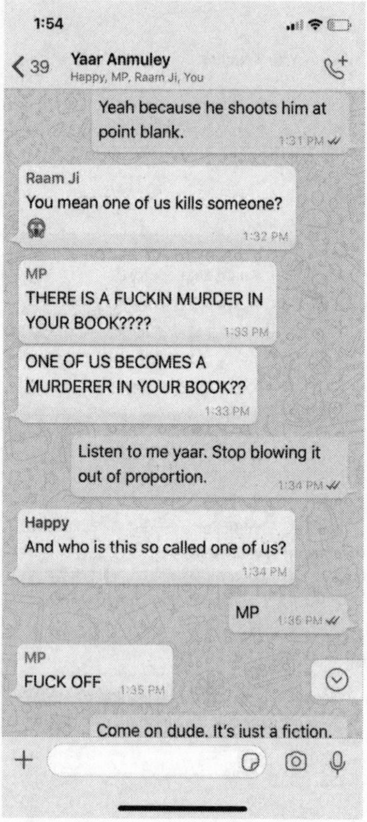

1:54

< 39 **Yaar Anmuley**
Happy, MP, Raam Ji, You

Yeah because he shoots him at point blank. 1:31 PM

Raam Ji
You mean one of us kills someone? 😱 1:32 PM

MP
THERE IS A FUCKIN MURDER IN YOUR BOOK???? 1:33 PM

ONE OF US BECOMES A MURDERER IN YOUR BOOK?? 1:33 PM

Listen to me yaar. Stop blowing it out of proportion. 1:34 PM

Happy
And who is this so called one of us? 1:34 PM

MP 1:35 PM

MP
FUCK OFF 1:35 PM

Come on dude. It's just a fiction.

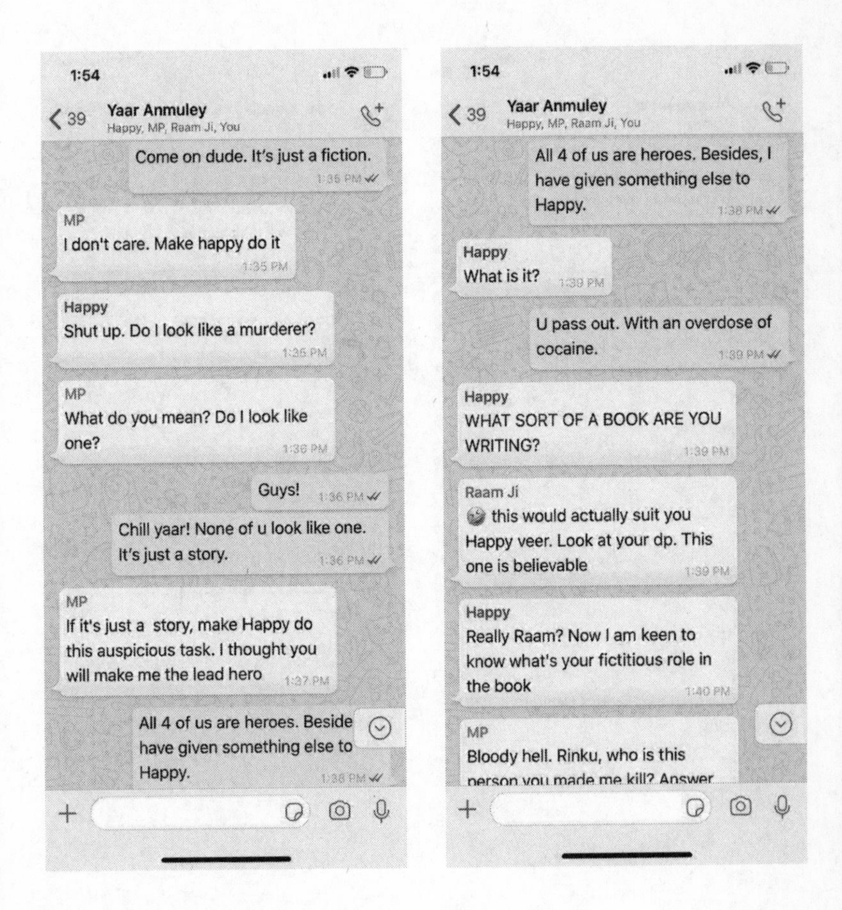
1:54
39
Yaar Anmuley
Happy, MP, Raam Ji, You
Come on dude. It's just a fiction.
1:35 PM
MP
I don't care. Make happy do it
1:35 PM
Happy
Shut up. Do I look like a murderer?
1:35 PM
MP
What do you mean? Do I look like one?
1:36 PM
Guys!
1:36 PM
Chill yaar! None of u look like one. It's just a story.
1:36 PM
MP
If it's just a story, make Happy do this auspicious task. I thought you will make me the lead hero
1:37 PM
All 4 of us are heroes. Beside have given something else to Happy.
1:38 PM
1:54
39
Yaar Anmuley
Happy, MP, Raam Ji, You
All 4 of us are heroes. Besides, I have given something else to Happy.
1:38 PM
Happy
What is it?
1:39 PM
U pass out. With an overdose of cocaine.
1:39 PM
Happy
WHAT SORT OF A BOOK ARE YOU WRITING?
1:39 PM
Raam Ji
this would actually suit you Happy veer. Look at your dp. This one is believable
1:39 PM
Happy
Really Raam? Now I am keen to know what's your fictitious role in the book
1:40 PM
MP
Bloody hell. Rinku, who is this

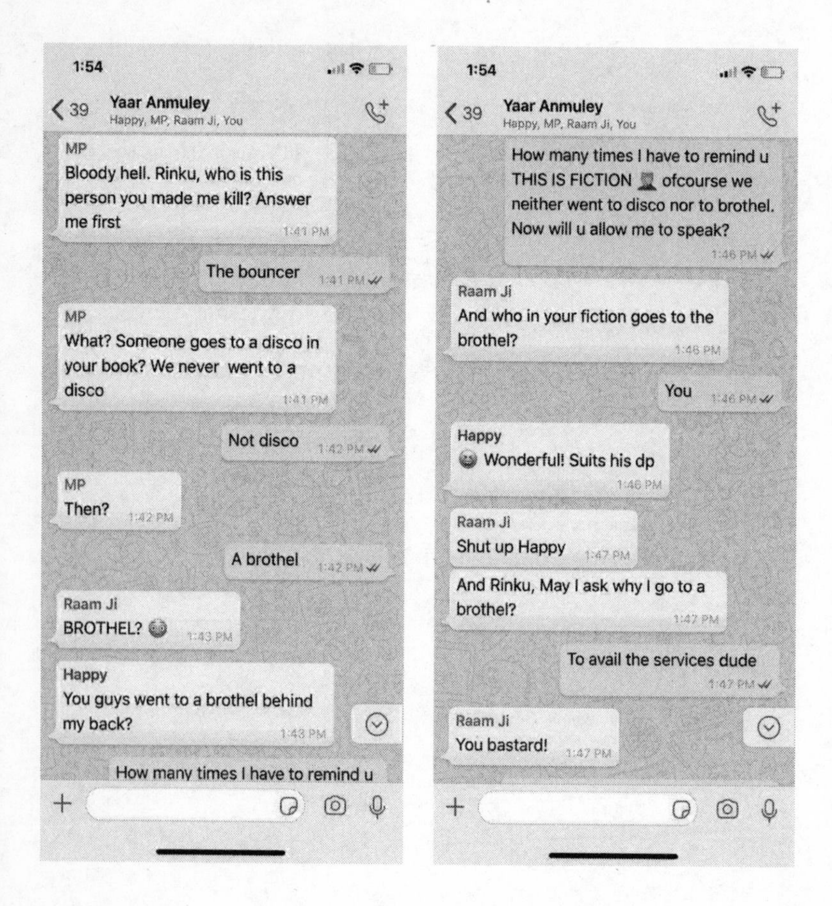
1:54
39
Yaar Anmuley
Happy, MP, Raam Ji, You
MP
Bloody hell. Rinku, who is this person you made me kill? Answer me first
1:41 PM
The bouncer
1:41 PM
MP
What? Someone goes to a disco in your book? We never went to a disco
1:41 PM
Not disco
1:42 PM
MP
Then?
1:42 PM
A brothel
1:42 PM
Raam Ji
BROTHEL?
1:43 PM
Happy
You guys went to a brothel behind my back?
1:43 PM
How many times I have to remind u
1:54
39
Yaar Anmuley
Happy, MP, Raam Ji, You
How many times I have to remind u THIS IS FICTION ofcourse we neither went to disco nor to brothel. Now will u allow me to speak?
1:46 PM
Raam Ji
And who in your fiction goes to the brothel?
1:46 PM
You
1:46 PM
Happy
Wonderful! Suits his dp
1:46 PM
Raam Ji
Shut up Happy
1:47 PM
And Rinku, May I ask why I go to a brothel?
1:47 PM
To avail the services dude
1:47 PM
Raam Ji
You bastard!
1:47 PM

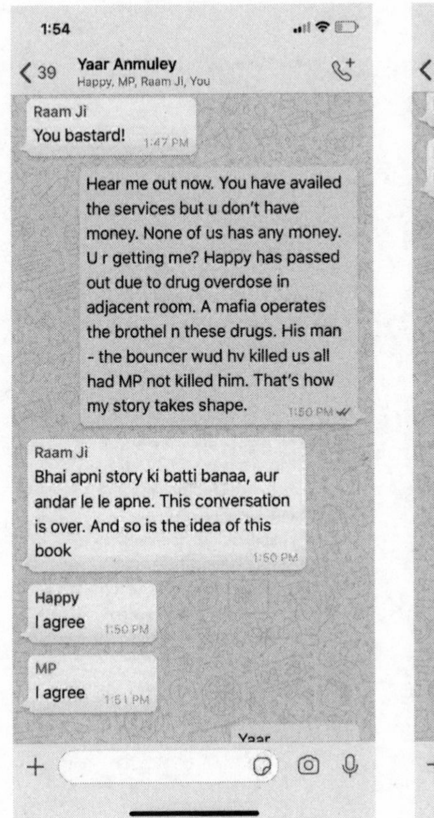
1:54
39
Yaar Anmuley
Happy, MP, Raam Ji, You
Raam Ji
You bastard! 1:47 PM
Hear me out now. You have availed the services but u don't have money. None of us has any money. U r getting me? Happy has passed out due to drug overdose in adjacent room. A mafia operates the brothel n these drugs. His man - the bouncer wud hv killed us all had MP not killed him. That's how my story takes shape. 1:50 PM
Raam Ji
Bhai apni story ki batti banaa, aur andar le le apne. This conversation is over. And so is the idea of this book 1:50 PM
Happy
I agree 1:50 PM
MP
I agree 1:51 PM

2:01
39
Yaar Anmuley
Happy, MP, Raam Ji, You
I agree 1:50 PM
MP
I agree 1:51 PM
Yaar 1:51 PM
Listen 1:51 PM
Guys..... 1:51 PM
There? 1:51 PM
1:51 PM
Saaalon 1:56 PM
Kameeeno 1:57 PM
Please yaar 1:59 PM
Alright then I m gonna call u 2:00 PM
All of u right now 2:00 PM
????? 2:00 PM
Bhaadd mein jao bc! 2:00 PM

A week later

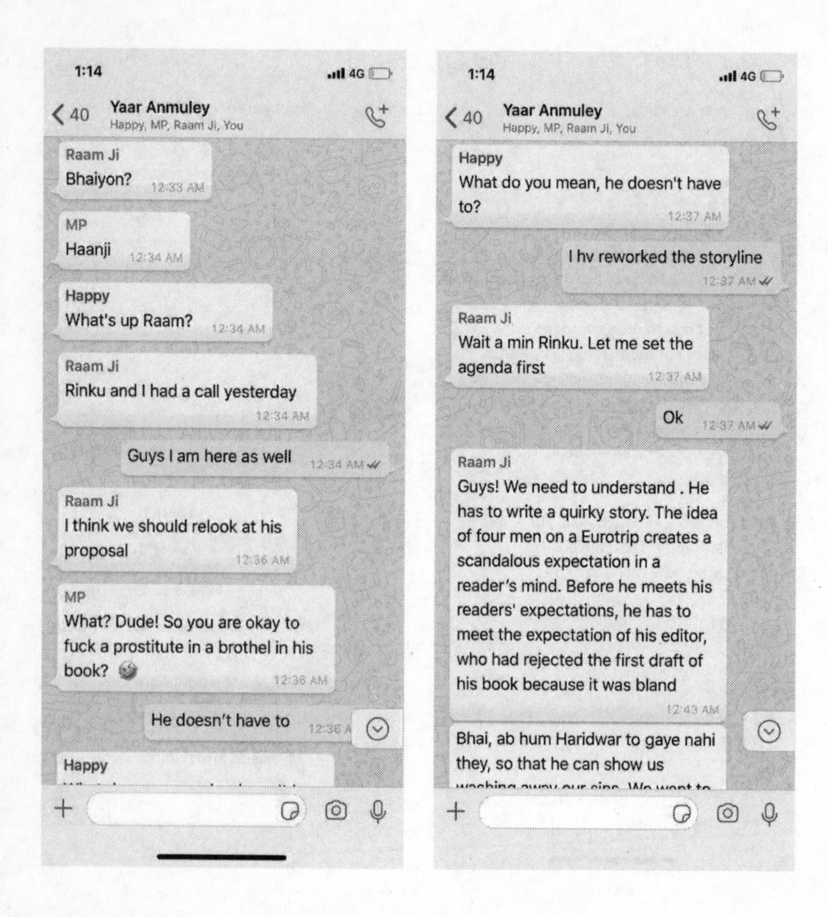
1:14
Yaar Anmuley
Happy, MP, Raam Ji, You
Raam Ji
Bhaiyon? 12:33 AM
MP
Haanji 12:34 AM
Happy
What's up Raam? 12:34 AM
Raam Ji
Rinku and I had a call yesterday 12:34 AM
Guys I am here as well 12:34 AM
Raam Ji
I think we should relook at his proposal 12:36 AM
MP
What? Dude! So you are okay to fuck a prostitute in a brothel in his book? 12:36 AM
He doesn't have to
Happy
1:14
Yaar Anmuley
Happy, MP, Raam Ji, You
Happy
What do you mean, he doesn't have to? 12:37 AM
I hv reworked the storyline 12:37 AM
Raam Ji
Wait a min Rinku. Let me set the agenda first 12:37 AM
Ok 12:37 AM
Raam Ji
Guys! We need to understand . He has to write a quirky story. The idea of four men on a Eurotrip creates a scandalous expectation in a reader's mind. Before he meets his readers' expectations, he has to meet the expectation of his editor, who had rejected the first draft of his book because it was bland 12:43 AM
Bhai, ab hum Haridwar to gaye nahi they, so that he can show us

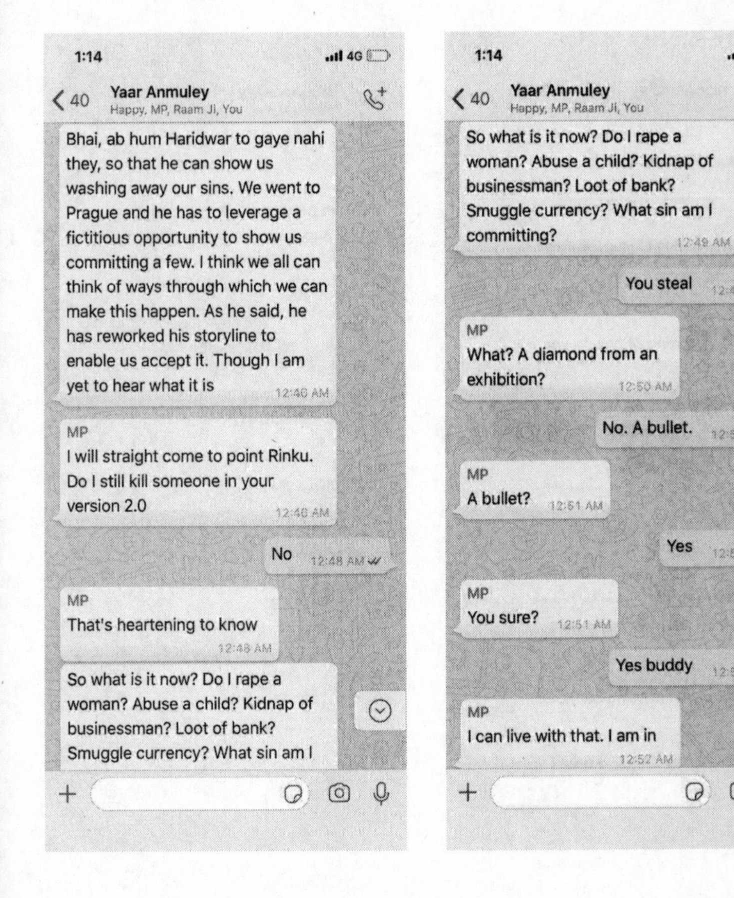
1:14
Yaar Anmuley
Happy, MP, Raam Ji, You
Bhai, ab hum Haridwar to gaye nahi they, so that he can show us washing away our sins. We went to Prague and he has to leverage a fictitious opportunity to show us committing a few. I think we all can think of ways through which we can make this happen. As he said, he has reworked his storyline to enable us accept it. Though I am yet to hear what it is
MP
I will straight come to point Rinku. Do I still kill someone in your version 2.0
No
MP
That's heartening to know
So what is it now? Do I rape a woman? Abuse a child? Kidnap of businessman? Loot of bank? Smuggle currency? What sin am I
1:14
Yaar Anmuley
Happy, MP, Raam Ji, You
So what is it now? Do I rape a woman? Abuse a child? Kidnap of businessman? Loot of bank? Smuggle currency? What sin am I committing?
You steal
MP
What? A diamond from an exhibition?
No. A bullet.
MP
A bullet?
Yes
MP
You sure?
Yes buddy
MP
I can live with that. I am in

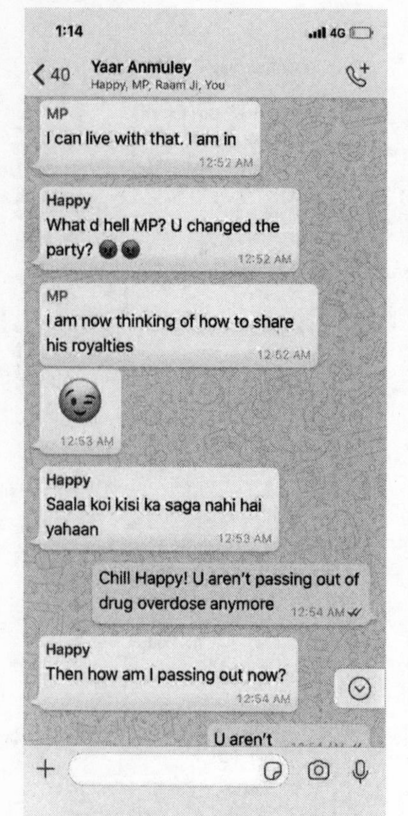
1:14
4G
40
Yaar Anmuley
Happy, MP, Raam Ji, You
MP
I can live with that. I am in
12:52 AM
Happy
What d hell MP? U changed the party?
12:52 AM
MP
I am now thinking of how to share his royalties
12:52 AM
12:53 AM
Happy
Saala koi kisi ka saga nahi hai yahaan
12:53 AM
Chill Happy! U aren't passing out of drug overdose anymore
12:54 AM
Happy
Then how am I passing out now?
12:54 AM
U aren't

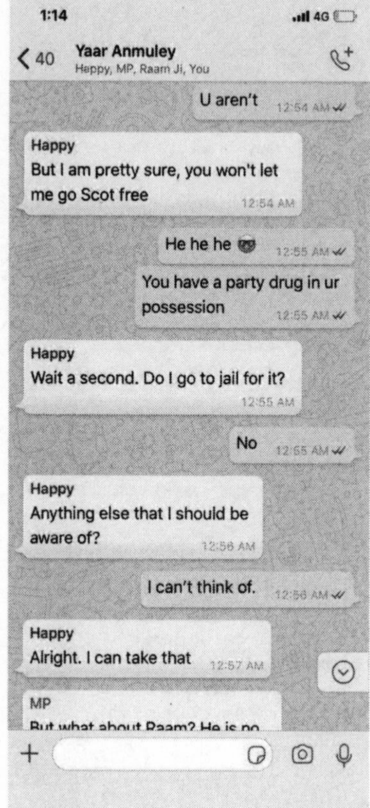
1:14
4G
40
Yaar Anmuley
Happy, MP, Raam Ji, You
U aren't
12:54 AM
Happy
But I am pretty sure, you won't let me go Scot free
12:54 AM
He he he
12:55 AM
You have a party drug in ur possession
12:55 AM
Happy
Wait a second. Do I go to jail for it?
12:55 AM
No
12:55 AM
Happy
Anything else that I should be aware of?
12:56 AM
I can't think of.
12:56 AM
Happy
Alright. I can take that
12:57 AM
MP

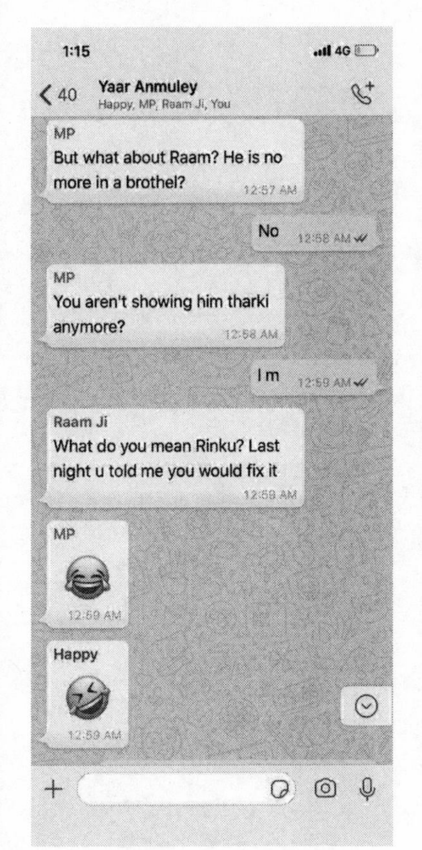
1:15
4G
40
Yaar Anmuley
Happy, MP, Raam Ji, You
MP
But what about Raam? He is no more in a brothel?
12:57 AM
No
12:58 AM
MP
You aren't showing him tharki anymore?
12:58 AM
I m
12:59 AM
Raam Ji
What do you mean Rinku? Last night u told me you would fix it
12:59 AM
MP
12:59 AM
Happy
12:59 AM

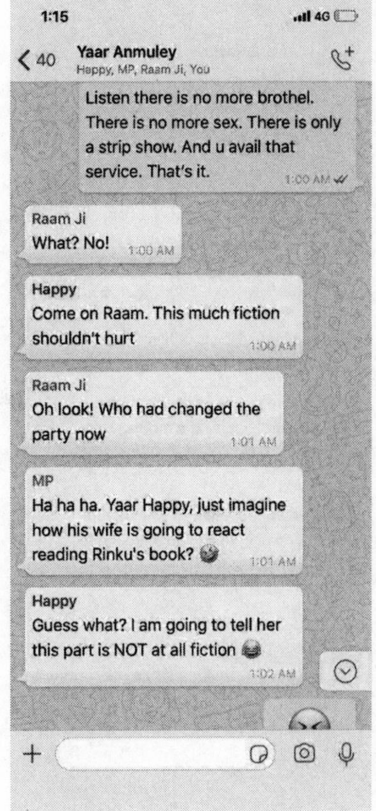
1:15
4G
40
Yaar Anmuley
Happy, MP, Raam Ji, You
Listen there is no more brothel. There is no more sex. There is only a strip show. And u avail that service. That's it.
1:00 AM
Raam Ji
What? No!
1:00 AM
Happy
Come on Raam. This much fiction shouldn't hurt
1:00 AM
Raam Ji
Oh look! Who had changed the party now
1:01 AM
MP
Ha ha ha. Yaar Happy, just imagine how his wife is going to react reading Rinku's book?
1:01 AM
Happy
Guess what? I am going to tell her this part is NOT at all fiction
1:02 AM

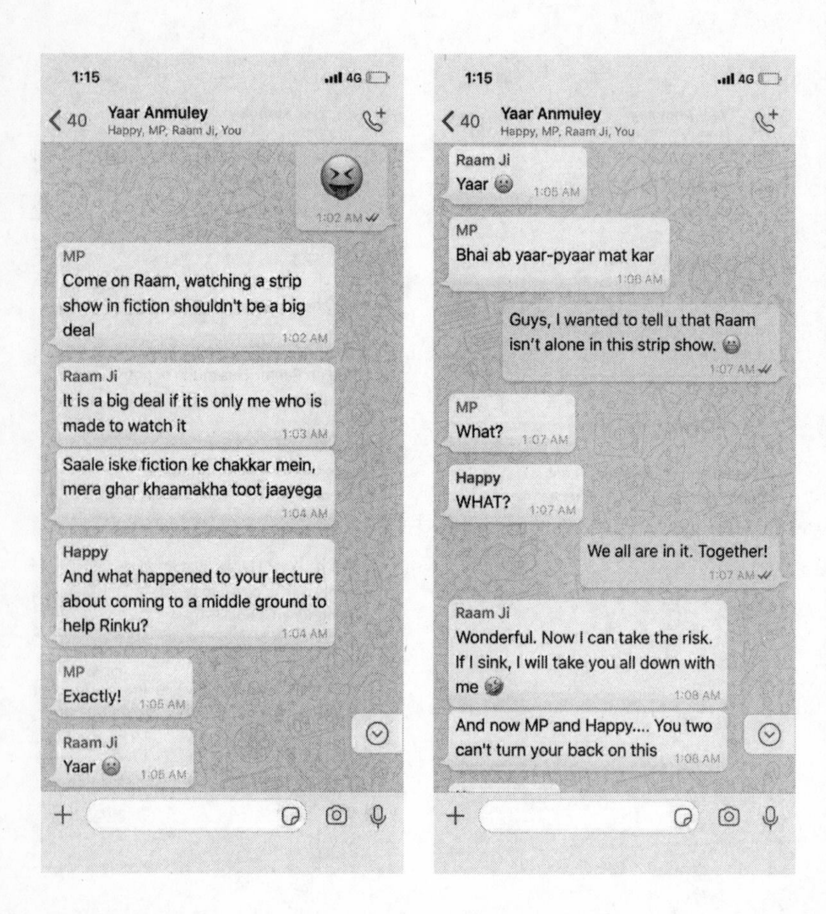
1:15
4G
40
Yaar Anmuley
Happy, MP, Raam Ji, You
1:02 AM
MP
Come on Raam, watching a strip show in fiction shouldn't be a big deal
1:02 AM
Raam Ji
It is a big deal if it is only me who is made to watch it
1:03 AM
Saale iske fiction ke chakkar mein, mera ghar khaamakha toot jaayega
1:04 AM
Happy
And what happened to your lecture about coming to a middle ground to help Rinku?
1:04 AM
MP
Exactly!
1:05 AM
Raam Ji
Yaar
1:06 AM
1:15
4G
40
Yaar Anmuley
Happy, MP, Raam Ji, You
Raam Ji
Yaar
1:06 AM
MP
Bhai ab yaar-pyaar mat kar
1:06 AM
Guys, I wanted to tell u that Raam isn't alone in this strip show.
1:07 AM
MP
What?
1:07 AM
Happy
WHAT?
1:07 AM
We all are in it. Together!
1:07 AM
Raam Ji
Wonderful. Now I can take the risk. If I sink, I will take you all down with me
1:08 AM
And now MP and Happy.... You two can't turn your back on this
1:08 AM

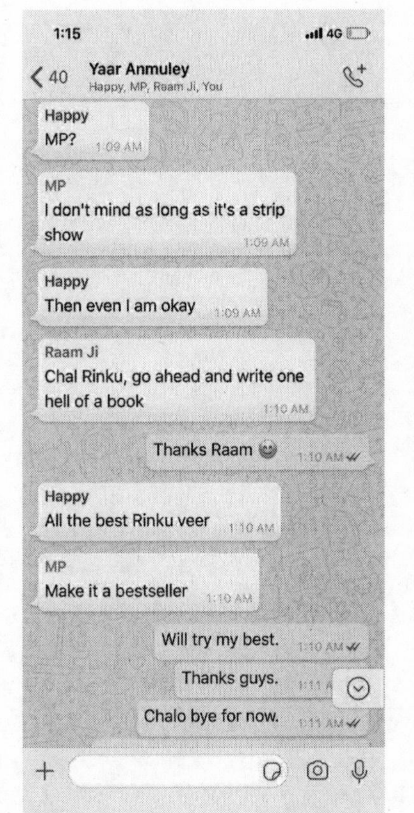
1:15
4G
40
Yaar Anmuley
Happy, MP, Raam Ji, You
Happy
MP?
1:09 AM
MP
I don't mind as long as it's a strip show
1:09 AM
Happy
Then even I am okay
1:09 AM
Raam Ji
Chal Rinku, go ahead and write one hell of a book
1:10 AM
Thanks Raam
1:10 AM
Happy
All the best Rinku veer
1:10 AM
MP
Make it a bestseller
1:10 AM
Will try my best.
1:10 AM
Thanks guys.
Chalo bye for now.
1:11 AM

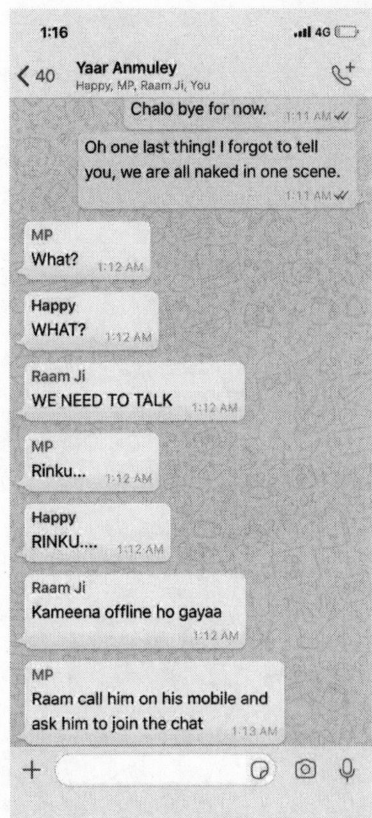
1:16
4G
40
Yaar Anmuley
Happy, MP, Raam Ji, You
Chalo bye for now.
1:11 AM
Oh one last thing! I forgot to tell you, we are all naked in one scene.
1:11 AM
MP
What?
1:12 AM
Happy
WHAT?
1:12 AM
Raam Ji
WE NEED TO TALK
1:12 AM
MP
Rinku...
1:12 AM
Happy
RINKU....
1:12 AM
Raam Ji
Kameena offline ho gayaa
1:12 AM
MP
Raam call him on his mobile and ask him to join the chat
1:13 AM